"Ride, Madelon. No matter what happens ride!"

She did not need to be told a second time. The wind whipped at her flowing cloak and sent it swirling behind as she galloped over the rocky Spanish plain.

Suddenly, one horseman, then two, appeared before her on the horizon. Dear God, she must not be captured! Wheeling her mount to the right, she headed for the distant mountains.

Her heart was frozen with fear. Her body was trembling with a violence she hadn't thought possible.

How she kept hold of the reins or endured the torturous ride she never knew....

Valentina Luellen
is also the author of
Harlequin Historical #6
Francesca

Francesca had been forced to marry
Raoul, a man who represented everything
she despised. But, unable to ignore her
growing attraction for him, she soon
found herself torn between a husband
she loved passionately and a brother to
whom she owed allegiance.

Her new home, the decadent court of
the ruthless Borgias, appalled her, and
she clung to her husband's professed
love. Surely she would be safe with him....

How was she to know she would soon
be brutally betrayed!

Madelon

VALENTINA LUELLEN

Harlequin Books

TORONTO • LONDON • NEW YORK • AMSTERDAM • SYDNEY

Harlequin Historical edition published March 1978
ISBN 0-373-05009-7

Originally published in 1970
by Robert Hale & Company

CHAPTER ONE

"MADELON, damn it! Where are you? I've been ready to leave for the past half hour."

Paco del Rivas y Montevides thrust aside the entrance of the silken pavilion and stormed inside, the angry expression on his handsome face deepening into a scowl as the soldier on guard tried to hide a smirk. Madelon's presence among the men was causing unrest, he would have to speak to her. She was too free with her smiles and favours. Well-bred young women did not acknowledge the common rabble. He stopped short on the threshold with a surprised oath.

"By Our Lady of Santalinas, what have you done to yourself?"

The girl standing before him was tall and reed-slender, her perfectly moulded figure displayed to full advantage in a sleeveless robe of white silk, trimmed with gold thread. A thin gold chain encircled a waist so small, it could be spanned by a man's two hands. Long fair hair streamed past her shoulders like a cloud of sunshine, reaching almost to the jewelled girdle. Her exquisitely beautiful face was perfection itself; the petal-soft skin flawlessly white despite the long days spent beneath a scorching sun, her mouth, full and soft, curving into a smile at her brother's surprised expression. Her eyes were a brilliant blue, as magnificent as the huge sapphire suspended around her neck.

"Alfonso and Sancho fight over kingdoms, but the fight of Kings will be nothing compared to the ones there will be over you, my sister. I should have left you in the convent for another year."

"Surely that would only have made matters worse," Madelon teased gently.

Paco feigned mock annoyance and walked slowly around her, scrutinizing her from head to toe.

"You look like an angel, but I suspect there is a devil in you somewhere, waiting to be released."

"Paco, really! I've only changed my dress. This is my first time at court in three years, I must look my best. Besides I thought you would want to marry me off as soon as possible."

Paco did not miss the bitterness which crept into her quiet tones.

"Father tried that. You were a precocious little girl three years ago and I thought marriage was the best thing for you, but you were mad enough to choose to remain in that grave-yard of a convent rather than agree to the man of father's choice."

"An old man, more than three times my age." Madelon's soft mouth curved in disgust. "I felt sick to have him look at me, let alone touch me."

"And what if I find a husband for you and he isn't to your liking?"

"I shall fight you as I fought our father," his sister replied stubbornly. "I still have a mind of my own and in the past three years I've grown up a lot more, Paco."

"So I see." Paco continued to gaze at her through narrow eyes. "Suddenly I find myself with a very beautiful sister and I'd like the chance to get to know you again."

"You could have visited me in the convent."

"I'm a soldier, I can't come and go when and where I please. Don Alfonso is a very zealous overlord, besides father gave orders I wasn't to be allowed in. He intended you to rot there until the day you died, you realize that, don't you? He never forgave you for disobeying him."

"You mean he never forgave me for being born a girl, not the second son he longed for and never had."

"He's dead now ... and you are free. I'll not chain you. But I must warn you about your familiarity with my men – especially my captain. You haven't been with me a week and yet I swear there are at least two young fools in love with you." Paco's eyes held hers for a moment and the look in them made him realize she was unaware of her beauty or the pitfalls such loveliness could bring. Beauty and innocence – rare combination among the women at Alfonso's court. She would be watched and envied and desired and suddenly he was afraid for her. "Madelon, you will be guided by me, won't you? You are so young – and vulnerable."

"Then why didn't you send me straight home?" Madelon swung away from him with an angry toss of her head that sent the loose cloud of hair swirling around the bare arms. With a soft expletive Paco grabbed her by the shoulders and swung her back to face him.

"Three years' solitude has dulled your wits. You are my sister and I want us to be together. . . ."

"But not at court?"

"You were at court for a month only before you exiled yourself. To a girl of sixteen, fresh from the country, it must have seemed very grand. But it isn't like that. There's ugliness and hate. Castilian spies are everywhere and as for morals – there are very few I know of. The women especially seem to take delight in taking lovers as soon as their husbands disappear from sight – some don't even wait for that."

"They can't all be bad or cousin Urraca would not have sanctioned my return," Madelon protested.

Paco released her with a heavy sigh.

"I've no more time to waste arguing, at this rate we won't reach Santa María de Carrion before the end of the week. I'm giving orders to strike camp in fifteen minutes – please have the goodness not to keep me waiting any longer."

"No, Paco," Madelon murmured. She knew her brother had inherited their father's impatient nature and she did not want to rouse him to anger, for it would only serve as an unnecessary reminder of the man who had parted her from her beloved mother when she was only a young girl and condemned her to a life of seclusion. He had hated her because she was a girl and had never tired of humiliating her.

Outside the tent she could hear her brother's authoritative

voice issuing orders to the soldiers. With a smile she sat down on one of the trunks containing the sumptuous array of clothes which had been made especially for her court début. Her first new clothes in almost three years. All the materials had been sent by the king's sister, Urraca, and brought by one of her own dressmakers and an escort of liveried servants. Doña Urraca would look after her, Madelon thought, but for her thoughtfulness she would have had to appear at court looking like a pauper.

One of Madelon's serving women brought her a white silk cloak which she placed around her mistress's shoulders, drawing the hood over her hair and face to protect them from the sun, but as soon as she was out in the open and she felt the warm sun on her cheeks, Madelon pushed it back. How wonderful it was to be able to do as she pleased without a disapproving look or rebuke from the sour-faced duenna her father had sent to the convent with her. She was free – and no longer under surveillance, for at the last moment the woman had decided she was too old to travel the countryside where the danger of attack from Moors and Christians alike was always imminent and she had remained in the peaceful convent. Madelon had been sent several serving women trained to anticipate her every wish by the Doña Urraca. They were young and inclined to be scatterbrained, but Madelon did not care. She could laugh with them and ask questions of the court. She knew far more of what went on there than her brother realized, but she had not enlightened him, knowing he would chide her for becoming friendly with her servants.

Paco was proud of his name and of the fact the Montevides family were related to the Kings of Leon and Castile. He was an alférez, a general in command of Alfonso's most skilled fighting men and he worshipped his king with a blind devotion both admired and ridiculed by his fellow officers.

Madelon wandered past the soldiers and servants busy dismantling the tents. It was not hard to pick out Paco's lean shape among the blue-liveried servants, for his voice, raised loudly in anger, led her to where he stood remonstrating his sergeant-at-arms. To her surprise she saw he had donned armour. It gleamed in the strong sunlight and made him look a different person. She had never known Paco, the soldier, as well as she had known Paco, the brother.

"It would not be wise to interrupt Don Paco at the moment, Doña Madelon," a voice remarked behind her.

She turned to look into the smiling face of her brother's second-in-command. Captain Rodriguez was in his late twenties, extremely handsome and with an eye for a pretty face as Madelon had discovered at an early stage, but she was still innocent enough to be flattered by his attentions without reading any ulterior motive into them. It was Paco who did that, on the second evening of their journey after he had discovered his captain kissing his sister's hand behind her tent. Madelon protested they had merely been talking, but still her brother lectured her until she thought her eardrums would burst. She could see nothing wrong in a little harmless conversation and after the solitude of the convent, with only the nuns or her duenna to talk to, or occasionally a learned tutor, she was grateful to anyone who took the trouble to be nice to her.

The man is a philandering rogue, Paco told her harshly. What defences do you think you have against his smooth tongue – you, a child fresh out of a convent? What do you, know of life? Madelon had no answer to the latter question for she had no knowledge of either love – or life beyond the walls of her prison until Paco came to fetch her, but as for the other, she assured him in no uncertain terms that she had not defied their father and his threats and received the ultimate whipping which had resulted in her being confined to bed for a month – or her three years of loneliness, to fall into the arms of the first man who smiled at her. She remembered her words as she stood looking at Captain Rodriguez, conscious of the admiration in his eyes and silently thrilled by it.

"Your horse is saddled and waiting, my lady."

The captain signalled a groom who came across to where they stood leading a chestnut mare. She had been a present from Paco to his sister, and Madelon, who had not ridden since she was in her early teens, took great delight in riding off alone, another offence which earned her the sharp end of Paco's tongue. Captain Rodriguez helped her to mount. Madelon suspected his hand lingered a moment longer than was necessary on hers, before he placed the reins in her hands and moved across to his own mount.

"You were disobeying me again." Paco was beside her, intent on adjusting one of the stirrups. When he looked up Madelon saw his brown eyes were hard and angry.

"Captain Rodriguez merely helped me to mount my horse," Madelon protested. "I didn't even speak to him. I am beginning to find your attitude rather childish, Paco. Your concern as my brother, I understand, but this goes beyond those bounds. I am as much a prisoner as if I'd stayed at the convent."

To her surprise she saw a flush steal over Paco's sunburnt features. The anger vanished instantly and he caught her hands in his with an apologetic smile.

"You are right, little one. Forgive me, but every time I see my captain or any of the men look at you, it makes my blood boil. All any of them have ever had are common peasant women or town whores. I'm a soldier too and I've had my share of women, so I know what I'm talking about and what they are thinking when their eyes follow you."

"Are you jealous?" Madelon asked, astounded.

"Why not? My little sister has grown into a woman of great beauty and I want you all to myself – to get close to you – as close as we were as children. Do you remember those times, Madelon, before father sent you away for the first time? You always came to me when he made you unhappy and I always let you join in my games because you were as sturdy as any boy and you didn't burst into tears every time I won a battle, like all the girls I knew."

Madelon nodded, her eyes growing misty at the remembrance of a childhood that had been both miserable and wonderful. Paco had made it wonderful for her and she had cried until she made herself ill when she had been parted from him at the age of ten. She did not see him again until her sixteenth birthday. The strict convent life had curbed her wild temper, tempered an impetuous nature into docility and produced a quiet, impeccably mannered lady from a wilful child.

Madelon had not been at home a week when her father announced her betrothal to the Count Don Fernando Gomez and all her hopes that her homecoming had been in an attempt to reconcile their differences, were dashed to the ground. She knew nothing of her future husband and had been disciplined sufficiently to accept the fact that she must marry whoever her father chose and be a good wife, whatever her own feelings in the matter, but the sight of the little, wizened man panting across the room to meet her on the night of her betrothal ball sent all the years of training spinning into the dark recesses of her mind. She could not marry that horrible creature. The apparition smiled and she saw he had no teeth – took her hand in his and kissed it and she felt as if she had been touched by death itself. As she ran from the room, pushing her way past startled, open-mouthed guests, shutting her ears to the angry roar of her father as he came after her, Madelon remembered thinking how much he must hate her.

No amount of threats on the part of her father, or persuasion by her tearful mother would induce her to go back downstairs. She was locked in her room for a week on a diet of bread and water, and allowed no visitors. Paco climbed up to her bedroom window with a basket full of fresh fruit and spent several hours trying to make her see reason, but Madelon was adamant, declaring she would spend the rest of her life in seclusion before surrendering herself to Count Don Fernando Gomez. Her father pleaded with her, for the good of their family name. Her conduct was bringing shame on them all, he told her. When the pleas ran out he threatened again and at last resorted to the whip. Had Paco not intervened, Madelon knew she would have died from that terrible beating. Even now she still bore several scars on her back which would remain with her for the rest of her life. It was Paco who reminded her of her vow to return to the convent rather than marry against her will. She knew he did it to warn her of the grim alternative; the thought of growing old, alone and unwanted, imprisoned within the same stone walls until the day she died and she could still recall to mind the look of pain on his face when she voiced her refusal to the marriage for the last time. He had expected her to give in.

From that day – until the day she left home a month later – Madelon had no contact with any of her family and she only glimpsed Paco for a brief moment as the litter bore her over the drawbridge, before the duenna closed the curtains and shut out sixteen years of her life.

Madelon drew a hand across her eyes to blot out the pain on her brother's face as he stepped back from her horse. Of course, now she understood! What an idiot she was. Paco blamed himself for her being sent away a second time, that was the reason for his possessiveness. He wanted to make up for those lost years.

Impulsively she leant down and kissed him on the forehead. "There was a bond between us when we were children, Paco, and it's still with us. No separation, however long, could erase the love I have for you. Be patient with me. I'm like a young bird who has just discovered it can fly. There are no walls about me any more and I can fly as far as I please. I've wanted to tell you how I feel, but it's difficult because you have never been cooped up the way I was – and the memory isn't exactly pleasant. Be patient, please."

The adoring look Paco gave her was sufficient to tell her he understood.

Night camp had been made on a hard sun-baked plateau accessible only by a steep path which rendered it invincible against a surprise attack. Several times Madelon had been awakened by the lusty howl of a wolf somewhere on the plains below.

It was past mid-day by the time the last horseman had

descended the narrow, rocky trail to the plains. Paco, riding out in front, paused to pick a handful of red poppies and daisies which he presented to his sister with great ceremony. Madelon thanked him and used the heavy silver brooch from her cloak to fasten a large daisy onto the blue tunic he wore over his chain mail.

"My God, the men will think I've taken leave of my senses," he said with a grimace.

Madelon reined in her horse and soaked her handkerchief in water from the goatskin bag tied around the pommel of the saddle. The cool touch of it on her burning face was heaven.

"Can't we rest for a while? We've been riding for hours," she begged. The sun was too hot for her to remove her cloak and risk burnt arms, and beneath the enveloping folds her dress clung uncomfortably to her perspiring body.

"In a while perhaps, if we can rid ourselves of our unwelcome guests. So far they have kept their distance, but if we make camp they may decide to pay us a visit."

Madelon turned in the saddle, her eyes following his pointing finger. Outlined against the skyline behind them was another band of horsemen.

"Moors," Paco said shortly.

"Moors!" She looked at him in horror. "What are they doing here?"

"Taking advantage of the unrest and petty squabbles which is driving Leon and Castile apart instead of uniting it. King Ferdinand was a fool to divide the kingdoms."

"But if he had given everything to Sancho, the eldest son, would you have served him as you serve Alfonso? I have never heard you speak well of him, even though he is our cousin."

"If he was my king, I'd respect him and give him my loyalty," Paco retorted, "even as I now give it to his brother. But he isn't my lord. He's a greedy, loudmouthed fool who can't be content with one kingdom, he has to try and steal his brother's as well. He's been making treaties with some of the Moors, making promises he has no intention of keeping, to get their armies on his side."

"Christians and Moslems fighting together, it's unheard of," Madelon said in disgust.

"To oust his brother from the throne of Leon, he will use any means in his power. I've heard it said he entertains the Moorish king of Badajoz at his court. If they join forces Leon will have enemies on both its borders. He even sends his alférez into their camps with gifts and offers of peace. Rodrigo Díaz, may he be cursed by heaven, has an army of Moorish soldiers he can call on at any time. They even call him El Seid – the Lord."

Madelon looked at him curiously. There was something odd in his tone when he mentioned that name. She watched his fingers roving over a jagged scar on one temple. She had noticed it before, but knew it would be tactless to ask how he got it.

"You are remarkably well informed, Paco."

"It's my job to know what goes on in Castile. Don Alfonso has ordered me to find out what allies his brother has among the Moors and then seek them out and persuade them to join us – or destroy them."

"Kill them . . . ?"

Paco's eyes narrowed at the disbelief in her voice.

"I too have grown up, little sister. I no longer play at war. Do you know what these Moorish dogs do with their captives? The men are sold as galley slaves. They die a slow death, chained to an oar they will not be free of until the day they die and their bodies are flung overboard. The women and children are sold in slave markets. Christian women fetch a good price on the auction block. Those that don't kill themselves when they are first taken, and many do, are bought for harems, where they are subjected to God only knows what kind of indignities. I've only known of one woman being found by her relatives after she'd been captured and that was the wife of one of my lieutenants. She was among a band of Moors we captured near the border, a year after her disappearance. She was twenty and she looked forty. She'd been sold four times and tortured beyond belief until she no longer cared

who her master was or what was done to her, so long as she
had enough food to eat. When she recognized her husband
and saw in his eyes what she had become, she killed herself."

"How awful." Madelon shivered, despite the heat. "Don
Sancho must be mad to enlist the aid of such terrible people."

"Greed turns men into animals," Paco told her gravely.
"Ride on and keep close to me. If we are attacked, ride as if
the devil was after you and stop for nothing."

Madelon tried to forget her brother's words and the horsemen dogging their rear whenever she glanced back over her
shoulder. Since leaving Salamanca, where they had stayed for
the first night after her departure from the convent, the
countryside had gradually grown more beautiful. On one side
of them was a huge grassy plain full of wild flowers and just
visible on the far horizon, a large flock of sheep grazing on
bare hills. To the west was Moorish Castile, the border marked
by a towering range of mountains. Shielding her eyes to study
them, Madelon was seized with a sudden sense of foreboding
at the sight of the formidable peaks. Beyond lay the kingdoms
of Toledo, Badajoz, Valencia and to the far south, Seville,
with their strange beliefs and barbaric customs. Slave ships
with their human cargoes bound for the slave markets,
seraglios crowded with scantily-clad women awaiting the
commands of their lords and masters, those swarthy-faced
men who considered them mere chattels, to be sold again at
will or disposed of in any way they chose. As Madelon dragged
her eyes away from the tall peaks she found herself thinking
her father must have had Moorish blood in him.

Spurring her horse to catch up with her brother, Madelon
marvelled at the hue of colours everywhere. The bright red
and white flowers against the green blanket of tall trees, falling
away to paler yellow-green slopes where the sheep grazed like
little black beetles. The brown mountains growing darker as
they soared upwards to pierce a cloudless blue sky. She had
watched the sun set the previous evening from the plateau
and caught her breath in wonder as the sky was set on fire by
the dying sun.

Captain Rodriguez galloping up to her brother, rudely cut short her pleasant thoughts. He was pointing ahead to the heavy cloud of smoke which hung over the far end of the valley they were just entering.

Paco swung round, issuing orders too swift for Madelon to catch. Motioning his squire to stay with the mules and luggage, he said tersely,

"Stay here, there may be trouble ahead."

"What kind of trouble?" Madelon began, but he was already riding away from her, taking with him all the soldiers, with the exception of four left to guard the women. Scarcely had they disappeared from sight over the hill, than one of Madelon's women let out a terrified scream.

The rebuke which rose to Madelon's lips was never uttered. Horsemen were converging on them from all sides. The sunlight flashed on long, curved swords and filled the hearts of the onlookers with a cold, numbing fear.

"Moors, my lady, what can we do?" Doña Elvira, the youngest of Madelon's maids cried out.

"After the soldiers – hurry – we'll be safe with them," Madelon shouted and spurred her horse into a gallop.

The thunder of hooves grew louder behind them and by the time the small party rode into the burning village, their pursuers were uncomfortably close. Wide-eyed, Madelon gazed at the bodies strewn on the ground before the drab, stone hovels, many of which were burning fiercely. With rising panic she noticed that the only women who had been killed were old or feeble and as such, were unrewarding prospects for the slave markets to which the other poor souls were undoubtedly heading.

"This way," Paco came out of the smoke and haze in front of her, gesticulating wildly for her to turn about. "It's a trap, there's no way out. They knew this would attract us and like a fool I fell for it."

"We can't go back," one of the women sobbed. "Dear heaven, we are all going to be killed."

Paco took one look at the frightened faces confronting him

and then reached forward and grabbed Madelon's bridle. Shouting to his men to follow, he urged his horse up a rocky slope, cursing profusely as it stumbled and almost toppled him from the saddle. Behind him Captain Rodriguez was shouting at the women to hurry and deploying the soldiers in a long line to cover their rear.

Paco and Madelon reached the top of the slope and were about to descend the other side when, behind them, came the ominous sound of steel clashing against steel and the screaming of women.

"Ride on," Paco ordered. "I must go back."

"No. If you stay, I do too."

Madelon swung her horse about to follow him back, but her brother's hand fastened over her arm and held her fast. The Moors had reached the village and the slopes below them were covered with fighting men. Madelon caught a glimpse of Captain Rodriguez, his face streaked with blood, battling with four of his men against an overwhelming number of Moors who were trying to reach the women. She shuddered and closed her eyes. When she opened them again, Elvira was lying prostrate on the ground with several bearded men tearing away her clothing. Another girl, who had managed to run a few yards, was overpowered and dragged back to where the Moors were examining their captives. Captain Rodriguez lay in a pool of blood, obviously dead.

With a moan, Madelon slumped forward over the saddle, near to fainting. Paco gripped her by the hair and jerked her upright and the pain restored her fading senses as he knew it would.

"Ride, Madelon. No matter what happens – ride."

She did not need to be told a second time. The wind whipped away her cloak and sent it swirling to the ground behind her as she galloped down the slope. Paco kept abreast with her, urging her on as one horseman, then two, appeared on the hill behind them. As they circled around and came past the entrance to the valley, half a dozen more rode out to meet them. Following Paco's frantic signals, Madelon wheeled her horse away towards the distant mountains. She rode with fear in her heart such as she had never known before. Not even the beating inflicted by her father had caused her to tremble so violently. She was shaking from head to toe and scarcely able to stay upright in the saddle. How she kept a tight hold on the reins or endured the tortuous ride she never knew.

No matter how mercilessly they spurred their horses or doubled back on their tracks in an effort to lose their pursuers, the Moors stayed doggedly behind them, growing closer with every mile. So too were the mountains ahead of them. It was in Madelon's mind they were being deliberately driven in this direction and once there, how many more of the cruel barbarians would be waiting for them.

Ahead of her Paco's horse stumbled, throwing him heavily to the ground. Staggering to his feet he pulled out his sword, waving her to ride on, but she went back calling to him urgently.

"We can ride together, quickly ..."

"The animal's too tired to carry both of us ... get out of here ..."

He was sent sprawling to the ground by the weight of the two Moors who flung themselves on him from their horses. Madelon screamed as she saw one of them plunge a dagger into her brother's body and then she too, was grabbed by numerous hands and dragged from the saddle. She kicked and bit and was cuffed so violently on the side of the head, she lost consciousness ...

She was brought back to her senses by the unpleasant sensation of someone's hands roaming in a crude fashion over her body. She was lying on a grassy spot at the foot of the mountains, surrounded at a distance by her Moorish captors. All their eyes to the last man were focused on the newest acquisition to what had so far been a profitable day and envying their leader who was examining her with great relish.

Madelon gave a scream as bony fingers fastened in the silk of her gown and tore it open, exposing her naked to the waist. Instinctively she tried to cover herself, but another blow to the head sent her crashing to the ground where she lay too stunned to move again or protest as the Moor ran his calloused hands over her breasts and shoulders, muttering to his men as he did so and evoking roars of laughter.

With a grunt of satisfaction he stood up, motioning to one man to remain with Madelon and issued orders to the remainder which sent them hurrying to their horses. Weakly Madelon sat up, trying to gather together the remnants of her bodice about her as best she could and looking around for Paco. When the Moors returned she had no doubt she would be on her way to a slave market. The thought made her feel sick and faint. To her right a weak voice called her name.

"Madelon, are you all right? I saw what that swine did ... Oh, God, if only I had a sword ..."

Madelon flung herself down beside her brother with a glad cry but the relief on her face turned to dismay as she saw his tunic was soaked with blood. The attack on him had been so savage, the surcoat of mail had served as little or no protection and he had received several wounds.

"Escape while you can," Paco urged.

"I won't leave you."

Somehow Madelon managed to tear away his tunic and fashion it into rough bandages which she packed under the blood-stained coat of mail as best she could. Her heart almost failed her as she looked into Paco's pain-ravaged face. He was too weak to move far and she would not go without him, but if they did not escape and reach a doctor quickly, he would surely die and she would become some man's bought slave. She checked the sob which rose to her lips, determined to show the bravery he expected from her, but realizing he had lapsed into unconsciousness, she slipped down in a pathetic huddle beside him, crying bitterly.

CHAPTER
TWO

A MUFFLED groan roused Madelon from near insensibility. Dazedly she pulled herself upright, wincing as a pain shot through her head and the bright sunlight seared her vision momentarily blinding her. Paco lay unconscious at her side – for a moment she had thought it had been he who moaned. And then she saw the Moor who had been left to guard her was sprawled on the ground and another man, enveloped from head to toe in a flowing white burnous similar to the ones worn by her captors, was rising to his feet. At the sound, slight though it was, the man spun around, his dagger raised. Beneath the shadow of his hood, Madelon glimpsed a sunburnt face and glittering pale green eyes which immediately betrayed the fact that he was no Moor. He laid a finger against his lips, warning her to be silent at the same time motioning to the second man slowly creeping up behind the leader of the Moors, who stood with his back to them, watching for the return of his men.

It was over in an instant and Madelon realized they had been rescued, but even as she opened her mouth to question her rescuers, her eyes fell on the two servants who had just come into view leading several horses. They were Moors. She and Paco were still prisoners. Desperately she looked about her for something to defend herself and her wounded brother. Half buried in the ground a few feet away lay a curved dagger. She pounced on it and stood over Paco's body, the weapon held high in the air, ready to strike the first man who came near enough.

"Put that down, we mean you no harm."

The man with the green eyes tossed aside his cloak. Beneath

he wore a pair of hide breeches and a dark-coloured shirt.
Over this was a tunic which had a huge eagle embroidered
on it. His blond hair was bleached almost white by the sun.
He was no Moor, Madelon thought, then why were those men
with him? He sounded sincere enough, but she kept a tight
hold on the knife just the same.

"Who are you? If you mean us no harm why do you travel
in the company of those murdering devils?" She nodded
towards the Moors.

The second man, having disposed of his victim, came across
to join his companion. From beneath the burnous emerged a
giant of a man with flaming red hair and a beard to match.
The eyes which swept over Madelon were bright with amusement and made her colour hotly and clutch more tightly at her
torn bodice.

"By all the saints, we have a firebrand here. Valentín is
right, gracious lady. If we meant to harm you we would not be
keeping our distance this way. Come now, stand aside and
let us see if we can help your husband."

"He's my brother, and neither of you is going to lay a finger
on him until I know who you are."

She swept the hair back from her face with a defiant gesture
that brought a soft whistle of admiration from the red-headed
man, as her bodice slipped away from milk-white shoulders.
His companion said nothing and his gaze, although it never
moved from Madelon's face, was unreadable. She did not
notice the way he was gradually sidling closer.

"Allow me to introduce us. My friend is Valentín Maratín
de Aguilas, quite a nice sort of fellow really," the giant said
with a smile which she supposed was meant to vanquish her
fears. "I am Rodrigo Díaz de Vivar ..."

A soft cry broke from Madelon's lips as her fast rising hopes
were dashed to pieces by his words. This was the man Paco
had spoken of with such venom in his voice ... the one the
Moors called 'the Lord'. These men were Castilians. As much
her enemies and her brother's as the Moors had been. Driven
almost out of her mind by fear she acted without thinking

and threw herself forward meaning to plunge the dagger into the heart of the man before her, but she was suddenly caught in a grip of steel and the weapon wrenched from her grasp. Her wrists were imprisoned behind her back by Valentín Maratín despite her frantic struggles and when she continued to fight, ignoring his warning to be still, he wound his hand in her loose hair and jerked her head back cruelly.

"Be still."

Madelon cried out in pain and instantly obeyed.

"That is no way to treat the poor girl," Rodrigo Díaz reproved, though he made no move to help her. He stood for a long while studying the sobbing, dishevelled girl whose long, blonde hair had fallen forward over her shoulders to cover her nakedness almost as effectively as a dress would have done, then he dropped on one knee beside the wounded Paco. Madelon heard him mutter a string of oaths and thinking the worst she tried to break free of the man restraining her, but the last of her strength was gone. Sensing her thoughts, Rodrigo Díaz looked up and shook his head.

"No, he isn't dead, but he'd prefer to die than have me help him."

"You know him?" his friend demanded. His voice sounded harsh and impatient.

"One of Alfonso's men – Paco del Rivas y Montevides. I killed his father in combat last month."

Madelon's legs gave way beneath her and she would have fallen but for the support of the man behind her. So that was how her father had met his death. Paco had told her no details and she had asked for none, she did not want to remember a man who hated her. Rodrigo turned and stared at her thoughtfully.

"You say you are his sister. I didn't know he had one."

"I – I have been away from home for a long time."

Rodrigo threw her a puzzled look, but she was too exhausted to answer any further questions and he seemed to sense this.

"Get him on to a horse and let's get away from here before

the others come back," Valentín Maratín said. Madelon found herself abruptly released. Brushing past her he stooped to pick up his cloak and then bent over her brother and wrapped it around him. "If he doesn't get attention he'll be dead by nightfall," he remarked calmly. "Yusuf's camp is the nearest."

Madelon suddenly found a reserve of energy and jumped in front of him, thrusting away the hands he stretched out to lift Paco.

"Where are you taking us? Who is Yusuf?"

"A friend of mine."

"A Moor?" There was a hysterical note in her voice and the two men exchanged glances.

"Yes. He has a doctor in his camp. Your brother will receive the best possible attention and when he's well you can both resume your journey," Valentín Maratín answered.

Once again the sincerity in his voice tempted Madelon to trust him, but the appearance of the two Moors at her elbow made her bend more protectingly over her brother.

Valentín Maratín uttered a sharp command in Arabic to his swarthy companions, who nodded silently and fell back. Madelon's eyes followed them apprehensively. She still had visions of herself on an auction block.

"Get up," Valentín ordered Madelon. "You can come with us or stay, the choice is yours. You should fetch a good price in the slave market with that golden hair. Some rich merchant will probably buy you for his harem and if you behave yourself, you have the looks to become his chief concubine."

"Doña Madelon, be sensible, for your brother's sake as well as your own," Rodrigo Díaz said gently.

When Madelon did not move, the man before her gave a shrug of his shoulders and turned away.

"Let the little fool stay where she is."

"No – please – help us."

It took the last of Madelon's courage to force the words through her stiff lips. Even as she said them she was afraid of what she had done. With a relieved sigh Rodrigo passed his friend the cloak he had been wearing. Valentín Maratín raised

Madelon to her feet and supporting her with one hand, as she was trembling so violently she could not stand by herself, he fastened the cloak around her, tucking her loose hair into the cowl, which he pulled well forward over her tear-streaked face.

"Poor little thing, you've had a bad time, haven't you," he murmured in a far different tone to any he had so far used with her. The harshness had gone out of his expression too and the smile he bestowed on her was almost friendly, although Madelon noticed it did not reach his hard, brilliant eyes. After his rough treatment of her, this unexpected kindness was too much for her to endure. She felt herself grasped firmly around the waist as she began to sway, then nothing ... as she slipped down, down into merciful oblivion.

The sound of voices made Madelon cautiously open her eyes. Still wrapped in the cloak, she found herself lying on a velvet-covered divan in a tent hung with silk drapes. A small table stood nearby, the carved top cleverly inlaid with gold and silver, and beyond, clustered around another divan were a group of men deep in conversation.

Rodrigo Díaz and his green-eyed companion she recognized instantly. The other two men were strangers. One was old and grey haired and wore a strange looking cap on his head, and sombre-coloured clothes. The other was tall and very good looking, dressed in white flowing robes. His black cloak was lined with yellow silk and fastened at the shoulder by a heavy jewelled brooch. A turban was wound around his head and jewels flashed at the front of this and on his fingers as he motioned to the slave girl hovering at his elbow to move back. He had a swarthy complexion, with dark piercing eyes which suddenly darted across to where Madelon lay studying him. She saw the flash of white teeth as he smiled and touched the arm of the man beside him.

"Your golden captive is awake, Valentín," he said quietly.

"For heaven's sake don't call her that or she'll be looking

around for another knife," Valentín Maratín laughed dryly.

As the men moved away from the divan Madelon saw they had hidden Paco from her view. His blood-streaked clothes had been removed and the knife wounds in his chest carefully bandaged. He lay still, deathlike beneath the multi-coloured blankets drawn up beneath his armpits. With a distressed cry she scrambled off the divan, only remembering at the last moment to clutch tightly at the cloak covering her state of undress, and fell on her knees beside her brother. How white he was and she could see no sign of breathing.

"He – he isn't – dead?" she faltered.

It was the tall Moor who raised her to her feet again, his eyes roving sympathetically over her ashen face.

"My own doctor is attending him. Everything possible has been done. You have had an unpleasant experience, but it is over now, thanks to the intervention of my two good friends. You must rest and forget it ever happened."

"While my brother lies so near death's door? You ask too much," Madelon said bitterly. "Had he not been wounded I would not have come here of my own free will. Today many fine men died and my serving women have either been killed or sold into slavery. You are a Moor and I shall never forget what I saw your people do – nor will I forgive them."

She heard a smothered oath behind her and saw the anger which flashed into the eyes of the Moor, but it vanished as quickly as it came. He touched his forehead, mouth and chest with his fingertips, which she took to be some kind of salutation, and bowed before her.

"I respect your feelings, golden one – and I admire your courage. My only regret is that it was not I who found you. Such beauty is wasted on my brother, Valentín. I alone, would fully appreciate it and in my arms you would soon have learned not all our hearts as as dark as our faces. As my company is so distasteful to you, I will leave. Will you join me, my lord Rodrigo? I have rather a fine young colt I would like to show you."

"Gladly."

Rodrigo de Vivar threw a half angry, half amused glance at Madelon and followed the Moor out of the tent, leaving her alone with Valentín Maratín and the old man.

"If you were a Moorish girl, Yusuf would have had you whipped for such rudeness," the former said coldly. "As his guest the least you can do is be civil."

"You could have taken us somewhere else," Madelon returned with a sudden flash of temper. She was desperately tired and wanting to sleep, but she would not show it to this hateful man.

"This camp was the nearest. Coming here kept your brother alive."

"I only have your word for that," Madelon said, although deep in her heart she knew it was the truth. "The word of a man who prefers the company of Moslems to Christians. If that wasn't bad enough, you are a friend of Rodrigo Díaz, my brother's enemy. You treat me little better than a servant girl and yet I am supposed to trust you with our lives."

"I'm not interested whether or not you condescend to trust me," the Castilian answered calmly. "As soon as your brother is fit to travel, we shall part company, but until then you will do as your are told, or it will give me great pleasure to put you over my knee and treat you as I do all spoilt children."

Madelon flushed to the roots of her hair, speechless with rage. While he had been speaking, his hardness of tone had not been unlike that of her father and unknowingly he had aroused unpleasant memories. At last she found her voice.

"Your lack of chivalry towards women is understandable, Don Valentín," she said with immense dignity and cast a look around at her surroundings to signify her point. "However I hope you will at least have the decency to leave me in peace with my brother. We have nothing further to say to each other."

"First you must rest. I'll have some clothes found for you."

Madelon's eyes rested on the silent girl at the foot of Paco's bed. Her clothes were thin, flimsy garments and Madelon instinctively wrapped herself more firmly in her cloak. The infuriating smile on the face of the Castilian told her he had guessed her thoughts.

"I will stay here with Paco. I want nothing from you."

Valentín Maratín shrugged carelessly and strode out of the tent. As the silken entrance closed behind him, Madelon became aware of the old man looking at her and shaking his head.

"When a man saves your life you do not reward him with harsh words and send him away," he murmured. "You are foolish to prefer a man like Valentín for an enemy rather than a friend. He told you the truth, you know, your brother's wounds are serious. Had he not received my assistance, he would have bled to death."

Madelon gazed a long time into the serene face before her. Aged though it was and lined with wrinkles, there was something about it which calmed her fears. She knew she had found a true friend.

"You are the doctor Don Rodrigo spoke of," she said.

"Yes. My name is Abraham ben Canaan."

"You are not a Moslem."

"I'm a Jew. Does it matter to you what I am as long as I can help your brother?" The soft voice was gently tinged with mockery.

Madelon shook her head.

"My brother is the most important person in my life – please don't let him die," she whispered.

The tears she had so successfully hidden from Valentín Maratín broke loose in a tumultuous flood and she slipped sobbing to the floor. She wept as she had never wept before as the pent up emotions of the last few hours swept over her. Shocked – frightened – too utterly weary to try and control the reaction which now claimed her, she lay on the richly patterned carpet oblivious to the doctor's urgent tones above her – and the hands which tried unsuccessfully to lift her from her pathetic huddle.

"Let me take her."

She knew the voice, but she could not put a face to it. She moaned as she was lifted upwards and the sudden movement caused a knife-like pain to sear across her temples.

"Too much sun," the voice said.

Madelon fought to hold on to her swiftly receding senses as she became aware of the protective cloak being drawn away and then her torn dress being gently removed from her bruised and aching body. Opening her eyes she discovered she was lying in a large bed. The face of Valentín Maratín hovered above her. She was resting in the crook of his arm and he was holding a goblet to her lips.

"Drink it, you little golden savage."

His green eyes burned into her colourless face, daring her to refuse. Worn out in both mind and body Madelon was in no condition to take up the challenge. Wordlessly she swallowed the contents of the cup, which were sweet and syrupy, with a taste reminiscent of spiced ginger. When she awoke, it was the following day . . .

For a long time she lay listening to the sound of shouting and laughing, mingled with the fierce thudding of horses' hooves which came from outside her tent. She was warm and still rather sleepy and in no hurry to leave the comfortable bed. She had been exhausted, Madelon thought, and unable to look at things in their right perspective, or she would have realized her foolishness in treating Valentín Maratín and his Moorish friend with such contempt. She and her brother were guests at the moment, but they could so easily turn into prisoners. Their relationship to the King of Leon would make them valuable captives, for although Sancho and Alfonso were brothers, the former had shown a positive dislike for the Montevides family at an early age and since his accession to the throne, had refused to acknowledge any kinship whatsoever between them. Until Paco was able to defend himself again, she would have to control her dislike of her rescuers. Somehow this morning their plight did not seem so terrible.

A slight movement by the entrance made her draw herself up on one elbow. A dark-haired girl came in carrying a tray which she set down on the stool beside the bed. She motioned to the array of delicious looking food with a shy smile.

"Valentín asked me to bring you some breakfast. He said you were probably starving."

"I am. I'm also in need of some clothes – not those awful flimsy things, something like yours perhaps." Madelon was looking at the girl's plain green sleeveless robe. It looked very cool and was not too revealing. She noticed this girl bore a striking resemblance to Abraham ben Canaan.

"I will find something for you."

"Wait, please." Stretching out her hand, Madelon caught the girl's arm. "Stay and talk to me for a while."

"I was told to let you rest, but – very well, for a little while then." The girl perched herself on the edge of the bed and helped herself to a sweetmeat from a silver dish on the tray. "My name is Rebecca. My father is looking after the man who was brought in yesterday, your brother isn't he?"

Madelon nodded.

"I am Madelon del Rivas y Montevides."

"I know," Rebecca said, with another shy smile. "Valentín has told me all about you. It was lucky he was out chasing Mahmud's raiders or you might never have been rescued."

Madelon took a tentative bite from one of the small sugared cakes near her and found to her delight they were quite delicious.

"Paco and I were lucky, I suppose."

"Luckier than the poor people in the village Mahmud raided – or your servants. Valentín said there were some women taken captive."

"Yes, four. They were alive when I last saw them, but now – " Madelon broke off with a shudder. "Yesterday I couldn't bear to think about it. I must have had a wonderful sleep."

"That was due to the sleeping potion Valentin gave you,"

Rebecca said cheerfully. "He said you were asleep before he left the tent last night."

Madelon was suddenly wide awake. With rising colour she remembered someone undressing her and putting her to bed.

"Don Valentín took care of me?" she managed to gasp at last.

"He wouldn't let anyone else near you. I was worried he wouldn't be able to quieten you, but Valentín has a way with him. He can be rough, but also very gentle. He is not an easy man to understand. You must not be embarrassed, he thought no more of putting you to bed, than he would one of his own men injured in battle," Rebecca added as Madelon's cheeks began to burn fiercely. She looked at the fair-haired girl curiously. "Did you really threaten poor Rodrigo with a dagger?"

"Please, don't remind me of that." Madelon grimaced, remembering how Valentín Maratín had seized hold of her. Looking down at her wrists she saw a small bruise on the inside of each where he had gripped them so tightly. "I thought they meant to harm Paco – Rodrigo Diaz killed our father," she added by way of explanation.

"I'm sorry," Rebecca murmured. "I had no idea. It is natural you should hate him."

"I don't hate him. I've only hated one man in my life and he's dead now," Madelon answered.

"Was he a cruel man?"

"Yes, he was my father." Seeing Rebecca's shocked expression, Madelon hastened to explain how she had been brought up in a convent because her father had not wanted a girl and of her refusal to marry an old man.

"Do you mean you have spent most of your life away from your family? What a terrible man he must have been. Why was it so important for you to marry this Count Gomez?"

Madelon shrugged her slim shoulders. She sat in the middle of the huge bed, her arms locked around her hunched-up knees.

"He was very rich, it would have been a good match as far

as my family was concerned, but I think it was because my father wanted to get rid of me. Anyway it's over now. When Paco is well we will join the king at Santa María de Carrion and I can forget I was ever unhappy."

"How I envy you," Rebecca breathed. "I would love to see all the beautiful women in their fine clothes and jewels. Rodrigo has promised to take me to court, but father will not allow it."

"Why not?" Madelon asked, wondering why the invitation had come from Rodrigo and not his arrogant companion.

"We are Jews. Twice we have been driven from our homes. Once by your King Alfonso, and then by his brother. Wherever we went people turned against us as they learned of our faith. We would be accused of awful things. Father was never able to practise medicine even though he is the finest doctor in Spain. In Castile he was accused of sorcery and we barely escaped with our lives. Yusuf and his men found us in the mountains, half starved, and took us in. That was three years ago. He offered us what no one else would – a place to make our home. Telhan, where we live, is ten miles from here. We have a small house and many friends. No one calls us dirty heretics or drives us out into the night."

Madelon felt an overwhelming compassion for Rebecca and her father. In many ways they were alike.

"Perhaps your father might let you come to court if I asked him?" she said.

Rebecca sprang off the bed with a soft laugh.

"No, I don't think so. Besides if all the women are as beautiful as you I should be terribly jealous."

"I'm not beautiful," Madelon said, stretching her long legs beneath the sheets. "My duenna always said my eyes were too large to be attractive, my skin was unhealthily pale and my hair too straight. I am also too thin, which, according to her, means I shall never be able to bear strong children. She's probably right too. My mother was very slender. She died giving birth to the second son my father wanted so much. He didn't live more than a few hours ..." Madelon's eyes filled with pain and she could not continue.

Rebecca made no comment on the other girl's description of herself. She could have told her how Valentín had praised her courage and of the undisguised admiration in his voice as he spoke of the large blue eyes which had burned with defiance as she threatened them with her knife. A half-naked little wildcat, with eyes that shone like sapphires and skin gleaming like alabaster in the sunlight, prepared to do hopeless battle to save her wounded brother. A golden savage – that had been the way he described her.

"You are very beautiful," she said quietly. "May it bring you the happiness you deserve. I'll go and fetch some clothes for you now before Valentín comes looking for me."

"He already has."

The tall frame of the Lord de Aguilas stooped through the entrance. Rebecca wondered if he had been standing outside listening to their conversation – and if so, for how long. Madelon looked as if she was thinking the same thing. She had drawn the sheets tightly around her and was stubbornly avoiding looking at the newcomer.

Valentín stopped beside the bed and picked up the tray.

"I'm glad to see you had an appetite, Doña Madelon," he said, handing it to Rebecca who caught his significant nod and left the tent. "You must build up your strength. We leave the day after tomorrow for my castle in the Sierra de Gredos."

Madelon looked at him blankly, then an expression of absolute horror flashed into her eyes as she immediately suspected the worst.

"Paco!"

Bending over the bed, Valentín caught her wrist in a firm grasp as if it were his intention to shake her if she became hysterical, but the agony in her cry had touched his hard heart and he said gently, reassuringly.

"I was with the doctor a few moments ago and he assures me your brother is recovering. In a week or so – "

"A week," Madelon broke in, "but we are on our way to join the king at Santa María de Carrion ..."

"Where two kings intend to resolve their differences once

and for all. Rodrigo and I will escort you both as soon as your brother is fit enough to ride."

"I don't understand you," Madelon said.

Valentín's fingers uncurled from her wrist. He stared for a moment at the bruise there and she saw him frown at the realization that he had made it.

"You were making a long journey through hostile territory merely for health reasons, I suppose," he retorted sarcastically. "Why the thought of watching men die in combat appeals to women I shall never know. Your cousin Urraca loves to see men fighting under her nose – usually over her."

"So you know who we are. Is that why you want to act as a so-called escort? We are really prisoners."

"The tournament at Golpejerra will prove Don Sancho's true claim to the thrones of Castile and Leon," Valentín said grimly, giving her a look which contained both puzzlement and suspicion. "Am I to understand you know nothing of what is to take place?"

Mutely Madelon shook her head.

"Six knights chosen by each brother will engage in combat on the fields of Golpejerra, until quarter is called for. When it is over and we Castilians have wiped the floor with your Leonese knights, Castile and Leon will be ruled by one king only."

And Paco would be one of Alfonso's chosen men, Madelon thought dazedly. That was why he had been so eager to reach their destination. She would hate every moment she was there, but it had been important enough for him to want her and so no matter what happened she must not let him know how worried she would be.

"Thank you for telling me, Don Valentín. I assure you I have no desire to watch men being hurt, but if it is Paco's wish I watch him fight, then I will."

"And if he loses, no doubt you will challenge the victor," Valentín mocked.

His remark brought to mind his words of the previous

evening. Somehow she forced herself to meet his searching gaze.

"Last night you called me – a – savage. Why?"

"A golden savage. Like a wild horse you have yet to be broken. The man who tames you will gain himself a great prize, but I fear there are no men capable of such a task at the court of Alfonso."

As Madelon sat with cheeks flaming, he bowed low before her and was gone before she could think of anything to say in answer.

The dress Rebecca brought for Madelon was of pale yellow material. It had the feel of silk and was pleasantly cool on her skin. A tasselled belt accentuated her tiny waist. Madelon stood regarding herself in the gilt-framed mirror suspended from one of the silken walls. She could see no sign of a savage in the reflection facing her, in fact the reverse seemed to apply more aptly. She looked paler than usual and the long days of travelling had caused her hair to lose its usual lustre.

"Am I really beautiful, Rebecca?"

The Jewish girl nodded, smiling at her uncertainty. They had known each other only a short while, but already they were friends.

"Valentín tells me you will be leaving soon. I was hoping we would be able to spend more time together. I don't see many other girls of my own age – not that I can talk to as you and I have talked, you understand."

"Don Valentín is taking us to his castle." Madelon began to braid her hair into one thick plait, which hung forward over her shoulder. "I would like us to remain friends too, Rebecca, but I hate it here. I can't wait to get away."

"Valentín realizes this, that's why he has made other arrangements," Rebecca answered. "He doesn't want you to worry over what happened."

"How can I help it? I shall see the faces of those horrible men in my dreams until the day I die. How can you live with them?"

"I understand them," the girl replied simply. "To you some of their ways may seem barbaric, but I don't find them any crueller than the men and women who burnt my home and stoned my mother to death." Rebecca placed an arm around Madelon's shoulders, and smiled at her. "Try to forget it. Come and see your brother, he is conscious now."

CHAPTER
THREE

THE Jewish doctor Abraham ben Canaan was with Madelon's brother when she slipped into the tent.

"Good morning, Doña Madelon, you are looking better this morning. You obviously slept well."

"Don Valentín had no right to drug me," Madelon protested. The effects of the sleeping potion were wearing off now and she was remembering, with apprehension, Valentín Maratín's intention to take her and Paco to his home and wondering why she had not questioned it.

"Come now, it has done you no harm – far from it. You speak of him drugging you as if you think he had designs on your person. Believe me, nothing was further from his mind. He gave you a drug to help you sleep, a strong one I admit, but you were in great distress. I prepared it myself and one for your brother too and as you can see he is greatly improved this morning."

Madelon moved closer to where Paco lay and saw his eyes were open and he was trying weakly to smile at her. His face, although still pale, had lost that awful greyish tint which had caused her so much alarm earlier.

"Please forgive my foolishness," Madelon said contritely. "I know you mean us no harm."

"You should direct your apology to Valentín, my dear child. Not only did he rescue you, but he sent men after the unfortunate women taken by Mahmud's raiders. Why you seem to think he is an ogre with two heads, I don't know."

"I question his being here in this encampment," Madelon said, aware her brother was taking in every word of the conversation. The smile had vanished from his features and she

wondered if he had connected the name Valentín with anyone he knew.

"Do you question my being here?" Abraham ben Canaan
asked with a frown.

"No Rebecca told me something of your past troubles."

"And that Yusuf gave us a home when everyone else spat in
our faces?"

"Yes – but I understand that. The faith of Jews and Moslems is not unalike."

The doctor's small brown eyes studied Madelon with new
interest.

"A woman of learning," he exclaimed with a smile. "You
and I must have a long talk sometime. You are right, the two
faiths are similar but whereas the Christians refuse to accept
the existence of any form of worship other than their own,
the Moslems are more liberal. They not only acknowledge
other faiths, but allow men and women to live in peace and go
their own way."

"How can you say that when Moorish hordes incessantly
cross the borders of both Leon and Castile to plunder and kill
the Christian 'dogs' they hate so much. Is this the acknowledgement of other faiths you speak of?"

"That is no question for someone of your obvious intelli-
gence," Abraham ben Canaan chided softly. "Iberians –
Phoenicians and Celts, of course, Romans and Visigoths have
all lived in Spain and given something of themselves to the
country whether we wish to acknowledge it or not. In A.D. 711,
it is your calendar I am referring to of course, not my own,
the Saracens under Tarik came in thousands and conquered
Spain. The Jews made peace with these newcomers who did
not want to persecute them as the ecclesiastical councils of
the Visigoths had done. Spaniards everywhere were allowed
a freedom they had never known before – even marriages
between the races was allowed. How many of the great Christian families today have a hint of Moorish blood in them?
By and large I should say the population prospered and could
have gone on doing so."

"I can't agree with you there," Madelon interposed.

"Are we better off now?" the doctor challenged. "On the throne of Castile we have Sancho, while ruling Leon is his brother Alfonso. Their greed drove them to imprison their younger brother and divide up his kingdom of Galicia between them. That wasn't enough and now they seek to take each other's – and enlist the help of the very men they have sworn to destroy to try and achieve this."

"I don't understand their reasoning either," Madelon had to confess.

"There will be much you don't understand in this world, Doña Madelon – much you will seek to learn, only to find the answers unsatisfactory. Your mind thirsts after knowledge, that much I have learned from our little talk."

Madelon wondered if Rebecca had told him of her life in the convent, but if so, he was obviously not going to mention it.

"I once had a great deal of time with nothing to do," she said smiling. "I used to sit in my room looking at the bare walls or sewing. One day I realized if I had to go on like that much longer I would go mad. My thirst for knowledge as you call it, began that day, I suppose. I have had several learned men as tutors. One was a Jew, like yourself – a philosopher. He too had lived many years among the Moslems. I don't profess to understand all the things he told me, he was much too wise and I was only seventeen, but he did teach me their language which I found fascinating and not as difficult as he said it would be. And then there was Father Lucien from Navarre. He taught me Latin and French – and how to grow flowers. When plague came to a nearby village, he was one of the first to go and nurse the sick. He caught it almost immediately and was dead within a week. His last wish was to be buried in the garden we both loved and when I last saw his grave, it was covered with the most beautiful flowers. I think he must be very happy living amid such splendour."

Abraham ben Canaan stared thoughtfully at the whimsical smile on Madelon's face, puzzled by this girl who spoke with such feeling for mere tutors, yet had not once mentioned her father or mother.

"Water – I'm thirsty." Paco's rude tones brought their conversation to an abrupt end.

Madelon saw the annoyance in the doctor's expression at the deliberate interruption and also resentment.

"I will leave you to talk to your brother alone," he said, "but for a few minutes only. If he is to make the journey to the Castle de Aguilas he will need all his strength."

Madelon nodded understandingly. The slave girl who always seemed to be hovering at Paco's side followed the doctor out of the tent.

"How are you feeling now, Paco, you look much better," Madelon said, bending over him.

"So your three years were not so lonely as you let me believe, or as wasted. No wonder our surroundings don't seem to bother you. What have you been doing since we were brought here – being cordial to our enemies?"

Madelon bit back the angry retort which rose to her lips. He was jealous again because she had shared a few moments with someone else and she could not reproach him.

"If by our enemies you mean the doctor whose skill and attention has saved your life, yes I was being cordial."

"What was that he said about my needing my strength?"

"We are leaving tomorrow for the home of Valentín Maratín in the mountains. Rebecca the doctor's daughter thinks he feels we will be more comfortable there and not feel so – so . . ."

"Trapped," Paco said grimly, "because that's what we are. Maratín did you say? What is the name of the other man who brought us here?"

"Rodrigo Díaz de Vivar."

"Sancho's men – his best. Cut-throats both of them."

"You are being unfair," Madelon protested.

"You don't know them as I do," Paco growled. "Rodrigo Díaz killed our father. Did he tell you that?"

"Yes. He didn't try to hide the fact."

"I'll wager he wasn't sorry either," her brother answered bleakly.

"He helped to save our lives. We are in his debt."

"I'd rather be dead than owe him anything." Paco pulled himself up on one elbow and motioned to their surroundings with a sweep of his arm that made him wince in pain. "What kind of men live like this – with Moorish heathen – and enjoy their way of life – have Moorish mistresses?"

Madelon thought of Rebecca and of the close relationship she shared with the two men. She was no Moslem, but was she the mistress of Valentín Maratín or perhaps Rodrigo, who wanted so much to take her to court? No, somehow she could not believe it of her new found friend,

"You have no right to say such a thing," she said fiercely. "You have no proof."

Paco's eyes narrowed as he saw the colour rising in her cheeks. Harshly he said,

"Valentín Maratín spent a year tracking down a Moorish girl – his mistress who was captured by the king's men on a raid into one of their border villages. The Moors had been crossing into Leon, pillaging and burning and carrying off our women as is their usual practice. This Castilian, you defend, challenged the officer to combat and killed him. The girl had been abused, I admit, but no more than Christian women in the same circumstances. He took the girl with him, in the process of which he murdered another three men. The girl was apparently wounded and it's rumoured she died soon afterwards. The Lord of the Eagles never lacks a woman by his side. He's planning to marry his ward, I believe. He'll probably use her money to buy a Moorish army, like his friend Díaz."

Madelon stood in a shocked silence until Paco demanded, "Well, do you still defend him?"

"I was doing nothing of the kind. I merely pointed out he and Rodrigo Díaz saved our lives. Whatever they have done in the past, no matter how they chose to live or what women they live with, we are in their debt."

"You disappoint me, Madelon."

"Perhaps you would have preferred to see me stripped naked and paraded on the auction block in some slave market for men to inspect and gloat over, while you were being led away to spend the rest of your life chained to an oar in a galley ship. Not that you would have lived long. The doctor said you would have died from loss of blood if he had not stopped the bleeding."

Paco lay back with a grimace. Then reaching out his hand he caught one of Madelon's and squeezed it.

"Remind me not to argue with you again, little sister. Your learned tutors instructed you well. Did they also give you that sharp edge to your tongue? It wasn't there as a child."

"The hatred of a man put it there. I'm going to use it on any man in the future who thinks because I am a woman I have no mind of my own, no opinions to voice, no will but the one men assert so forcefully over the weaker sex."

"My God, weaker did you say? Carry on like this, and I'll find a suit of armour for you and you can fight alongside me," her brother chuckled.

Madelon drew away from him, embarrassed she had allowed herself to give way to some of her most secret thoughts.

"I must let you rest."

"Where are you going?"

"Back to my tent. Try to sleep and don't worry."

As she pushed aside the entrance and stepped out into the hot mid-day sun, the slave girl slipped past her, carrying the drink Paco had demanded, and resumed her position at the foot of his bed. There was no denying her brother was well cared for, she mused.

No one took much notice of her as she wandered through the encampment. It was too hot to return to her tent and she was driven by a curiosity to see more of the Moors for herself. The doctor had aroused her interest more than he cared to admit. Groups of men clustered around fires talking, broke off their conversations to watch her pass by, but no one made any attempt to detain her. At a nearby stream veiled women were busy washing clothes. Madelon had not been watching them long when a cold voice behind her demanded.

"Have you taken leave of your senses, Doña Madelon? What are you doing wandering around alone?"

Madelon turned and looked up into the angry face of Valentín Maratín.

"Are these people not your friends?" she asked quietly. "Come now, Don Valentín, what possible harm could they do me without arousing the anger of their own leader. Unless of course, you are not what you seem and my brother and I are prisoners after all – as he is inclined to believe."

Her companion stood regarding her with his hands on his hips, an amused smile playing around his lean mouth. The white burnous he wore billowed out behind him in the wind. He was much taller than Madelon – the top of her head barely came up to his shoulders and his arrogant stance made her feel like a child in his presence.

"It is customary for women to be veiled outside the harem – only prostitutes leave their faces uncovered," Valentín said casting a quick glance over her flushed cheeks. "As you are a guest here, your conduct may be overlooked, but not forgiven. You may have those lovely eyes scratched out by one of Yusuf's women."

"Does he have many slaves in his harem?" Madelon asked in a low voice. Now she looked more closely at the women about her she did catch sight of enmity, even hatred blazing out of some of the eyes just visible above the flimsy veils.

"Slaves no. Women he has purchased in the markets and who now live a life of ease and comfort – yes, around fifty or sixty, I believe. They are all Moslems, I assure you," he added as he saw the questioning look in her eyes.

"And you call this man your friend?" she asked in amazement.

"More than that, he is like a brother to me. Come, I will escort you back to your tent."

Madelon walked with him in silence for a few yards, then plucking up her courage, she said suddenly,

"I have been speaking to Rebecca and it seems I may have misjudged you, Don Valentín. In fact I made rather a fool of myself yesterday, didn't I?"

"What woman doesn't when faced with circumstances she can't talk her way out of," Valentín answered in a dry tone. "I've seen tears before and I take little notice of them. I thank God the women in my family are not prone to such dramatics."

Madelon caught her breath in anger. Here she was trying to make peace between them and in return he was insulting her again.

"I'm trying to apologize," she said.

"And as you have made the effort, the least I can do is accept, although I assure you it wasn't necessary. I would have done the same for any woman."

"Moorish women as well?" Madelon asked with iced sweetness.

The remark shot home and she saw his green eyes gleam with sudden malice.

"So you've heard that story, have you? Well, it's true. Now I suppose I have confirmed the unpleasant opinion you have of me?"

"And you really killed four men over – over a Moorish girl?"

The look of anger which crossed Valentín's face was so frightening, Madelon stepped back in alarm, beginning to wish she had never mentioned the subject.

"Who gave you the right to stand in judgement over me? Perhaps if you had been violated with the same brutality as Yasmin, you'd have more understanding – and compassion. But then you are only a child and in need of a good thrashing at that. She was no slave girl, Doña Madelon, but a princess in her own right ..." he broke off with a fierce expletive. "Why should I bother to explain to you?"

He strode off and Madelon followed, oddly disturbed by the depth of the emotions she had unwittingly aroused in him. He must have loved her very much, she thought. Yasmin, it was a pretty name and conjured to mind a dark-eyed girl, beautiful – proud – and seductive enough to have captured the stony heart of Valentín Maratín, Lord of the Eagles.

Valentín had reached her tent and was waiting for her to catch up with him.

"You are to be Yusuf's guest at dinner this evening," he said as she drew level. "Please have the goodness to be ready when I send for you."

"I have no intention of being put on show to amuse your heathen friends," Madelon said stiffly and brushed past him. He did not follow and chose to ignore the way she sat down on the divan with her back deliberately towards him as if to signal their conversation was at an end.

"To refuse the hospitality of your host will be the worst of insults. Must I remind you your brother would be dead but for the help of Yusuf's doctor. You are obligated to him whether you like it or not."

"It is an obligation I refuse to accept," Madelon retorted. "I refuse to stir from this tent until Paco and I leave with you in the morning."

She expected further argument, but when she turned around, Valentín Maratín had gone.

Madelon slept throughout the hottest part of the day, awakening towards evening to find a tray of food had been left beside the bed. She drank the cup of cool sweet wine, but only nibbled at the platter of sweetmeats. Her encounter with Valentín Maratín had taken away her appetite. If his home was in the nearby range of mountains where she and Paco had been captured by Mahmud's raiders, it must be extremely close to the border and so she could understand why he chose to be friends with his Moorish neighbours, but his close relationship to Yusuf, regarding him as a brother, not just a friend or ally – this puzzled her. And the girl Yasmin. Why should he have sought a Moorish mistress when he was to marry his rich ward? And yet why not, she thought with sudden bitterness, he was a man. She had been a little girl of nine when she had come across her father entertaining a servant girl in his bed.

Awakening from a bad nightmare she had run terrified to seek comfort from her mother and had found another in her mother's place, a faceless, cringing creature who had obeyed her master, not out of pleasure, or what she might gain from the liaison, but out of fear. Madelon was to learn what fear really meant in the weeks to follow. Her mother's fear which made her submit without a murmur, to every degradation heaped on her head by the man she had married, and the fear which kept her brother from voicing the disgust and hatred he felt every time he saw fresh bruises on his mother's face.

Madelon did not keep silent and her passionate outbursts in defence of the only two people she loved resulted in her sudden departure to a convent.

Valentín Maratín reminded her of her father. They were the kind of men who made their own laws, over-riding other people's human rights in pursuit of their own selfish pleasures and lust for power. Paco was probably right, she thought, most likely both Valentín Maratín and his friend Rodrigo had mistresses in the encampment. She could not wait to be free of them and reach her cousin at Santa María de Carrion.

To her surprise she discovered a large chest at the foot of the bed which had not been there when she fell asleep. It was one of those containing her clothes. With a glad cry she fell on her knees beside it and threw back the lid, giving a thankful sigh to find the dresses inside had not been disturbed in any way. The search party must have found it. Had they found her poor serving women too?

With great care she took out the many unworn gowns and laid them across the bed, searching for something suitable to wear the following day. Nestled between the folds of one of them, she found the dagger her duenna had placed there and the sight of it brought a smile to her lips. They had never been friends, yet at the last, the old woman had still tried to give her some protection now she was alone in the outside world.

Beside the weapon Madelon found the ring she herself

had carefully hidden. It was by far the most precious piece of jewellery she possessed. Her smile became sad as she sat back on her heels and watched the cluster of stones sparkling in the light of the taper above her head. Emeralds, sapphires, diamonds, all mounted together in a heavy gold setting. The inside of the ring was highly polished and inscribed with Moorish inscriptions which she could not understand. She never knew how such a strange ornament came to be in her mother's keeping, and had taken it for granted that her father had brought it back from one of his many campaigns as a souvenir. It was not important. It was the only thing she possessed which had belonged to her mother. She had been given it on her tenth birthday – the same day she had been torn from her home for the first time, not destined to see it again for six long years.

The soft rustle of the entrance behind her being disturbed made her look up. She had the glimpse of wide brown eyes rolling in terror and a tear-streaked face before the girl prostrated herself at Madelon's feet.

"Save me, save me," she cried in Arabic. "Oh, gracious lady, don't let the black executioner take me. Help me and I'll be your faithful slave. As Allah is my witness, I will worship you until the day I die."

"Enough! Get up and start again from the beginning," Madelon answered in the girl's tongue. It had been a long time since she had conversed in Arabic and she felt rather proud as her companion's dusky face lit up with hope.

"You understand. Oh, Allah has surely guided my footsteps here so that you may save me."

"From what?"

"Death, my lady. My master warned me what would happen if my loose tongue ran away with me again, but I forgot and when he ordered me to entertain him, I called him a pig and ran away. Now he has ordered my tongue and my eyes to be cut out and I am to be left behind to fend for myself when the camp returns to Telhan. Don't let them take me, I implore you."

Madelon stood up and helped the girl to her feet, studying her as she did so. She could not have been more than sixteen years old. Glossy hair hung thick and black over her dark brown shoulders. She was dressed in the usual flimsy garments Madelon was accustomed to seeing in the camp – a type of blouse which barely covered the bosom and left the arms and midriff bare and long, full trousers. This girl's costume was covered by a large amount of coins. A gold coin on a fine chain adorned the centre of her forehead and her wrists and ankles were weighed down with coloured bangles. She was a most colourful character, Madelon mused, and also a very frightened one. The next moment she discovered why.

The entrance to the tent was filled by a huge negro brandishing a deadly-looking scimitar which was pointed in the direction of the slave girl. The latter gave a frightened squeal and ducked out of sight behind Madelon. In a flash Madelon had seized the dagger from the trunk.

"Stay where you are. How dare you enter without permission." Her authoritative tone, coupled with the fact she addressed the newcomer in Arabic, stopped that man in his tracks. He glared at her, his lips moving soundlessly, and then the scimitar was drawn back menacingly.

"Wait, Bula!" Yusuf appeared behind the negro, Valentín Maratín at his side. At the sight of Madelon defying the armed giant, the latter stepped quickly between them.

"Don't interfere," he warned quietly. "Let Bula take the girl."

"To have her blinded and her tongue cut out and then left to die? Never! I'll use this on the first man who tries to touch her," Madelon swore.

Valentín's eyes fastened on the dagger in her hand and the gleam which entered his eyes told her he was remembering the last time she had threatened him. He had disarmed her then, was he about to do so now? Suddenly behind him, Yusuf threw back his head and roared with laughter.

"By Allah! Did you ever see such a spirit in a woman? She is worth twenty, no forty slaves. Give her to me?"

"I cannot do that, old friend, much as I would like to at this moment. Let me buy this slave girl instead."

"I'll give her to you if you promise to let me feast my eyes on your golden savage some more."

"You will have that chance this evening. Doña Madelon has accepted your dinner invitation, have you not?" Valentín asked glaring at Madelon. She knew if she refused it would mean the death of the trembling girl behind her, but still she hesitated, her blue eyes blazing defiance.

Yusuf's hawk-like eyes flickered from the bronzed features of his friend to that of the girl confronting him. They were like soldiers measuring each other before a battle, silently calculating the enemy's worth and determined not to give way one iota. He sensed hidden strength in Madelon. She would not go lightly to the bed of any man who asked her, only to that of her husband, and Valentín had so far eluded the chains of matrimony. If it was his intention to make this girl his mistress and Yusuf could see no reason why he should not – he had after all saved her life, a little love in return would be a small price to pay – he would have a fight on his hands.

A stifled sob from Madelon's charge spurred her to take up the challenge.

"How can I, a mere woman, not be honoured by such an invitation? Of course I have accepted," she said softly.

Yusuf dismissed the negro with a curt nod of his head. Advancing to where Madelon stood he bowed before her, smiling broadly.

"I can hardly wait, golden one. As for you – " he fixed the little slave girl peeping under Madelon's arm with a frown that made both girls inwardly shudder. "Allah in his great mercy has given you another chance. You will serve the *sitt* faithfully or I will slit your throat myself and feed your remains to my dogs."

"My wayward tongue has been stilled, generous lord."

The girl prostrated herself before Yusuf and did not rise again until he had quitted the tent. Madelon thought her easy

capitulation was going to earn her a sarcastic comment from
Valentín Maratín, but he simply bowed politely and followed
the Moor.

Madelon learned the name of the slave girl was Diya. Her
mother had been a Persian dancer and her father a well-to-do
Moorish merchant who had bought her in Valencia. Diya
had been sold as soon as she was old enough, to a eunuch
from the harem of the Sultan of Cordova. As she was barely
twelve and not pretty enough for the harem, she had become a
dancer. Luckily she had inherited her mother's talent.

"I am a good dancer too," Diya pouted, "but – alas – I talk
too much."

She had been sold three times. In each case it was because
she had spoken thoughtlessly in front of her master or a tactless
remark had been overheard by a servant eager to curry favour.
A month before when the town where she lived had been
raided, she was captured and sold in a local market to the
man in charge of Yusuf's horses.

"He is a pig," Diya said after she had described her master.
"Always he is drunk and he smells of sweat and horses. Ugh!
Perhaps if I find favour in the eyes of my new mistress, she
will tell the lord Yusuf what a good dancer I am."

"At the moment I am more concerned that I don't find
favour in your lord's eyes," Madelon said with a grimace.
There was a certain boldness in the way Yusuf looked at her
and he had had the effrontery to ask Valentín Maratín to give
her to him – as if she was a slave like Diya and the other
women in the encampment. Suddenly she was afraid. Not
the numbing fear that had overwhelmed her when she and
Paco had been captured by Mahmud's raiders, but the fear of
knowing she was desired by a man and helpless to do anything
about it. In fact she was probably making matters worse by
dining with him, but that was Valentín Maratín's fault. He
had forced her into this predicament and if things became
difficult, she would blame him.

"Are you not honoured the lord Yusuf has looked at you and

found you pleasing?" Diya asked in puzzlement.

"I am not." Madelon looked at the dresses strewn across the bed. "I must wear something quite plain and not too revealing."

The little Persian gave a distressed cry at her words.

"Oh, no, mistress, you must dazzle him with your beauty. Make him unable to refuse any request you make. He must remember this night for the rest of his life, so that when you go you will leave a friend, behind, not a dissatisfied lover."

While Madelon looked at her in open-mouthed surprise, Diya sorted through the clothes on the bed until she came to the one dress Madelon had intended to wear on her first day at court. It was of cloth of gold, designed with great simplicity.

"Let me make you more beautiful than you have ever looked before," Diya pleaded, clutching the dress to her. "I will make every man who dares to look at you tonight your slave."

"Why not," Madelon laughed softly.

She was flattered by the compliments, although she did not believe a word. Diya would be right in one respect however, Madelon thought. To run away from Yusuf and the attraction he had for her – if indeed he was attracted to her and it was not her imagination – could only make matters worse. She would dine with him and be herself, talk to him as she used to with her old tutors, for she suspected a keen intellect lurked behind that lazy smile. No harm could come from that and if she made a friend of him, perhaps she would also gain another ally for her cousin Alfonso – despite his friendship with the two Castilians.

The gold dress moulded seductively to Madelon's figure as she turned to and fro in front of the mirror. She wore no jewellery against her white throat for it had all been stolen with her other clothes. Even the sapphire pendant Paco had given her on her departure from the convent had been lost in her desperate flight to avoid capture. After some hesitation she slipped her mother's ring on to her finger.

With various dyes and powders Diya used as a dancer, she

skilfully accentuated the beautiful blue colouring of Madelon's eyes and smoothed a faint pink colour into the finely structured cheekbones. Brushing the long fair tresses until they shone, she arranged them in a thick coil on the top of her mistress's head. The added height set off the lovely face to perfection. She was a golden goddess, unaware of the power at her fingertips, of the men who would desire her or of the turbulent passions unawakened within herself which were to raise her to the heights of ecstasy and bring her to the brink of destruction.

It was growing dark as Madelon followed the scarlet tunicked negro sent to fetch her through the almost deserted camp to where Yusuf's blue and white striped tent stood several hundred yards away from the others, guarded by impassive-faced Moors, each armed with a deadly-looking scimitar. These were only four of the large army of bodyguards who accompanied Yusuf wherever he went, Diya whispered in her mistress's ear. She pointed to a smaller tent a few yards away, equally well guarded, and added that that was where the harem women were kept.

The entrance to the massive tent had been thrown back to allow the cool night air into the interior. It also allowed the many spectators gathered outside to have an unobstructed view of the entertainment which would accompany the feasting.

The crowd fell back allowing Madelon and her escort to pass. She stood on the threshold aware of the sudden lull of voices beyond. On each side of her, two and three deep, sat more than a hundred of the cream of Yusuf's fighting men in their crimson and blue robes. In front of them were long, low tables loaded with food and large copper bowls filled to the brim with wine. Before her was a raised dais covered with a Persian carpet. A long table, covered with a more sumptuous array of food than on all the other tables combined, stood in front of three velvet couches. Resplendent in blue and gold robes, a huge ruby glistening in the front of his turban, sat Yusuf, Sultan of Telhan, Shadow of Allah, with Valentín

Maratín and Rodrigo Díaz on his right and Abraham ben Canaan and Rebecca on his left.

The negro at Madelon's side stepped back so that she could approach the dais. As she did so she could feel hundreds of eyes boring into her back. Rodrigo Díaz turned his head and whispered something to his companion, but Valentín did not answer, his interest focused on the approaching figure enveloped from head to toe in yellow silk. Only a pair of tiny jewelled slippers showed beneath the cloak Diya had so meticulously wrapped around her mistress. Madelon could not take her eyes off Yusuf, the Moor. In his eyes she saw a look she had seen many times in her father's when he saw an attractive woman, servant or lady, the lusting glances were still the same.

Her steps faltered. She wanted to turn and run back to the sanctuary of her own tent, but it was too late. Yusuf had risen to his feet and was descending from the dais to greet her. His action was not without meaning in the eyes of many of his people and even Valentín Maritín was suddenly frowning.

To hide her apprehension, Madelon swept down into a deep curtsey, to show respect of his rank. As she rose Diya slipped off the cloak. It was a perfect piece of timing. She knew by the stunned look on Yusuf's face and the murmur which ran around the tent that she had kept her promise and made Madelon look more beautiful than ever before.

Slowly Madelon became aware her hand was being taken. As if she was a queen, Yusuf led her up on to the dais and seated her beside him.

"If I die tomorrow, Allah will receive a happy man," he murmured, bending his dark head towards her. She caught the perfume of roses about him and another, more heady, which she did not know. She blushed and heard him laugh as he saw the fierce colour flooding into her cheeks. "A woman of great beauty – and modest too. This is unusual, but most pleasing. Have you found yourself one of the angels you Christians swear reside in heaven, Valentín?"

Madelon stiffened. She had forgotten who was sitting at her

side. His voice, like the hidden barb in his answer, had the taste of bitterness in it.

"Beware the angel of destruction, Yusuf. One hand outstretched in peace, the other clutching a knife."

The reference to the knife greatly amused both Yusuf and Rodrigo Díaz who chuckled for an infuriatingly long time while Madelon sat seething.

"Enough! Let us show our guest some Moorish hospitality." Yusuf clapped his hands several times as a signal the feast was to begin.

CHAPTER
FOUR

IT was like a dream, Madelon thought. Only a month ago her evening would have been spent sitting in her tiny whitewashed cell sewing or reading. Her old duenna would be dozing in a nearby chair after their simple evening meal which would have consisted of broth, a few vegetables and a small piece of some kind of meat and plain bread, baked in the convent kitchens. No wonder she was thin. Until tonight she had forgotten how wonderful food could look – and taste. On the table before her were roast chickens on golden platters, dishes piled high with pretty little sugared cakes, sweetmeats and fruit, oranges and lemons and grapes. Her plate had been covered first with chicken, then tender slices of roast mutton roasted in wine, both had been eaten with equal relish. A slave girl held out a tiny silver bowl containing water for Madelon to rinse her fingers before sampling the luscious grapes a black eunuch had just placed before her.

Yusuf clapped his hands and immediately the goblet at Madelon's side was filled to the brim with wine the colour of honey.

"Taste it and tell me if it is to your liking," he murmured.

Madelon sipped her drink, trying not to appear too cautious. Except for a strong herbal brew which she had taken for a severe chill the year before, no wine had passed her lips since the night of her betrothal ball. The wine not only looked like honey, but tasted very similar and was strongly spiced, but it went down well and left a pleasant taste in her throat.

"Your wine, like everything here tonight, is excellent. I have never tasted better," she said, and saw the Moor's dark eyes glow with pleasure at her flattering answer.

"How is your brother today, Doña Madelon?" Rodrigo Díaz asked, leaning past Valentín to engage her in conversation.

Paco! Madelon suddenly felt ashamed. Here she was enjoying herself while he lay alone and in pain, probably worrying about her. She would go to him as soon as possible and reassure him all was well. Looking into Rodrigo's bearded face she managed a smile.

"He is a little stronger." Then, with a sidelong glance at the silent man at her side, "But I don't think he can be moved yet."

"Don't worry, everything has been arranged," Rodrigo assured her. He too, looked at Valentín Maratín as if his friend's continued silence surprised him. "We are borrowing a litter from Yusuf to save your brother the painful task of trying to stay on a horse. The doctor will be coming with us too."

Madelon turned to seek confirmation from Abraham ben Canaan. He nodded and his daughter smiled and said,

"I shall come and visit you too – if you wish?"

"I should like it very much, but I don't really have a say in the matter."

"Rebecca knows my house is always open to her," Valentín's quiet drawl sounded close to Madelon's ear.

"I have never known the Lord of the Eagles to close his castle doors to any friend," Yusuf said, beckoning a slave to refill his guests' empty goblets. Madelon stared at the wine being poured into hers. Had she drunk it already? She stretched out long, slender fingers and explored the intricate design on the goblet.

"You own many beautiful things, my lord," she said in admiration.

"Do you like it? It's yours," Yusuf said, flashing a bright smile at her. "Beside your beauty it is dull and uninteresting."

"You are too kind, but I – I couldn't take it," Madelon faltered.

"You must or I shall be offended. Perhaps each time you use it you will remember the time you spent with – my people."

Madelon caught the slight hesitation before the last words and knew he had meant to say 'with me', but obviously had been deterred by the presence of the other guests. His eyes caught and held hers. The primitive passion there alarmed her – yet intrigued her. Was Rebecca right – was she beautiful? Had Diya really made her look lovely – desirable enough to attract this Moor who looked at her so longingly that she felt weak at the knees?

Her convent upbringing had been strict. So vigorous it had curbed all her high spirits before callously surrendering her to the father who intended to marry her off once and for all. During the last three years the only men she had seen had been her ageing tutors or the gardener who tended the gardens with loving care – and he had been well past seventy. No man had ever told her she was beautiful until Paco spoke the words not so many days ago. "My little sister has grown into a beautiful woman and I want you all to myself." But she did not want to be stifled, she had had enough of being a prisoner. Now she wanted to try out her wings – to fly high – to reach unknown heights – to feel the touch of a man's lips on hers, firing her blood with passion.

With a horrified start she became aware of the smile on Yusuf's dark features. He knew what she was thinking! Was she out of her mind? Whatever had made her dwell on such disgusting thoughts? It could only be the wine, she decided, and resolved not to drink any more.

Yusuf's piercing black eyes dwelt for a long time on the exquisite face slowly flushing with colour under the boldness of his gaze.

So, she was a woman beneath that fine air of ladylike respectability. A soft, feline creature like all the others in his harem – and more beautiful – far more desirable. She was a queen and he, Yusuf, knew how to treat her, both as a queen and a woman.

He made a signal to one of the huge black eunuchs waiting by the entrance to the tent and moments later a dozen or more dancing girls came running in to entertain them.

Madelon's eyes fastened on the whirling twisting figures before her. Their diaphanous costumes were more for decoration than concealment. Many wore gold bangles on their arms and ankles and their long hair swirled loosely around their shoulders. She saw pale golden skins, some dark brown, others as black as night – all oiled and glistening in the flickering light of the hundreds of tapers burning all around them. She felt a shiver go through her as she watched the men leaning forward, some breathing heavily, others glassy-eyed as they gazed at the slender seductive figures passing them. At another signal from Yusuf, the dancers turned and ran from the tent and in their place came a solitary dancer whose appearance caused a growl of appreciation to come from the crowd of onlookers.

The girl came in covered from head to toe in a scarlet satin mantle which she immediately discarded to reveal a dusky skin oiled and so heavily perfumed Madelon could smell the odour of musk even where she sat. She wore a transparent skirt, cut away to reveal her long legs and over her hips hundreds of tiny coins jangled and glittered. A heavy necklace of coins covered almost all of her shoulders, finishing just above the rise of her full breasts. Apart from these, she was naked.

Madelon caught sight of a proud, almost scornful expression on the brown face as the girl paid her respects to her master. She was barbaric, she thought, and yet was fascinated as the girl began to dance – slowly – undulating every part of her body in a fashion that made her grow hot with embarrassment. Every movement was a deliberate enticement for the impassive-faced Moor seated beside Madelon. The girl's eyes always came back to his face as if searching for some sign of approval.

"Are you shocked?" Yusuf's bantering tone brought Madelon back out of a near trance.

"Shocked? No – not exactly," she confessed truthfully.

"A little afraid then?"

"No. Fear comes from lack of understanding. Tonight I think I have learned much about you and your people. Shall we say instead, I am not used to seeing young women in such a state of undress."

Madelon heard an amused chuckle come from Rodrigo Díaz and even Abraham ben Canaan was smiling. They were used to such sights, she thought. The clothes she had worn at the convent had been mended countless times and had been of the plainest material and sombre colours. Her hair had always been hidden beneath a coif. The gown she was wearing now would probably make her duenna throw up her hands in horror and start praying for the soul of her lost charge.

"They are pleasing men with the gifts Allah gave them," Yusuf laughed.

"Forced to do as their masters order them under fear of a whipping or torture," Madelon said and she was thinking of Diya as she spoke. "Woman was not created merely to please man, my lord."

"Was she not? Can you think of anything she does better? No, perhaps you can't, but then you don't think like a Moorish woman who is taught to please others, not herself."

Madelon whirled around abruptly as Valentín's mocking voice sounded behind her. How distasteful his presence was to her. Was his love of Moorish women so great he could not bear to be near any other? When he was not treating her like a child, he was hurling insults and barbed remarks. Madelon's stay in the camp had served as a strong reminder that, although she was free, there would always be men like her father who considered women merely as objects of amusement or for the purpose of childbearing. The slave girls she had seen and especially the one dancing before her now, made Madelon ashamed to be a woman. She would kill herself rather than become a man's plaything.

She fixed her tormentor with a disdainful look, hating the

way his eyes remained unwaveringly on her face, making her stumble nervously over her words.

"I am – a – a free woman. I have no master. I come and – and go as I please. I dress to please myself . . ."

"And sleep alone at night. How lonely you must be," Valentín sneered.

A silence descended over the dais at the scornful jibe. Rodrigo glanced in dismay at Madelon's shocked face and muttered something she did not hear, probably trying to get his friend to apologize.

"Women and love are like the sun and the moon – one must surely follow the other," Yusuf said smoothly. "Valentín has lived so long amongst us he understands this, but for you it must be strange, Doña Madelon."

It was the first time he had addressed her so formally, Madelon realized. Was it a hint to remind his friend she was not only a guest, but cousin to the kings of Leon and Castile. The relationship was probably not to their liking, but it could not be ignored. Her position demanded not only respect, but courtesy – the kind she had so far not received from Valentín, Lord of the Eagles. What a strange title that was, she thought. Who had bestowed it on him – his Moorish friends?

Ignoring him she turned to Yusuf with a greatful smile.

"Strange – yes," she admitted, "but exciting and instructive. Perhaps the hospitality I have received here can be returned at my cousin's court, my lord Yusuf. When I tell him of your kindness, I know he will want to extend his gratitude to you himself."

Yusuf's eyebrows rose quizzically at the suggestion.

"Soldiers of your King Alfonso have been raiding my camps and villages for the past two years, since I refused to become his vassal. In return my men have crossed into Leon. I have two Leonese women in my harem in Telhan. Do you still think he will offer me the hand of friendship?"

"Perhaps – if I talked with him."

Yusuf leaned forward and refilled her goblet himself,

waving aside the eunuch who ran forward to do such a menial task.

"Let us drink a toast," he murmured. "To your hopes that I shall become your cousin's ally – that is what you intend, isn't it?" And while Madelon sat realizing he had completely misconstrued her good intentions, he added, "And to the hope you will some day find your way into my harem."

They toasted each other oblivious of the glances passing between Valentín and Rodrigo. As much as she had disliked Yusuf's last words, Madelon realized she could not refuse to drink and had heard a soft exclamation of annoyance from Valentín as she raised her drink to her lips.

"Our friend Yusuf has fallen for her," Rodrigo said, helping himself to a handful of sweet grapes.

"Don't you believe it. Yusuf's no fool, besides I warned him what her game was," Valentín returned, his face growing noticeably grimmer as Madelon's soft laughter reached him.

"Did you now?" Rodrigo looked at him blankly. "Perhaps you wouldn't mind telling me what it is."

"It's obvious surely. What were Paco Montevides and his sister doing so far south when the whole court has gone to Santa María de Carrion?"

"They were crossing into Castile."

"Why not nearer Salamanca, that's where they live," Valentín said, frowning fiercely. "You know Montevides, Rodrigo, he's Alfonso's right hand, or should I say the Doña Urraca's. She's got the young fool under her thumb. Two months ago he followed Yusuf's hunting party almost to Toledo trying to get an audience with him. Last month he was at Badajoz at a meeting of border chiefs. Only one promised men, but that's another hundred men at least we've lost."

"And you think he was making a last attempt to see Yusuf and get his support before joining the king?" Rodrigo breathed. "My God, he's a fool. He knows Yusuf is with us. What could he offer him?"

Valentín's green eyes blazed with such fury his friend was taken aback. His voice was low, dangerously calm.

"His sister, perhaps?"

"Have you taken leave of your senses? She's a child, anyone can see that. What have you got against her?"

"She's Urraca's cousin. You know the lady in question better than most people, you were raised with her. You, Sancho, Alfonso and Urraca. How old was she when she first took a man into her bed to bend him to her will – fifteen, wasn't it? Since then she's used her body not only as an instrument of pleasure, but as a means of effectively binding men to her. Young Carlos, for instance. He was one of my best men until he was captured at Vañez. The Doña Urraca herself tended his wounds and now he leads men against his one-time friends. Would you like me to name more?"

"No, old friend, you are right, but to accuse the Doña Madelon of such a terrible thing! She has the look of an angel about her."

"The angel of destruction," Valentín mocked. "She is far more beautiful than Urraca and no doubt more skilled in the subtle arts. You heard her offer to talk to Alfonso on Yusuf's behalf. She's dangerous, Rodrigo."

The slave girl had finished dancing. She came forward to the dais looking up at Yusuf expectantly. Valentín knew her name was Aiya and she was the favourite in Yusuf's harem. Whenever there was entertaining of guests, she performed for them and then her master would take her hand and sit her at his side or on the cushions at his feet, to show everyone she held the place of honour in his heart.

Tonight however there was no outstretched hand. Yusuf looked down at her, smiled and dismissed her with a wave of his hand. Aiya looked stunned. Her eyes fastened on Madelon and Valentín saw the intense hatred which flashed into them at the sight of her master paying so much attention to this white-skinned vision of loveliness. It meant only one thing to the slave girl. She had been replaced by another. She had been ousted from the favourite's position – she who at that very moment was carrying her master's child.

She moved with the speed of a snake, but Valentín who had

been expecting a reaction of some kind, moved even faster.
As she flung herself forward, her long painted nails aimed
straight at her rival's eyes, he jumped between them and
struck her across the face. The blow knocked her to the ground.
Madelon gave a cry of horror at what she thought to be an
unnecessarily brutal act and her distress grew as two armed
guards picked Aiya up between them and dragged her out
of the tent. Her screams rang in Madelon's ears and the sight
of the hatred distorting the face of the slave girl made her
inwardly tremble.

"Do not upset yourself, she will be suitably punished,"
Yusuf assured her. If the incident had perturbed him, it did
now show. "Had Valentín not intervened, my guards would
have killed her."

"But why?" Madelon cried.

"She meant to claw your eyes out. She believes you have
found favour in her master's eyes and she will no longer be
attractive to him," Rodrigo told her, his expression strangely
troubled.

"She had no reason to think that." As Valentín's lips
curved into a contemptuous smile, she turned appealingly to
Yusuf. "The girl was mistaken, my lord – it was a silly mistake, but she is so obviously fond of you, could you not forgo
the punishment you spoke of . . ."

Further words died in her throat at the coldness of Yusuf's
expression. The enjoyable evening was suddenly spoilt. She
felt afraid to stay beside this Moor any longer. She had said
nothing – done nothing to make him want her. The favourable
impression she was beginning to have of him was rudely
shattered by the realization he was willing to have the dancing
girl punished merely for being jealous, despite all the pleasant,
perhaps tender moments he must have shared with her.

"If you do not object, my lord, I will take my leave of you.
I am feeling a little tired . . ."

Yusuf looked angry at the sudden hostility in her voice, but
this was quickly replaced by a smile.

"I am desolate you are leaving me so early."

Diya materialized behind Madelon and draped her cloak over the golden figure.

"Will you walk with me to my brother's tent, I would like to see how he is before I retire?" Madelon asked Rebecca.

The Jewish girl nodded and rose to her feet, despite what seemed to be a disapproving look from her father.

Madelon took her leave of the other guests with a slight nod of her head which was meant to include everyone.

"By Allah! What a woman," Yusuf breathed as she vanished from sight amid the crowd outside the tent. "Did you see how those eyes defied me?"

"I saw a woman of great beauty who possesses a heart of ice and a calculating mind to match that of her cousins," Valentín sneered. He was wise enough not to ask what would happen to Aiya. He guessed she would be whipped, perhaps tortured, it depended on how deeply Madelon had impressed her host – the least that would happen to her would be expulsion from the harem.

Watching him, Rodrigo wondered at the dislike he held for a girl he hardly knew. Women, however lovely or talented, never moved him to passion and hardly ever to anger – at least not such intensive vibrant feelings as had broken loose since Madelon del Rivas y Montevides had entered his life, waving her curved saracen dagger. A smile touched Rodrigo's weatherbeaten face. Was Valentín's concern for Yusuf, or because he was afraid he himself might be susceptible to the angel innocence of Doña Madelon? He was, after all, only a man.

"What will happen to that poor girl?" Madelon asked Rebecca. She was conscious of something being terribly wrong in the camp. Curious eyes no longer watched her. Men turned their backs and women stood silent as she passed, without looking at her.

"She tried to attack you and for that she must be punished."

"But I wasn't harmed," Madelon protested. "Besides didn't Don Valentín say she was Yusuf's favourite wife?"

"His favourite concubine," Rebecca corrected quietly.

"Yusuf has been married only once. When his wife died he vowed never to take another. Aiya was bought for him in Valencia last year. He was happy with her – until he saw you."

Madelon flinched at the reproach in the girl's voice.

"Are you blaming me for what happened? I didn't ask to come here. I was brought. I didn't want to dine with Yusuf tonight, but Don Valentín forced me to."

"Oh, and how did he do that?" Rebecca asked curiously.

Madelon related how Diya had come seeking sanctuary in her tent and to protect her and keep her as her maid, she had agreed to be Yusuf's guest.

"How like Valentín to turn the moment to his advantage," the Jewish girl said amusedly. "I was wrong to blame you, please forgive me. Life here must appear very barbaric after being in a convent for so long?"

"Yes, it is," Madelon admitted. She could not wait to leave the Moorish camp and return to civilization. The Castle de Aguilas was not her choice, but at least she would be among people of her own kind again. Rebecca laughed softly when she said this, but did not enlighten her as to the cause of her mirth.

At Paco's tent the two girls parted. Rebecca promised to see Madelon before she left in the morning and walked off towards the striped tent she shared with her father.

Madelon found her brother was asleep. His colour was steadily improving and after questioning the slave girl at his side and assuring herself he had improved since her last visit, she left him.

Walking slowly back through the camp to her own tent, Madelon was seized with a desire to stay in the Moorish camp until her brother was fully recovered. If only Yusuf had not taken a liking to her. The Moors could be kind, she reasoned, and she had been treated with respect and courtesy, more so than by her Christian rescuers. The camp was quiet. Most of the fires had been quenched except for one some way in front of her and she found it easy to forget many soldiers had died and the poor Elvira and her serving women had been dragged off into slavery by these people. Men, women and children slept in the tents on either side of her, ordinary human beings – a dog ran across her path barking noisily – somewhere a baby was crying. Life went on here the same as in Christian villages. Were the two peoples so vastly different after all?

A scream pierced the stillness of the night – an agonizing cry for mercy which was abruptly curtailed by . . . she did not know what. She stopped and quickly crossed herself, demanding of Diya, "What was that?"

"Alas, I fear it was Aiya," the Persian girl replied calmly.

"Do you mean the dancing girl?"

"Yes, mistress."

"In heaven's name what is happening to her?" Madelon's eyes searched the darkened tents surrounding her and came to rest on one where a fire still burned. She could see a light flickering inside and started towards it. Diya gave a wail and hung on to her arm.

"No, stay here. You must not interfere. She must be punished for what she did."

Madelon shook her off and headed determinedly in the direction of the fire.

"She did nothing except show a little jealousy," she retorted.

There was no guard outside the tent. With Diya continually lamenting the fearful consequences which would befall her mistress if she interfered, Madelon flung aside the entrance. The scene within kept her transfixed in horror on the threshold.

In the centre of the tent stood a brazier with glowing coals filling it to the brim. The heat was so intense it made her cringe, and the fumes were suffocating. Her eyes widened at the sight of a curved sabre embedded in the flaming coals. Beside the brazier stood the negro who had pursued Diya into Madelon's tent – Bula – the executioner. He was naked except for a piece of cloth tied around his loins and in the intense heat the sweat ran in rivulets down his black body. He looked like something from another world.

Steeling herself to look further, Madelon switched her gaze to the far side of the tent. There, chained to a large wooden post was the slave girl Aiya. Her wrists were shackled above her head and she had obviously been beaten by the state of the skin on her back.

Madelon brushed aside Diya's frightened warning and stepped inside, her eyes fastening scornfully on the tall, impassive-faced Moor standing at Aiya's side.

"Order her to be released this instant."

Yusuf's face broke into a sardonic smile, but realizing she was serious, the smile was replaced by a look of intense anger.

"Unless you wish to see how I deal with ungrateful slaves, I suggest you return to your tent," he said coldly.

"Yes, mistress, please come away," Diya begged plucking at Madelon's arm with nerveless fingers.

"You showed me kindness when I expected almost anything, including rape and torture," Madelon said, holding her ground. "Your own doctor tends my brother, but for him Paco would have died. You have treated me as an honoured guest and shown me Moslems and Christians can be friends and when I begin to trust you, you do this – " she motioned to the whipped girl who was staring at her as if she had taken leave of her senses. Did she think she had come to gloat, Madelon wondered, and hoped Aiya could understand a little of what was being said. "What kind of man can stand by and watch a woman being treated like this? She must mean something to you, if you have chosen her as your favourite."

"Your heart is too soft, she would have scratched out your eyes," Yusuf interrupted. "This lesson will prove to her it is she who is the slave, not I. Will you return to your tent, Doña Madelon, or must I summon men to have you taken there by force?"

Instead of suppressing Madelon's wild desire to help the unfortunate slave girl, his words gave her fresh courage.

Yusuf was amazed to see her advance closer to where he stood, with eyes blazing and defiance written all over her face. The flames from the brazier made the gold of her dress glitter so much it hurt his eyes to look at her, but painful as it was he could not drag them away. She was magnificent – truly a golden savage. Only now did he realize how accurate Valentín's description of her had been. The ice had melted and he was confronted by a woman such as he had never known before, and the upsurge of admiration helped to quell the anger of being told what to do by a mere woman. There was fire in her eyes, her face, her heart. She would no more bend to his will than she would accept his faith and for the first time, Yusuf, Prince of Telhan, Shadow of Allah, bowed to the wishes of a woman.

"Go and fetch some women to take care of Aiya," he ordered Diya. The little Persian was gone before the words were all out of his mouth. She had been standing in the background trembling, certain not only her mistress, but she herself, would end up in a slave market for daring to interfere.

"As much as I enjoy your company – and admire your spirit, Doña Madelon – I hope you will not make a practice of interfering in my affairs. The next time you might find yourself in Aiya's place with me administering the lashes." He came around the brazier to where she stood, unable to believe she had really won. "No, perhaps a whipping would not break you, but there are other ways. Some of them you would find most unpleasant."

Madelon followed him outside into the refreshing night air, her cheeks flaming.

"What will happen to Aiya now?"

"She will not give way to her feelings so foolishly again. I have forgiven her. When she is well she will take her place in my favour again. I am really quite fond of the girl."

Madelon almost choked at the indifference in his voice.

Half a dozen heavily veiled women passed them and went into the tent where Aiya was chained. Madelon could hear sobbing and moaning as she hurried back to her tent. She had

left Yusuf without a word, but the proprieties of their host
and guest relationship had suddenly become farcical. She
realized now he looked on her as another acquisition to his
harem and only the presence of Valentín Maratín and his
friend kept him from asserting his authority over her. She did
not like her rescuers, but at least they had saved her from the
unwelcome attentions of this arrogant Moor.

A shadowy figure loomed up out of the darkness as she
reached her tent. For a moment she thought Yusuf had
followed her and was panic stricken, then in the bright moonlight she recognized the Lord of the Eagles.

"I thought you were tired, Doña Madelon?"

At any other time the sarcasm in his voice would have
aroused Madelon's fighting instinct, but at the moment she
was far too weary to be bothered by it.

"Yes, I am. If you will please allow me to pass."

His tall frame blocked her way and she saw he was looking
over her shoulder to where Yusuf stood watching Aiya being
carried to the harem enclosure.

"So your curiosity got the better of you, did it? Well, did
you enjoy seeing the poor girl suffer because of you?"

Madelon fell back with a soft cry.

"What are you saying? I am not to blame – Diya said it was
not my fault."

"Diya's a woman, I should expect her to side with one of
her own," came the angry retort. "Of course you were to
blame. I told you to wear a veil, but you preferred to flaunt
yourself like a shameless whore before everyone. You knew
how Yusuf would react, you counted on it, didn't you?"
When Madelon did not answer he caught her by the wrist
and dragged her against him until her face almost touched his.
"That's why you are in this part of the country, isn't it? Alfonso and Urraca's two little spies. You fool, did you think the
promise of your body would make Yusuf change sides? I'd
already told him what to expect."

"You – told – " Madelon searched in vain for the right
words but none came. Perhaps he was drunk, or was she going

mad? She cried out as he released her, only to seize her by the shoulders, holding her so tightly the pain made her feel faint.

"If it's a man you want, Doña Madelon, what's wrong with a Christian one? Me!"

Madelon had never been kissed before. In her dreams she had always imagined it would be something wonderful – a tender moment to cherish for the rest of her life. Valentín Maratín rudely shattered the illusion. His mouth on hers was unbelievably cruel, bruising her soft lips while she writhed and twisted in his arms in a desperate, unsuccessful attempt to free herself. Helpless, she was forced to endure the torturous embrace until he chose to release her. Madelon swayed back from him, panting heavily, her eyes dilated, almost on the verge of fainting. Was this what she would have had to endure at the hands of the man her father had wanted her to marry? The convent had been a blessed sanctuary after all.

"When you next see your cousin Urraca, tell her her pupil is in need of further instruction. A great deal more," Valentín said scornfully.

Madelon fled into the tent and flung herself across the huge canopied bed, convulsed with sobs. With a contemptuous gesture, the man dropped the silken entrance into place and turned away. A few long strides took him to where Rebecca stood. How long she had been there he did not know – or care. He had taught Madelon del Rivas y Montevides a well-deserved lesson and it gave him great satisfaction to know she was crying her heart out. A child had set out to entrap a man, he thought. God! She acted as if she had never been kissed before.

"How is Aiya?" he asked.

"Father is giving her a sleeping potion." Rebecca looked past him to Madelon's tent, puzzled by the incident she had just witnessed. She had left the women tending Aiya, who had told her what had happened and had come to thank Madelon for her intervention. Until she saw her run into the tent in obvious distress, she thought Valentín had preceded her.

"Forget what you saw," Valentín growled, glancing behind him. "She'll not cause any more trouble."

In a flash Rebecca understood. With a sigh she took Valentín by the hand.

"Come with me. I have something to tell you."

CHAPTER
FIVE

MADELON was awakened the following morning, as she had been the previous day, by the sound of great activity going on outside her tent. She lay for a while in her luxurious surroundings allowing her mind to go back over the incidents which had taken place since her arrival at the Moorish camp. She knew in Rebecca she had found not only a friend, but a staunch ally to whom she would always be able to turn to in times of need. Abraham ben Canaan, her father she surmized, was also another good friend, despite his disapproval of her attitude at the disastrous dinner.

Yusuf, the Moorish leader, she suspected, should the opportunity arise, would take great pleasure in revenging himself on her for obtaining Aiya's release. He had given in too easily – as if confident their paths would cross again and the next time she would not have as many advantages. Somewhat against her will she liked him, with the same kind of reluctance with which she liked Rodrigo Díaz. The latter had, after all, saved Paco's life and her own and he had behaved well towards her.

Rolling over on to her side Madelon saw Diya had brought her a light breakfast. While she ate, the maid repacked her mistress's dresses into a trunk, after a suitable one had been chosen to wear on the journey, and then waited patiently beside the bed to help Madelon to dress.

Madelon's head ached abominably and her throat was very dry, probably from too much wine, she thought ruefully. However after a wash in crystal-clear spring water which Diya had fetched earlier from the other side of the camp, she began to improve. Attired in a pale blue travelling dress with long, full sleeves reaching almost to her wrists and a cowl to tuck her hair inside, Madelon inspected herself for the last time in the gilt-framed mirror. Despite hours of crying her eyes were no longer red and her mouth, although it felt bruised and swollen, did not look it. She was merely a little pale.

Behind her, Diya gave a heavy sigh and Madelon turned and looked at her in surprise.

"What is it? Why do you sigh like that?"

"Alas, my lady, I wish I was coming with you."

"But aren't you? I thought the lord Yusuf had given you to me?"

"Only for the duration of your stay here." Diya's face began to brighten. "Oh, my lady, would you take me with you? I will be no trouble. I will be so silent you will not notice my presence."

"I doubt that very much," Madelon laughed, "but you are competent and I have no servants to attend me until I reach court. I will speak with the lord Yusuf."

When she left the tent, Madelon found a band of horsemen assembled outside, among them Rodrigo Díaz on a velvety black stallion and Valentín Maratín mounted on a white charger, issuing orders to the three men busy fixing a litter between two mules. On a bed of cushions, apparently unconscious, Madelon glimpsed her brother's white face and ran to him

"He is under heavy sedation," Abraham ben Canaan assured her as she called his name in vain. "When he awakes he will be in a comfortable bed, none the worse for the journey. I, myself, will be riding one of these mules so I shall be close to him at all times. Don't look so worried, dear child, he is mending nicely."

"The good doctor is right, Doña Madelon," Rodrigo called out cheerfully and Madelon moved back, convinced.

A boy brought a docile white-stockinged bay for her and helped her to mount. As she did so, Yusuf came striding through the crowd of onlookers towards them, Rebecca running to keep up with him. He touched his forehead, mouth and chest with his fingertips as he bowed before the two Castilians, while the Jewish girl went to say her farewells to her friends.

"Goodbye, my friends, may Allah guide your footsteps to the Castle of the Eagles. Let me know how you fare at Golpejerra, Valentín."

Valentín Maratín nodded. There was no answering smile on his face as he turned his horse about to draw level with Madelon and she was struck by the graveness of his expression. He merely nodded in her direction, acknowledging her presence, nothing more. After their stormy encounter the previous evening, she had expected at least one insult.

"He's feeling rather ashamed of himself," Rebecca whispered gleefully, leaning up on tip-toe so that her words did not carry beyond her friend. "I told him how mistaken he was about you. Don't be surprized if he apologizes."

"I don't want his beastly apologies, I hate him," Madelon said fiercely.

"Nonsense. Once you get to know him, he's really very sweet."

Madelon did not answer. No matter how "sweet" he was to her, she could never forgive the terrible humiliation he had forced her to endure. The memory of the way he had kissed her was still so vivid in her mind, she dared not look at him lest the colour in her cheeks gave away her thoughts.

"Doña Madelon, I am in your debt."

Yusuf was standing beside her horse, staring up at her with his black eyes dancing with wicked lights. Madelon blinked at him dazedly. Had she heard aright?

"My – my lord?" she stammered.

"Aiya is with child. Had I continued with her punishment, she would have lost it. Last night I was angry with you. Today I call upon Allah to pour down his blessings on your head. Will you accept this barbarian's good wishes for your journey?"

Madelon smiled and nodded.

"Thank you, my lord. May Allah in his infinite mercy grant you a son," she said quietly.

Seated on one of the mules a few feet away, the Jewish

doctor smiled at her simple but effective answer. Yusuf's expression was delighted as he stepped back to allow the horses to pass.

"My lord, I would ask a favour of you." Madelon suddenly turned on him, her expression pleading. She had seen Diya hovering in the background and was angry for having forgotten the promise she had made. "The slave girl who has cared for me. What will happen to her?"

"As she has pleased you, she may live," Yusuf said. "I will see she is returned to her old master."

"Would you give her to me instead? I have taken a liking to her."

"Will you risk the animosity of your own people merely because the girl has pleased you? She shall have her freedom if you wish it. Will that satisfy you?"

Reluctantly Madelon nodded. At least Diya would not have to return to the evil-smelling man she hated. But the next moment Diya flung herself in front of Madelon's horse, screaming she would rather die than be parted from the mistress who had saved her life. One of the Moorish guards came forward to remove her, but on seeing the distressed look on Madelon's face, Yusuf waved him aside and motioned Diya to get up.

"Take her, she is yours," he said to Madelon. "She is a good-for-nothing chatterbox and would serve you better with her tongue cut out but that is up to you now."

"She can ride the other mule, here with me," Abraham ben Canaan called out, and Madelon nodded gratefully in his direction.

"May I ride beside my brother?" she asked the stony-faced Lord of the Eagles as he passed her.

"At times the way is both steep and treacherous. There is not enough room for two horses to stay abreast. Please ride behind him, Doña Madelon."

He looked at her only briefly, then after a last salute to his friend, Yusuf, he led the way out of the camp.

After they had been riding for some time, ascending all the

while on to higher ground, Madelon reined in her horse and looked behind her. The camp was a blur in the distance and without knowing why she felt strangely miserable.

Her mood did not leave her. Soon they came in sight of the towering range of mountains where she and Paco had been captured by Mahmud and his raiders. They passed quite close to the spot where their rescuers had found them and took a narrow trail between two enormous rocks which seemed to lead the way into the very heart of the frightening peaks. As they rode deeper and the mountains closed in around them Madelon was unable to suppress a shudder. Here, where the sun could not penetrate it was suddenly cold – and she was growing more apprehensive as the journey progressed.

"You have nothing to fear." Valentín Maratín's quiet tones sounded in her ear. With a start she realized she had allowed her horse to slow its pace and she was some considerable way behind the others. Her companion had obviously come to hurry her up.

"I am not afraid," she snapped, ignoring the sudden friendliness in his voice.

"A little apprehensive, perhaps, but that's understandable."

"Is your home up there?" Madelon asked, looking at the path stretching ahead of them.

"Yes. My father built the castle in the midst of these mountains. He wanted an impenetrable fortress and that's what it is. Many men have laid siege to it and fallen dead at its walls without dislodging a single stone."

He was proud of his home, Madelon thought and if it was as magnificent as the pride in his voice proclaimed, he had every right.

When they had ridden on a little way Valentín stretched out his arm, pointing upwards.

"Look!"

Shielding her eyes against an unexpected flood of sunshine which came streaming through a break in the rocks before them, Madelon followed his outflung hand. The Castle de Aguilas stood on a plateau high above her – the only access to it, a narrow track, wild and desolate, twisting out of a thick wood, on the outskirts of which was a small village, with a river encircling it.

Madelon caught her breath in awe. The whole place looked as if it had been hewn out of the solid rock against which it stood. She could just make out the battlements along the top of the inside wall and a large crenellated tower. The outside wall had battlements also and strong looking towers at each corner. They did not look heavily fortified, but there was no reason for them to be for on each side of the plateau was a gorge of terrifying steepness. The sunlight flashed on steel, probably the weapon of a guard, she thought. As she continued to peer upwards, small figures, looking like coloured dots, appeared on the battlements.

"Will you ride with me – ahead of the others?" Valentín asked quietly.

The disdainful answer which rose to Madelon's lips died away as she looked into his green eyes. What was it she saw there? Self reproach – a hint of apology – interest perhaps? Whatever it was those eyes commanded her respect. His outrageous treatment of her was no longer important.

"My brother . . ." she began.

"He will sleep until the doctor has put him to bed in the castle," Valentín answered, a hint of impatience creeping into his tone. "Come, Doña Madelon, forget your wounded pride. You shall have an apology for my rudeness as soon as we can find a suitable moment to talk alone. Now I am asking you to forget our differences and ride beside me to my home. I have sent word ahead to my mother to expect us. She is waiting to greet a guest – not a subdued prisoner. You are not a prisoner, you know that, don't you?"

"Yes, Don Valentín, I know," Madelon said and she even managed a rather shy smile. "I will ride with you."

Rodrigo Díaz, riding ahead of Abraham ben Canaan smiled behind his red beard as the two riders passed him and entered the village. Thank God you didn't see them, he mused with a backwards glance at Paco.

Madelon guided her horse carefully over the well-worn stone bridge, which as far as she could see, was the only access to the village and the castle beyond. The water did not look too deep, but the river widened further downstream and no attacking army could cross it unseen. By the time it had been forded, the alarm would have been raised in the castle. The home of the Maratín family was indeed a fortress.

There were less than twelve houses in the village. Most were of drab brown stone with tiled roofs, but here and there some had been painted white and the roofs stained with some kind of red colouring. People poured out to greet then, lining both sides of the narrow street, their eager shouts proclaiming how glad they were to see their lord returning safe and well. With a shock of surprise Madelon saw among the weather-beaten faces of the peasants, a few swarthy countenances that were most familiar. A Moorish girl in a brightly coloured dress and wearing an elaborate belt of coins ran alongside Valentín's horse and tossed him a large red apple from the basket of fresh fruit hung on her arm. The Lord of the Eagles caught it with a laugh and waved his thanks.

So this was why Rebecca had been so amused when Madelon had voiced her relief at leaving the Moors behind her, she thought with renewed bitterness. Obviously there had been intermarriage between the villagers and people from Yusuf's town.

The village was behind them now and they were entering the forest. There was an almost unearthly stillness in the midst of the tall trees which allowed no light to penetrate their thick, intertwined branches. Madelon did not hear a single bird or animal. And then they came out into the open again and began to ascend the winding trail to the plateau.

As they progressed Madelon discovered the rocky crevasses were filled with pretty little flowers; pink columbines and white daisies, multi-coloured wild roses and purple thrift and the higher they went, there were different coloured hues to be seen in the rock formations. From the valley she had thought the large, somewhat clumsy-looking place as bleak and forbidding as the mighty wall of rock behind it, but as they reached the plateau, the castle had lost most of its menacing appearance. A moat, the usual first line of defence, had not been necessary when the Castle of the Eagles was built for it was unlikely any attacking army would successfully scale the trail, whilst being under attack from above at the same time.

Madelon reined in her horse beside her companion giving a soft exclamation of delight at the magnificent view of the surrounding countryside, but she was not allowed to stay and enjoy it for long. Valentín motioned her to follow him and urged his stallion across the drawbridge which had been lowered to give access to the castle. The inner courtyard was huge and a hive of activity. Outside the massive stables, a smithy was busy at his trade. Behind him Madelon glimpsed a fine selection of animals, Arab stallions most of them as was the one the Lord of the Eagles rode. Pages in dark green livery, their tunics emblazoned with golden eagles hurried to and fro, obviously making preparations for the new arrivals. Two richly dressed young women, Madelon guessed they were ladies-in-waiting, were standing on the top of the steps in front of two massive iron-hinged doors. In the centre panels of each were golden eagles, their wings outstretched in flight.

Madelon allowed her gaze to drift upwards, past the window embrasures where curious faces were clustered, to the archers on the battlements high above. Oh, well, I'm here now, she thought, and until Paco is well, I shall just have to make the best of it.

A freckle-faced boy in the dress of a squire came forward and took the bridle of Valentín Maratín's horse.

"Welcome home, my lord. We expected you yesterday."

"I was detained," his master said with a smile – and a side-long glance at Madelon. Sliding from his horse he came around to where she sat. "Let me help you down."

For the brief moment his arms were around her as he lifted her from the saddle, Madelon was reminded of the other side of his nature. Not quiet and reserved as he was now, but wild and rough, forcing his kisses on her unwilling mouth. Two fierce spots of colour burned on her cheeks and she quickly averted her gaze from his face. As his hands fell away from her, she saw once again the strangely shaped birthmark on his right hand – it was almost a perfect five-pointed star. She had seen it several times since their first meeting, but it was not ladylike to ask too many questions and she had kept silent. Now, however, overcome with curiosity, she raised her head, only to have Valentín anticipate her question.

"For generations men of the Maratín family have borne a similar mark. Only the men, never the women. My father had one on his back, my brother's was identical to mine. Unfortunately it helped to betray them while they were escaping from a besieged town. That and the treachery of a man they had thought to be their friend." His green eyes glittered suddenly as he looked at her. "We Maratíns have always been cursed by having treacherous friends. I prefer an enemy I can see and fight. Traitors and spies are the lowest form of human life and I treat them accordingly."

Madelon had the horrible suspicion his words were meant as a warning and she felt her old dislike of him returning. Further conversation was curtailed by the arrival of Paco's litter and the Moorish escort led by Rodrigo Díaz. Behind them came a stream of villagers bringing home-made produce, fruit and suchlike, and driving before them several plump sheep and pigs.

"The villagers are pleased to see you return safely, my lord," Stephen said, his freckled face breaking into a grin as one of the pigs broke loose from its owner and dashed squealing across the courtyard. "Is it true Mahmud and his men have dared to return to our lands?"

"They left rather suddenly." Valentín looked down at Madelon, his expression troubled. "Yusuf's men chased them over the border, but I regret they were unable to catch up with the main party who had captured your serving women."

"What will happen to them ... the slave markets?" she asked in a trembling voice.

"Probably, but don't dwell on their fates, Doña Madelon, you escaped. Be grateful and forget."

It was a callous attitude, but a realistic one, Madelon realised. If only her women had not been so young and pretty ... so full of life ...

Valentín looked around him at the villagers and the Moorish soldiers mingling together and nodded slowly.

"Tonight we celebrate, Stephen. Doña Madelon has been entertained by lord Yusuf, now it is our turn. We must show her our Moorish friends are not the only ones who know how to enjoy themselves. Tell Joseph to open the storerooms and use whatever we need."

"Valentín! Thank God you have come back unharmed."

The man turned with a soft expletive and leapt up the stairs two at a time to the side of the exquisitely dressed woman in the open doorway. Her gown was of richly patterned grey damask, the hem of the skirt and the edges of the long sleeves trimmed with sable fur. A head-dress of some wispy white material concealed most of her auburn hair, just beginning to turn grey at the temples. Madelon knew who she was. The pale green eyes glowing with pleasure as Valentín took her face between his hands and kissed her on both cheeks, betrayed her immediately.

"Mother, surely you weren't worried?" he teased gently.

"How could I not worry, my son, when word came from the village that Mahmud was in the area. I was afraid you two would meet."

"We did," Valentín answered, "that's how we have acquired two guests."

"Your message said one was wounded." Pale eyes, so like those of the man beside her, came to rest on Madelon. Valentín indicated the litter being unloaded under the careful supervision of the doctor and Diya. Then he beckoned and she joined him on the stairs.

"Mother, this is Madelon del Rivas y Montevides. It is her brother who is hurt, though with Abraham's skilful tending he'll be on his feet again in no time. Don't you think we've cheated Mahmud of a valuable piece of merchandise?" As the colour surged into Madelon's face, he said, "Doña Madelon, my mother, Francesca Maratín."

Madelon, who had been brought up to show the greatest respect for her elders, curtseyed before the imposing figure of Doña Francesca.

"You have had a lucky escape, my dear," Valentín's mother said as the young girl straightened. "I hope you will enjoy your stay with us. You need have no fears for your safety here, my late husband built this castle to enable us to live in peace, untroubled by Moors or Christians alike and apart from the odd incident, we are very happy."

Madelon glanced into Valentín's expressionless face. Obviously the messenger he had sent ahead had omitted a great many details.

"Before you welcome me so readily, Doña Francesca, I must tell you my brother and I are cousins to King Alfonso of Leon and the Doña Urraca. If you wish to refuse us your hospitality now I shall understand."

Francesca Maratín looked at her son. He nodded, indicating what had been said was true, but he made no comment.

"Your kinship to the people you have mentioned must surely mean you are also related to our gracious Sancho of Castile. As my son fights beneath his banner, you are doubly welcome."

"Cousin Sancho hates my family," Madelon said. "It may go ill with Don Valentín if he learns you have given us shelter."

"Valentín has brought you here and I do not question his judgement," Valentín's mother replied, and took Madelon by the arm. "Come, you must be in need of refreshment after the journey. Don't worry about your brother, rooms have been prepared and servants are waiting to attend him."

With a last glance at the litter being carried across the courtyard, Madelon allowed herself to be led into the castle.

The large, two curved window embrasures in the Great Hall

of the Castle of the Eagles, looked out over one of the deep gorges Madelon had seen earlier. She was just able to make out a thin silver ribbon of water winding its way in the valley below, probably the same one which circled the village. She sat on one of the window benches while Valentín, sprawled in a huge sheepskin-covered chair, was relating to his mother what had passed since his departure a week ago.

The interior of the castle had taken Madelon completely by surprise. The Great Hall where she sat was enormous – over a hundred feet long and half as wide and so richly furnished it was more like a palace than the home of a mere knight. If all the other rooms were as comfortable, the Maratín family lived in better style than the King of Leon, she mused. Across the room from her was a huge arched fireplace, set into the grey brickwork. The design was undoubtedly Moorish, as were the tapestries hanging on either side. At the far end of the hall was a raised dais, covered in sheepskin rugs, dyed various colours, with a long trestle table on it. The chairs and stools were made of seasoned timber and stained with dark colouring. More and more Madelon was reminded of the Moorish camp as she stared about her. The heavy velvet drapes hanging beside the windows which would be pulled across at night to shut out the sight of the wooden shutters covering the embrasures; the many brightly coloured cushions scattered everywhere, just as they had been in her tent. Wealth and comfort were denoted wherever she looked. Either Valentín Maratín had an unlimited supply of riches or he was being handsomely paid by someone other than his royal master. It was an ugly thought, but what other answer was there?

Madelon saw him suddenly sit up and look around as if realizing the absence of someone important.

"Where's Teresa?" she heard him ask.

"In bed with a badly bruised ankle. Really, Valentín, you must give her a severe talking to," Francesca Maratín said sternly. "Despite all my protests and warnings she tried to ride Conquistador."

"Then she's lucky to get away with mere bruises," came the

dry retort. "You are right, it's time I had a word with her."
Valentín looked across to where Madelon sat trying not to
appear as if she was listening to their conversation. "Where are
you putting Doña Madelon?"

"In the South Tower, where Teresa can't get at her. The
poor girl looks as if she needs a good sleep."

Valentín smiled and rose to his feet.

"I will show you to your room, Doña Madelon. You will
want to rest before the feast tonight. On the way I'll introduce
you to the plague of my life, my young sister, Teresa."

Madelon took her leave of Francesca Maratín and followed
her host through a door at the far end of the hall and up a
winding flight of stairs to the upper part of the castle. As
they climbed she often paused to look out at the countryside
spread out below. It was breathtakingly beautiful.

"After I've seen Teresa, I'll take you on to the battlements,"
Valentín said, as she stopped yet again to watch an eagle
circling the craggy peaks.

"Has your sister had a riding accident?" Madelon asked.

"You could put it that way," Valentín halted before a brass-
studded door and pushed it open. A gasp came from the
scantily clad red-headed girl leaning up on tip-toe by the
window. As he stood in the doorway, hands on hips, she gave
a squeal of dismay and scrambled back into bed.

"Teresa, sister or not, I ought to put you over my knee.
How many times have I told you Conquistador will obey only
me? You could have been seriously hurt – even killed."

His voice was so fierce even Madelon wondered if he was
about to drag the girl from the bed and administer a sound
spanking – as he had once threatened to do with her – but as
she moved further into the room, she saw the wicked amusement glinting in his eyes.

"I'm sorry, Valentín. I didn't mean any harm. Mother said
you would be furious, but you aren't – are you? Oh, you
beast, you are teasing me." Teresa Maratín sat up in bed and
threw a badly-aimed cushion at her brother's head. It missed
him completely and hit Madelon full in the face.

"Not only do you disobey all my instructions, but now you insult our guest as well," Valentín said with mock severity.

"Oh, Doña Madelon, I'm so sorry," Teresa's cheeks grew almost as bright as her hair, "but my brother is such an unfeeling brute. Here I am nursing bruises in all kinds of uncomfortable places and all he cares about is his wretched horse. My name is Teresa – I'm much nicer than Valentín, so please stay and talk to me. I expect he'll want to go and inspect his horse after my disastrous ride."

"Not at all – I'm confident he expelled you from his back before you could do him any harm. Besides, Doña Madelon has had a long ride and wants to rest," Valentín answered.

"You've only come from Yusuf's camp, that isn't far," Teresa pouted. "I made Stephen tell me all about you."

She was a very pretty girl, Madelon decided. Not strikingly beautiful, for she did not have her brother and mother's green eyes – hers were grey but the combination of the fiery tresses cascading down her back and a softly-tanned skin, a slightly turned-up little nose and an appealing smile, were more than enough to rate her as pretty. It was obvious brother and sister adored each other, despite Teresa's recent escapade. Madelon found herself envying this other girl who had grown up in the safety and comfort of this huge castle, loved and wanted by mother, father and brother. Something of her thoughts must have showed in her expression for Valentín abruptly took her arm and turned her towards the door.

"If you are well enough to join us for dinner, young woman, you can ask all the questions you want then," he said.

Madelon allowed him to lead her along the corridor and up another flight of stairs which brought them onto the battlements. Not until they came to the edge of the wall, did he release her arm and point down into the valley.

"There's the village. Can you see it on the edge of the trees?"

Madelon peered down. She could just make out the river and a few white blotches amid the dark green foliage of the forest. Her eyes swept over the gorge on the far side of them

and she felt everything begin to reel around her. Heights had
never appealed to her and the sight of the terrifying drop was
making her feel faint.

"Don't look down," Valentín said sharply. When she
swayed back from the edge he slid an arm around her waist and
drew her against him. "Look beyond the mountains and
tell me what you see."

"The – the sun's shining on something near that other
range of mountains. It must be many miles away."

"Those are the towers of the minarets of Toledo. The town
is built on a rocky bluff almost as high as these mountains. To
the right of it is Telhan, but that's on much lower ground.
What did Teresa say to upset you?"

His question was so unexpected Madelon could only stare
at him in silence.

"There was envy on your face," Valentín said. "Why?
What could you with your great beauty begrudge poor little
Teresa? Certainly not her looks – or her clothes – or her
surroundings even. At times this place is a mausoleum for a
young, high-spirited girl. What put that look of desperate
longing into your eyes, Madelon?"

She hardly realized he had used her first name so intimately.
Her whole being cried out against confiding her thoughts,
her longings to this man who was her brother's enemy. With
deliberate slowness Valentín turned her to face him and
before the searching gaze of his green eyes, she faltered.

"You ask what I begrudge her, Don Valentín, then I shall
tell you, not that you will understand. Her family – a mother
and a father who loved her." Ashen-faced, she broke free of
him, hating herself for giving away to the weakness of a
moment. "I am very tired, will you please show me to my
room now?"

Valentín's face darkened at the hostility which had returned
to her voice. For a moment he thought he had penetrated her
defences.

"Very well, Doña Madelon. As you wish."

CHAPTER
SIX

MADELON awoke from a deep sleep towards the late afternoon.
After she had been shown to her room and left alone, she
had thrown herself across the bed and fallen asleep immediately. Sleepily sitting up she looked around her. Apart from
the large wooden bed where she lay, two brass-bound coffers
and a carved window seat were the only other pieces of fur-
niture, but it was nevertheless a comfortable room. Sheepskin
rugs covered the floor and fresh rushes perfumed the air and
everywhere there was an abundance of brightly coloured
cushions – as in the Great Hall.

From outside came a hub-bub of voices and she remembered
preparations were going on for the feast that evening. As she
slipped off the bed and went to look out of the window
curiously, Diya, who had been dozing by one of the coffers,
sprang to her feet.

"Did you sleep well, my lady?"

"Very well. Who is making all that noise below?"

"Everyone is watching the acrobats practising," Diya
replied. "A band of them staying in the village heard of the
feast and offered to perform for lord Valentín. They are very
good, I was watching them earlier."

Madelon returned to the bed and sat down with a sigh.

"I wish I didn't have to be there tonight, I don't feel in a
feasting mood." She saw the Persian girl look at her quickly
and wondered if she had guessed Valentín Maratín was the
reason for her reluctance. Diya's alert brown eyes gave
Madelon the impression they missed nothing, however trivial.

"Are you worried about the lord Paco? He was sleeping
soundly when I left him. El Hakim said I was to tell you he
would soon be able to travel."

How soon was soon, Madelon wondered? A few days – a week? How much longer of being under the inscrutable gaze of a man she had come to fear? Madelon shuddered. Why she feared him was a complete mystery to her, he meant her no harm, after all and yet, whenever she was near him he made her feel unsure of herself. Either she was shy and lost for words or the exact opposite, when she found it difficult to control her temper. When he looks at me, Madelon thought, it's as if he sees something I do not.

"Which gown will you wear tonight?" the maid asked with a saucy smile.

"You little minx, I should box your ears," Madelon cried. "Are you planning to make me look beautiful for the Lord of the Eagles too?"

"If you wish it."

"Well, I don't. Come and brush my hair, it feels a mess. I will decide what to wear later."

Diya had just begun to brush the tangles from her mistress's hair when the door opened and Francesca Maratín came in. With her was a maid whose arms were full of clothes which she laid down on the bed and then went away again.

"I thought you might be in need of a few things, my dear. Valentín told me almost all of your own luggage has been lost."

"Yes, I'm afraid it was. A few of my court gowns were saved, but they are hardly suitable for everyday wear. All I really have is this." Madelon touched the blue travelling gown she wore, badly creased where she had slept in it.

"You and I are nearly the same build. The dresses may be a little long, but your maid will be able to do something about that," Doña Francesca said with a smile. "If you need anything else, please send your girl to tell me. I want your stay here to be a pleasant one."

"Thank you. Doña Francesca, you are very kind." Madelon's heart warmed towards the older woman. She had none of Valentín's curtness about her and it was apparent she did not regard her guest with the same suspicions as her son.

"You have met my daughter, Teresa, I believe. She is to be married soon to Cristóbal de Altamiras, one of Valentín's cavalry captains. The sooner the better, my son often says. She's driving us quite mad with the wedding plans. No doubt you will hear all about them tonight. We don't have many visitors here and Teresa will make the most of having someone to talk to, especially someone as young and lovely as you. Please try to be patient with her."

"I am accustomed to being patient," Madelon said quietly. "Don Valentín obviously has not told you I have lived most of my life in a convent. Until only a few weeks ago, in fact. I shall have as many questions for Teresa as she has to ask me."

Francesca Maratín did not comment on Madelon's surprising statement, but her expression betrayed the astonishment she felt. It was usual for girls of Madelon's age to have been married several years. Her looks and the name of Montevides were more than sufficient to have suitors clamouring for her hand. The traditional dowry would count very little compared to the prestige of being related through marriage to the royal houses of Leon and Castile.

Valentín's mother wondered, but she contained her curiosity. If her son did not know the answers, there would be time enough to prise them in a gentle fashion from Madelon herself during her stay. She had liked this blonde-haired girl from the first moment they met. Her frankness about her relationship with Alfonso and Urraca had been impressing. Francesca Maratín was a woman who respected honesty and demanded it from those about her. She had raised two stalwart sons secure in the knowledge they would never break their given word or lie. She had lost a husband and one of those sons through treachery and had watched Valentín grow more embittered as the years passed, because of treacherous acts by friends and enemies alike and wondered if she had not demanded too much of him. He had become a man alone – a man of strange, unpredictable moods. It was not unusual for him to spend days hunting with only his squire Stephen for company, or to disappear inside the walled city of Telhan on a visit to his childhood friend Yusuf. He would come back loaded down with presents for his mother and sister, but after only a few days, Francesca would see the old restlessness returning to his eyes – the impatient gestures which always preceded a sudden departure. She had tactfully suggested he found himself a wife, but he had only smiled and replied he had the company of his horse whenever he was lonely – and then seeing the angry look on her face, he had laughed and added, he also had the services of a very captivating mistress. Francesca never discovered who she was or if she was the only woman in his life, but the subject was never mentioned again. It had not even entered her head until she saw Madelon.

After she had gone, Madelon inspected her new clothes. There was a warm woollen dress in a beautiful shade of green, a yellow one in heavy damask, the skirt embroidered with silver thread and one in black velvet. There were silk nightgowns too, delicately embroidered, stockings and delightful little velvet shoes with silver buckles. Madelon had been grateful to her cousin Urraca for the new gowns she had provided, knowing the material had come from her own wardrobe, but towards Valentín's mother who had parted so willingly with such lovely things to a perfect stranger, she felt a different kind of gratitude. No matter what she felt for Valentín Maratín, she would go out of her way to be pleasant to his mother and try to find some way to repay her kindness.

Madelon eventually decided to wear the yellow damask that evening. It was a trifle too long, but she found if she took extra care when walking, it would not be necessary to make any alterations. Otherwise it fitted perfectly and was cut in such a way as to make her waist appear even smaller and her breasts fuller. Inspecting herself in a mirror Diya had managed to borrow, Madelon had to admit not even Urraca's marvellous clothes had made her look this attractive.

Diya brushed her mistress's hair until it shone and left it

loose about her shoulders. The simplicity of styling, coupled with the lack of jewellery and the close-fitting gown, produced a stunning effect.

Stephen, the young squire, came to conduct Madelon downstairs. The look of admiration on his face gave her the courage she needed to enter the Great Hall without showing a trace of the nervousness she felt.

"Why, the dress is a perfect fit," Francesca Maratín exclaimed as Madelon mounted the dais. "You were right, Valentín, yellow is her colour."

Madelon's eyes met those of Valentín, who sat on the left of his mother and her cheeks flamed at the realization that he had chosen the selection of dresses. Stephen pulled out a carved chair for her beside his master and she sat down without a word. Her father had always dictated what her mother should wear. She remembered the dresses had always been demure in style, in grey or black or some other dark colour. Never anything bright which would have exploited the beauty his wife possessed.

The Great Hall blazed with lights from hundreds of torches and wax tapers suspended from the walls. In the fireplace, cooks and kitchen maids were busy basting the enormous ox slowly roasting on the spit over the flames. The smell wafting from it was delicious. At a smaller table sat the more important villagers, stewards of the castle and some ladies-in-waiting. Teresa sat beside Madelon and Rodrigo Díaz, who had greeted Madelon with great enthusiasm when she entered, was seated beside Doña Francesca.

Disturbingly handsome in dark green velvet, the golden eagle of his family woven into his doublet, Valentín lounged in the chair beside Madelon. Despite the fact that she was carrying on a conversation with his sister, she was acutely conscious of his presence, but as the evening wore on, she discovered she was enjoying herself so much, it did not matter.

Teresa's excited chatter was endless. Madelon learned the man she was to marry, Cristóbal de Altamiras, was of a Castilian father and a French mother, both of whom were now dead.

She described him as being exceedingly handsome and the kindest, gentlest man in the whole world. Were there men who could be kind and gentle and loving? Madelon wondered. Her only knowledge of men was what her father had given her – cruelty – hatred – and lust, in place of love. Valentín Maratín was like her father, arrogant and proud, giving orders and expecting immediate obedience without question. Perhaps that was why he had taken a Moorish mistress. And then she remembered Paco had told her he was to be married to his rich ward, Raquel Vargas. She scanned the sea of faces around her, but none of the women at the lower table looked elegant enough, besides she would have been sitting on the dais, beside her betrothed.

"If you are looking for the doctor, he is with your brother," Teresa murmured. "Isn't he a marvellous old man? Valentín says he's the wisest man I'm ever likely to meet in the whole of my lifetime."

"He may be right," Madelon answered, recalling to mind her conversation with Abraham ben Canaan. It would be nice to talk to him again, he was the only man she did not look down on and when with him, she was herself. It was likely Rebecca had told not only Valentín but her father and possibly Rodrigo Díaz of her convent background.

She stole a sidelong glance at her companions along the table. Valentín was intent on watching the wonderful tricks of the jugglers. Madelon studied his profile for a moment, realizing for the first time how handsome he was. Handsome – and dangerous, she decided. She had noticed when he smiled, which was very rarely, his eyes remained cold, as if completely detached from the rest of him and the lean, firm mouth, had a hint of cruelty about it.

Beyond him, Rodrigo Díaz was also watching the jugglers, at intermittent intervals applauding loudly and flinging coins into the midst of the delighted performers. With a start Madelon realized Francesca Maratín was watching her. Their eyes met and then Madelon quickly looked away.

Francesa sat back in her chair with a slow smile. Her

fingers toyed with the necklace of lapis lazuli around her slender throat.

"What do you think of Doña Madelon, Rodrigo?" she asked softly.

The man beside her looked surprised at the sudden question. "You know me, gracious lady, I appreciate beauty and the lady in question is very beautiful."

"Yes, she is, isn't she. Her frankness is quite refreshing too. Tell me truthfully, what is your opinion of her?"

Rodrigo looked at the woman quizzingly. She had successfully arranged a match for her daughter, was she once more attempting to arrange one for her son?

"I find her utterly charming," he replied honestly, "despite the fact she tried to kill me once."

Francesca laughed amusedly.

"Yes, I heard about that. A spirited girl by all accounts." Francesca noticed Valentín was listening intently to the conversation, although he appeared to be concentrating on the jugglers. Unconcerned, she asked Rodrigo, "Do you think Paco Montevideś took his sister into Yusuf's territory deliberately? Is she as innocent as she appears, or, as my son thinks, a clever seductress like her cousin Urraca?"

"Doña Francesca, just because she's beautiful, that doesn't make her like her cousin," Rodrigo said fiercely. "Valentín is wrong and I've told him so. If he wasn't such a pig-headed fool he'd admit it."

Valentín turned and fixed him with a piercing gaze. His voice, too low to carry to Madelon's ears, was heavy with sarcasm.

"If she wasn't such an exquisite little creature, would you still trust her so implicitly, my gallant red-beard?"

"Yes. She is a fine young woman, despite her relationship to the King of Leon."

"Well said, Rodrigo," Francesca laughed, "but you are wrong about one thing. Madelon is not yet a woman. She is a girl, unaware of her loveliness, unaware too, of what lies ahead of her. In a way Valentín is nearer the truth than he realizes.

She is not yet a pawn, but she could be and I think that is why she is being taken to court. Maybe her brother knows the truth, but I doubt it, he loves Urraca too deeply to believe she would use his own sister, but I know better. I would not like to see such a lovely young girl turned into something ugly – as ugly as Urraca."

"In heaven's name, why should you care?" Valentín demanded in a fierce whisper.

Francesa ignored the anger burning in his eyes.

"I had a long talk with the doctor this afternoon. The girl has talents you know nothing of." Valentín's mouth curved into a mocking smile, but he said nothing. "Did you know she can speak and write not only Latin, but Arabic and French and has been well schooled in the Arts? Abraham was most impressed with her. He feels, as I do, that she will be wasted at court. She has an active mind and a will of her own."

"Not if Urraca has her way," Rodrigo muttered. "Believe me, Doña Francesca, that witch can captivate any man merely by looking at him. If what you suspect is true and this girl is as innocent as you hope, she will stand no chance against her cousin. Their kinship is a close tie to begin with and court life to a girl fresh from a convent will be most appealing."

"You are taking it for granted, Madelon will be satisfied with that kind of life, I am not," Francesa declared. "When the tournaments at Golpejerra are over, I intend asking her to return here and stay a while."

So the old lady was playing matchmaker after all, Rodrigo thought with a silent chuckle. Valentín looked furious. He knew it too, but there was nothing he could do about it. His mother was twice as stubborn as he was.

It was well into the early hours of the morning before the feasting began to die down and Madelon said good night to her hosts and was escorted back to her room by Stephen. Diya was curled up at the foot of the bed, fast asleep, her black hair spread out around her dusky face like a black cloud. With a smile Madelon stepped over her and began to undress, but scarcely had she started, than her attention was drawn to the lightening sky outside. She had often watched the dawn before from her tiny room at the convent, for the days were long there and sleep did not come easily. As soon as the sky began to grow light she would awaken and lie in her bed until it was time to get up and make herself ready for mass.

With a smile she refastened her dress, opened the door of her room and slipped out into the corridor. Silently she stole up the staircase at the far end and out on to the battlements, shivering at the keenness of the early morning air. Below her the courtyard was silent. Several fires still burned and she could just make out the shapes of the sleeping villagers and soldiers. They too had been celebrating with equal enthusiasm and the sound of their revelry had often drifted into the Great Hall.

Life had not been dull since leaving the convent, Madelon thought. She had been re-united with Paco and almost lost him again in death. She had come close to being sold into slavery or a Moorish harem and a Moslem prince had wanted to buy her. Behind her were years of unhappiness – ahead lay the court of her cousins. She need never look back on those terrible years again.

She stood drinking in the beauty of the dawn as the darkness slipped away from the heavens and the sun slowly rose into view, tinting the clouds a delicate shade of pink. With a heavy sigh she hugged her arms about her and lifting her face to the pale sky she closed her eyes. How wonderful it was to feel the wind on her face. She was free . . . free . . . free . . .

The man watching her from the other end of the battlements caught his breath as the wind stirred her hair so that it played out around her shoulders. She looked like some pagan goddess about to offer up a prayer to the sunrise. In the half-light her face was pale, almost ethereal, and there was a faint smile on her features as she dwelt on thoughts he knew nothing of and probably never would. The first rays of sunlight streamed down on to the plateau. Sunshine merged with the blonde hair and softly-coloured dress of the girl and for an instant, before a cloud obscured the sun, she stood bathed in a golden glow of light. Then suddenly she shivered and the spell was broken.

"The morning air is inclined to be cold at these heights, Doña Madelon," Valentín said, stepping forward. "Take my cloak if you intend to stay out here."

Not waiting for an answer he flung the green velvet cloak he had been wearing around her shoulders and fastened the gold chain beneath her throat.

"Thank you." Madelon wondered how long he had been watching her and why he had followed her in the first place.

"I have come this way to reach my own rooms," he said, reading her thoughts. She had noticed before he seemed to achieve this easily and with remarkable accuracy. "I too like to watch the dawn. I prefer to see it from here than from the battlefield where I always find myself wondering if it will be my last day."

"Somehow I don't think you are afraid of death," Madelon said.

"Of death? No. Of the manner in which I die – that is a different matter," Valentín returned quickly and she realized he had a fear of dying like his father and brother, betrayed by treachery. She nodded understandingly. Valentín leaned back against the stone balustrade beside her, his eyes intent on the sun rising as he asked, "Why were you looking so solemn just now?"

"Was I?"

"Are you feeling guilty because you have been enjoying yourself, while your brother lies ill?"

"Yes." It was partly the truth, Madelon thought and it might stop him from questioning her further.

"My dear child, forget him. He's done more than his fair share of enjoying life with your cousin Urraca over the past two years while you were entombed in that damned convent." At the blank look on Madelon's face, he added, "I don't suppose that kind of gossip ever reached you. I still don't understand why such a lovely creature chose to live that way instead of marrying."

"In my case, marriage or entombment, amounted to the

same thing. You did not see the man my father wanted me to marry," Madelon replied, her face wrinkling into a grimace.

"Rebecca did enlighten me on some of the facts. But what did his age matter, or if he was as ugly as sin, men would still have flocked around you as bees to honey, whether you were wed or not?"

Madelon stared at him with growing amazement. The open mockery in his expression stirred her to spring to her own defence. Coldly she said:

"If you mean I should have taken a husband and a lover, I consider the suggestion insulting, Don Valentín. You don't have a very high opinion of women, do you?"

Valentín gave a low, amused laugh.

"I know your sex too well and I don't endow them with saintly virtues they don't possess. Beauty and innocence – both of which you appear to have, go well together, but I'm inclined to regard anyone possessing them with suspicion. Doubtless you have been told many times you are an attractive young woman. In a short space of time you have not only Rodrigo falling at your feet, but my mother too. She's got it firmly fixed in her head that Doña Urraca has special plans for you."

"It's true my cousin has taken an interest in me," Madelon confessed, "but to read any ulterior motive into her actions is unjust – and despicable."

Valentín's eyes gleamed at the cross look on her face.

"I prefer you when you are angry. The little-girl pose drops and then I have a glimpse of the real you."

Madelon felt a chill of fear run through her. For some reason he distrusted her. It involved both Paco and Urraca Madelon knew little about her cousins, only of the great love Urraca held for her brother, Alfonso, and she supposed Paco had spoken of their own close relationship and so forged a common bond between them all. Of his personal life, Paco had said nothing and she had not had the time to question him on it before their journey was so rudely and unpleasantly interrupted.

"What did you mean about my brother and cousin Urraca?" she asked in a disapproving tone.

"Why don't you ask him – if you don't already know?" Valentín retorted.

She turned to face him, her lips quivering slightly. Whether it was from anger, or distress, he was not sure and it was not important. Spy or innocent dupe – whore or angel, she was the most exciting woman he had ever met and he wanted her. The realization so shocked him he could only stand and stare into her lovely face and wonder at this woman who had entered his life so forcefully.

"Your insinuation that there is an unpleasant liaison between Paco and my cousin is in bad taste," Madelon said. "I demand you withdraw your words, or explain them."

"Your cousin collects men as enthusiastically as I collect horses – and I have a stable full below. Does that answer you?"

He saw her eyes cloud with pain and felt his heart lurch unsteadily. Was he wrong after all? It was true she had been reared in seclusion, but that did not necessarily mean she was an innocent. He remembered when Urraca had been given the lordship of several monasteries instead of lands by her father, Ferdinand, first King of Leon and Emperor of Castile, she had been so disgusted with the life he intended she should lead, she had threatened to give herself to any man who took her fancy. To Moors, who would have to pay gold – to Christians for nothing. She had retired to one of the monasteries taking with her a large collection of women attendants and courtiers and had held such scandalous courts behind the dignified walls that Ferdinand, in desperation, had also given her the town of Zamora. Urraca's behaviour afterwards, though no less scandalous, at least did not profane the sancity of holy ground. And these two women were cousins, Valentín thought to himself. He had known many women, most of them attractive in one way or another, but only towards one had he ever felt affection. He had never been in love and cared too much about his freedom to be worried by the fact.

"Are you saying my brother is one of Urraca's lovers?"

Madelon asked in a small voice. It could not be true – he could not be her father all over again. And yet why not – they were of the same blood. So was she . . .

"She has nurtured him for the past two years. He was a captain when she first took an interest in him – in a very short while he was promoted. Now he has command of four times as many men. He is entrusted with secret missions by Alfonso and he has his own apartments – in the royal palace at Burgos directly below those of your cousin. Most of her lovers last only a few months – one lasted a whole year. Your brother has kept her favours for double that time. I wonder why? What does he have to do to earn them, ask yourself that? Why, after all these years has she suddenly taken an interest in you? Why not three years ago? She saw you at court then, didn't she?"

Madelon nodded mutely. She had no answers to his questions and was growing terribly afraid. Had her future been planned for her after all? Was she not as free as she believed? No, it was not the truth. Stubbornly she fought down the urge to believe that Paco had deliberately tricked her. If anyone was trying to do that, it was the man before her.

"You seem to be remarkably well informed of my brother's personal life," she said scornfully.

"The information came from Rodrigo Díaz originally. He was sent by our king to make arrangements for the tournaments at Golpejerra. He grew up with the infantas, you must know that?"

Madelon nodded. That much she did know.

"I have little inclination to trust his word, or that of a man who forsakes his own kind for the friendship of a Moorish prince," she answered bleakly and then, spurred on recklessly by the sardonic twist to his mouth, "Perhaps the friendship is merely a facade to cover the true nature of your relationship. Who is your real master, my Lord of the Eagles? The King of Castile, under whose banner you profess to fight, or Yusuf, Prince of Telhan? You speak so often to me of treachery. I accuse you of it."

Valentín straightened, his green eyes glittering with a strange light. She expected anger, but none came. There was no expression on his face. It was like a stone mask, inscrutable – frightening.

He moved towards her, his eyes intent on her ashen face, and Madelon became aware, once again, of their strange compulsion. She knew she had gone too far. She wanted to turn and run, but she was rooted to where she stood, as if held by heavy chains. Reaching out his hand, Valentín touched her cheeks with his fingers, then her hair. His caress was as light as a breath of wind.

"And I accuse you of not being the innocent you seem, little golden savage. Once and for all I am going to prove I'm right about you."

In a choked-off voice Madelon heard herself cry out.

"Don't. Please don't touch me."

Her plea fell on deaf ears. One of Valentín's arms closed around her waist and she was held immobile. His free hand fastened at the nape of her neck, forcing back her head to take possession of her mouth. He ground his lips into hers with the same cruelty as he had used once before until she stopped resisting him and went limp in his arms. Then they were no longer cruel, but unbelievably gentle, exploring hers with the expertize of a man knowledgeable in the ways of women. In that moment Madelon knew she was lost. He took possession not only of her lips, but her body too. She could hardly breathe – she felt drugged – unable to think for herself – only obey the command of the man who held her. The silent command to surrender and belong to him.

Her fingertips touched his velvet doublet and then tightened about his shoulders as something wild, almost primitive was unleashed inside her. She heard herself moan softly as he rained kisses on her face and neck and was ashamed of her lack of control, but she was helpless against the fire rapidly consuming her body – against the overwhelming desire to submit to the ecstasy of the moment.

Valentín was murmuring endearments in her ear as he

caressed her body beneath the cloak and Madelon was brought almost to insensibility with the pleasure his touch brought, when she suddenly remembered the last man who had paid attention to her. Not in this fashion, but a friend, who might have become more. It had been the unfortunate Captain Rodriguez, who had died defending her serving women from Mahmud's raiders. The memory was enough to shock her back to reality.

She looked up into Valentín's face and instantly grew rigid in his embrace as she saw his eyes. She had been lured into something false – almost disastrous by the touch of his hands and the sound of his voice whispering tender words no man had ever said before – but his eyes were cold, calculating, watching her as she allowed herself to be drawn towards the brink of disaster. Disaster for her – and triumph for him. Deliberately he had set out to entrap her, and succeeded.

Releasing her he stood silent. The colour ebbed from Madelon's cheeks leaving them ashen, only to flood back again in a scarlet wave as he said heavily,

"My God, I was right. You are the angel of destruction."

His words broke the last remaining threads of Madelon's composure and she struck him across his marble features.

Deliberately Valentín raised his hand and struck her across both cheeks. The blows rocked her on her feet, but she knew they had been controlled. She had felt his strength before and she knew if he had wanted to, he could have slapped her to the ground with ease. A humourless smile touched Valentín's lips at her shocked expression.

"Like the Moors, I consider wilfulness in a woman should be curbed. In your case, perhaps it was little more than an outburst of childish temper, but the lesson to be learned is the same. If it matters at all, I believe you now," he said, stepping back from her. "There is not the slightest possibility of Urraca using you the way I suspected – you don't have the talent for it."

And with that parting shot he left her.

CHAPTER
SEVEN

It did not seem long to Madelon that she had closed her eyes, before a whirlwind invaded her room in the form of Teresa Maratín. While she lay dazedly trying to gather her senses, Teresa unbarred the shutters from the windows and flooded the room with sunshine. With a groan Madelon buried her head beneath the bedclothes, but they were immediately pulled away again.

"Don't go back to sleep, I want you to come and see my wedding clothes. You did promise, remember?" Teresa asked gaily, throwing herself on the bed with such force Madelon thought it would collapse. She nodded and said she did recall the promise, but she didn't. There was only one thing she remembered from the previous evening and the memory of it made her grow hot with shame.

"Have you been crying?" Teresa asked, staring at the other girl's red-rimmed eyes. "I suppose you are still worried about your brother, but there's no need, honestly. Please don't upset yourself over him any more, Madelon, he's getting well and mother and I so want you to enjoy your stay here."

I could, Madelon thought miserably, if only your insufferable brother would leave me alone. She sat up, smoothing back her dishevelled hair and forced a smile to her stiff features.

"I am enjoying myself – it's just that – well, I suppose I was overtired last night."

"You watched the sun come up, didn't you?" Teresa asked, her grey eyes growing wide with amusement.

"Why, yes, I did. How did you know?"

"I'll show you." Madelon climbed out of bed and followed

Teresa to the window. The latter pointed to the tower at the far end of the battlements. "My room is over there. I have the same view as you almost."

Madelon looked down and saw the spot where she had been the night before. A man was standing directly in her line of vision, a hooded eagle resting on the wide leather strap around his left wrist. Before she could move out of sight, Valentín looked up and saw her framed in the window embrasure in only her nightdress, her hair streaming down over the rich abundance of lace concealing her breasts.

Teresa leaned out to talk to him, giving Madelon the chance to step back. How dare he looked at her so boldly. What did he think she was? Paco – please hurry and get well, she thought distractedly. I must get away from this place. The thought of another incident like the last one brought her almost to the doint of panic.

"Why, Madelon, you are blushing." Teresa was looking at her and laughing. "Valentín wants us to join him. Shall I wait for you?"

"No. I mean – I don't feel very energetic this morning. Go down without me, perhaps I will join you later when I have visited my brother," Madelon replied. Nothing on earth would induce her to spend more time than was necessary in Valentín's detestable company.

"What an idiot I am. You want to be alone with him," Teresa murmured.

"What!" Madelon was astounded by the girl's words. "Whatever put that idea into your head?"

"You are forgetting the view from my window. I saw you with him last night. I went to bed feeling very happy."

"You retired a little too early, or you would have seen me slap his face," Madelon said. "I'm sorry, Teresa, but your brother, far from being attracted to me, considers me one of the lowest creatures on earth. The feeling is mutual, believe me." At the look of dismay on Teresa's face, she hastened to soften the blow. "Perhaps I exaggerate a little, but we could never be anything other than friends. We have different allegiances to begin with, besides, your brother is to marry his ward isn't he?"

"Raquel? – Ugh!" Teresa pulled a most unladylike face. "That ended long ago. Valentín made her father a promise to take care of her and marriage was the only way he could really carry it out. He thought – as we all did, that Raquel needed taking care of. We soon found how wrong we were. There was some kind of scandal after she had been at court only a few weeks and Valentín was forced to kill a man who insulted her. She deserved it, mind you, but there was nothing else he could do. After that he gave her an allowance on the condition she never came back here. You'll probably see her at Golpejerra. Just look for the woman who has the most men around her and that will be Raquel."

Will it? Madelon wondered. If she was to believe all she had been told, the woman would be her cousin Urraca.

"Does it make any difference to you and Valentín?" Teresa asked hopefully and was disappointed when Madelon shook her head. "It's a pity, you would be good for him. He needs a strong woman, someone as stubborn as he is."

What would he do with a stubborn woman, Madelon wondered, beat her with a whip when she argued with him?

Teresa stayed with her while Diya dressed her mistress, talking of the fabulous array of materials which had arrived that morning from Yusuf. They were part of his wedding gifts to the betrothed couple and were accompanied by a small, silver casket containing an assortment of aromatic perfumes, a string of flawless pearls and a magnificent stallion for the prospective groom.

When she went to join her brother, Madelon quickly made her excuses and went towards Paco's room. He was in one not unlike her own propped up in bed and looking greatly improved. Madelon threw herself into his arms and cried tears of relief until Paco put her from him with an astonished look on his face.

"Were you that worried about me, little one?"

"Of course I was. When those horrible men first took us

I thought you would die. If we hadn't been rescued, I think you would have bled to death before my very eyes. Oh, Paco!"

Her brother gingerly touched his chest. It still hurt like hell, but soon he would be able to ride and then he and Madelon could put the Castle de Aguilas far behind them. His sister looked concerned when he voiced his intention of getting up that afternoon.

"Did the doctor say you could? You can't be strong enough yet. Please, take care, Paco, and take his advice."

"Advice be damned," Paco growled. "If I'd known what he was, I'd never have let him touch me. Jews!" His unshaven face wrinkled into an expression of disgust. "Filthy pigs! Do you know they use the blood of new-born Christian babes in their devilish rites? To think I've been touched by hands that have slit the throats of children."

"Have you never killed a child? A Moorish child perhaps?" Madelon demanded.

At the anger in her voice Paco looked at her in astonishment. "What did you say?"

"What you say is not true, it's superstitious nonsense. Abraham ben Canaan is a wonderful man and without his skill as a doctor you would not be alive."

"Are you defending him?"

"Yes. I won't have you saying such terrible things about him. I can't stop you thinking them, but at least have the decency to keep them to yourself."

Paco fell back onto his pillows, staring at her as if she had taken leave of her senses. Slowly his eyes wandered over the dress she wore. Today she had chosen the green wool, which was inclined to fit her even more snugly than the yellow one had. The tight fitting sleeves had a band of ermine at the wrists and a wider band softened the severity of the high neckline.

"I see you are being well taken care of," he said harshly. "I understand you were at a banquet last night. It seems to be becoming quite a habit. Do I take it you have become friends with our enemies?"

"I have been courteous to the men who saved our lives and the woman who has given us the hospitality of her house. Paco, what is the matter with you, why do you reproach me so? Do you want me to stay in my room until you are well enough to leave? If you ask it of me, I will, but please don't continue to treat me as if I am behaving like a shameless whore."

Paco gave an amused laugh and catching her by the wrist, he pulled her down beside him.

"I'm a bear, aren't I? Blame it on to being cooped up in bed for so long. Forgive me and go and enjoy yourself while you can – I intend leaving soon. No arguments, Madelon. I'm not foolish enough to believe Valentín Maratín has given us shelter out of the goodness of his heart – he doesn't have one. How do you think cousin Alfonso is going to react when we arrive at Santa María de Carrion, prisoners of one of his brother's alferez?"

"But we are not prisoners, I have Don Valentín's word on it," Madelon protested. "I believe him."

"My dear little sister, you are far too naïve for your own good. Maratín and Rodrigo Díaz command the cream of Sancho's army and are at his right hand. The land and power they possess is equalled by no other man in Castile. Should the contest at Golpejerra turn in favour of their king, I have no doubt I shall be flung into the deepest dungeon they can find and the key thrown away. Exile would be out of the question, I know too much."

"Don Valentín is under the impression you were not on your way to Santa María de Carrion, but were in this part of the country searching for Prince Yusuf." Madelon saw a tiny nerve twitch at the side of Paco's mouth and grew apprehensive. "Is that true? Don't lie to me – it's important I know the truth."

"Very well, he speaks true. We could have been at our destination on the day we were attacked had I taken a direct route. I had orders to try and contact the Moor."

"And bribe him to come over to our side," Madelon said

slowly. "I understand now. We were not brought here for our comfort alone. Don Valentín has also prevented you from talking to your man."

"At last you are beginning to understand Maratín is dangerous to us. He will not be content with letting us go, Madelon."

Madelon drew back from him, determined not to be swayed from her course now she was so near the truth.

"Who suggested I should leave the convent and join you? Was it our cousin Urraca, or did you decide on it?"

Paco threw her a puzzled look. She had grown pale and he saw her hands were locked together in her lap.

"As it happens, Urraca suggested it. Why do you ask?"

"Did she also suggest I should accompany you in your search for Yusuf and perhaps allow myself to be seduced in order to win his allegiance?"

Paco interrupted her with a string of violent oaths and she knew that if it had been her cousin's intention to use her – and she was still highly sceptical about it – Paco had known nothing. Somewhat shamefaced she told him of Valentín's suspicions. Paco cursed softly as she spoke and his face became grey and drawn.

"You believed him, didn't you?" The pain in his eyes brought tears to Madelon's. Mutely she nodded. He covered his face with his hands and was silent for a long while.

"When I am well again, I swear he'll pay for the bitter words he's caused between us. Have you told me everything?"

"No." Madelon's voice was so low he could scarcely hear it. "He said you were Urraca's lover."

Paco looked uncomfortable.

"If by that he implies I'm in love with her, he's right. I'm not ashamed of it – or that she is my mistress. It was her own wish. It only hurts me to know he told you and made it sound so sordid."

"I knew it couldn't be as horrible as he made it sound. He described Urraca as something resembling a vulture – always waiting to pounce on some poor unsuspecting men."

So great was her relief, Madelon did not notice the bitter smile which briefly crossed her brother's face.

"For love of Urraca there is nothing I would not do," Paco told her quietly. "She has given me great happiness during the past two years, Madelon. I pray, you too, will someday find someone to give you equal happiness. I love her, not only with my body, but my soul, my mind. Every little part of me belongs to her. Without her I am nothing – I have nothing. Do you understand? No, of course, you couldn't."

Madelon thought of how the touch of Valentín's lips on hers had brought her to the heights of ecstasy. Yes, she thought sadly, I do understand, but I can never admit it to you or you will know how deeply I have betrayed your trust.

The arrival of Abraham ben Canaan brought their conversation to an abrupt end. Paco refused to talk in front of him as if he regarded him as a spy. Madelon said she would come back later in the day and left them alone.

That evening she did not dine in the Great Hall with her hosts and sent Diya with a message that she had retired to bed plagued by a nauseating headache. She lay awake for hours listening to the various sounds from the courtyard below. As she closed her eyes, at last growing drowsy, she heard the creak of the drawbridge being lowered and wondered who was arriving – or leaving – at such a late hour. The sharp staccato of horses' hooves on the rocky plateau followed her into the realms of sleep.

The following morning, Madelon's headache had become reality. She was taking the air on the battlements, cautiously keeping a wary eye out for the Lord of the Eagles, when she heard someone calling her name and Rebecca appeared at the top of the steps. Madelon was immediately struck by the paleness of her face. She looked as if she was greatly upset.

"Teresa said I might find you here," she said breathlessly. "My, you do look a grand lady in that green dress."

"Thank you. It belongs to the Doña Francesca. She has been very kind to me."

"Father has told me your brother will be able to travel in a few days. He's much stronger than we imagined."

"If he has his way, he'll have us leaving tomorrow," Madelon answered. "You look unwell, Rebecca. Can I do anything?"

"I've been crying – silly of me, wasn't it? I'm not usually so foolish."

"Come and talk to me in my room," Madelon insisted.

"I can't, I have to get back to camp." Rebecca motioned to a dozen or more Moorish riders gathered near the drawbridge. "My escort is ready to leave. They brought Doña Teresa her wedding presents and I came along for the ride and to say good-bye before you leave here. I don't suppose we will ever meet again. I tried to see you last night, but Diya said you had gone to bed with a bad headache."

Madelon felt a deep pang of regret. She had grown fond of the Jewish girl, and was annoyed not to have seen her earlier. She noticed Rebecca looking towards the main entrance and leaned over the wall curiously to see who – or what was attracting her attention. Rodrigo Díaz stood on the steps looking up at them and then abruptly he spun around on his heel and disappeared inside. Madelon looked around in time to see the intense longing in Rebecca's eyes and instantly guessed what had upset the other girl.

"You and Rodrigo," she breathed. "What an idiot I am not to have realized you are in love with him."

Rebecca nodded with a sad smile.

"Everyone seems to know except Rodrigo himself. He's asked me to go to Golpejerra but of course I can't."

Remembering Paco's unreasonable attitude towards Jews, Madelon has not need to ask why. Gradually her own enthusiasm to reach the royal court was diminishing. She had been plunged into a life totally different from the one she had led at the convent and was just beginning to realize how little she knew of the world.

"Don't be too hard on him, men are inclined to be blind sometimes," Madelon said gently. How experienced she sounded and yet she knew nothing of love. Paco's feelings for Urraca made him risk his life in her brother's cause – the love of Rebecca for a man she could not have was breaking her heart. If love brought such misery, she would take care never to lose her heart, she decided.

"I wish you would stay a while longer," she pleaded. "I'm sure your father won't mind."

"But – don't you know? He returned to camp last night. He quarrelled with your brother and decided to leave. Valentín went with him."

Madelon realized she had heard them riding away.

"What did they argue about, do you know?"

"Father is a Jew, what other reason do you need," Rebecca said bitterly. Composing herself, she stepped back from Madelon. "Thank you for listening to my troubles, but there is nothing you can do. Good-bye, Madelon, I will pray for your safety."

Madelon watched her walking away with growing anger. How dare Paco insult the man who had saved his life – there was no excuse for such a bad display of manners. It was too late for him to apologize and so she would have to do it for him, even if it meant riding out to the Moorish camp to do it.

"Wait," she called and picking up her skirts, ran after Rebecca.

Francesca Maratín was surprised when her guest asked permission to borrow a horse to ride back with Rebecca, but when she heard the reason for the journey, she silently congratulated herself on making a correct assessment of Madelon's character and ordered one to be saddled. She told her Valentín was at the camp and would probably want to escort her back. Also that she would tell Paco where his sister had gone, but only if he asked. Madelon realized the woman was only too aware of the doctor's reason for leaving unexpectedly.

Madelon's decision to accompany Rebecca seemed to revive her flagging spirits and for most of the journey, she rode close to her friend, talking about the many homes she and her father had made in different places and lost through the hatred of people of another faith. Madelon listened and wondered if she would have accepted such a life so calmly. Somehow she knew she could ever endure the life of an outcast, and yet they were not completely so. Yusuf had given them a home and a new lease of life. Whatever other faults he possessed, she admired him for that.

The camp was strangely deserted when they rode in. Only the women watched them from behind their veils, or old men, sitting beside their fires. Abraham ben Canaan came out of his tent to greet them, his face breaking into a warm smile as he saw the unexpected arrival and explained Valentín and Yusuf had gone hunting and taken most of the men with them.

Madelon followed the doctor and his daughter into the pleasantly cool interior of their tent and sat down on the couch, unconscious of the soft sigh which escaped her lips.

"You look tired," Abraham ben Canaan said quietly. "Did you not sleep last night?"

"Not really. I have a bad headache."

"I have just the thing to refresh you. Rebecca ..."

His daughter nodded, apparently understanding. She went away to return carrying a large tray which she set down before them. On it was a platter of sweetmeats and sugared fruits and a large silver samovar and two wafer thin gold cups. She smiled briefly at Madelon, made the excuse she wanted to change out of her dusty riding clothes and disappeared through the silken curtain which partitioned the tent into two rooms.

Madelon watched curiously as the Jew picked up the samovar and poured a dark, syrupy looking liquid into the cups.

"Be careful, it's hot," he warned as she stretched out her hand to pick up one.

"What is it?"

"The Arabs call it kahwi – coffee. Sip it slowly. I don't think you will find it unpleasant."

After allowing it to cool for a while, Madelon took a tentative sip of the kahwi. It was terribly strong and very sweet, but after two or three mouthfuls, she decided she quite liked it. Certainly it had a reviving effect on her.

"Something is worrying you," Abraham ben Canaan said, with a glance into her pale features. "Am I right in assuming you are having a conflict of emotions?"

"Why do you say that?"

"As you probably know by now, your brother and I quarrelled. He said many unpleasant things to me, but I have heard them all before and I bear him no grudge, but it makes me sad to think he may direct his anger to you when he finds out you have come here to see me. He said you defended me? Why did you do that?"

"I respect you. Apart from my brother, you are the only other man I respect."

"Rebecca told me you did not have an easy childhood. Would you care to tell me a little more, if it isn't too painful?"

Madelon found herself pouring out her heart to the wise old doctor who sat sipping his kahwi and nodding from time to time. He did not interrupt once. When she had drained herself of memories and bitter feelings, some of which she had not been aware of until she started talking, she laid her head back amid the cushions and said quietly:

"Do you know I actually feel better now?"

"It is good to talk sometimes – to rid your mind of harmful thoughts."

Madelon looked at him curiously.

"Why do you speak of them as harmful?"

"Aren't they? Not all men are like your father, but you consider them so."

"I have good reason."

"Come now, is that really true? Who, apart from your brother, do you know – only Rodrigo and Valentín, unless of course, you took to entertaining visitors in your convent as seems to be a certain Castilian custom?"

Madelon coloured at the reference to her cousin's behaviour. So Valentín had spoken the truth about that at least. She was sure the doctor would not have mentioned it otherwise.

"The resemblance between Don Valentín and my father grows stronger every day," she replied and went on to explain why. Her companion smiled to himself as she described her shameless behaviour that night on the battlements. She was so young and had much to learn of life and love.

"Valentín has not confided in me," Abraham said, "but that is not unusual. He is a man alone."

"As wild and free as the eagles which live above the castle. I saw him with them the other day. Teresa tells me he tames them with the greatest of ease. He is like them in so many ways. Now I understand why he is called the Lord of the Eagles."

"Exactly, but if you are honest with him, he will be your friend and you will never find a truer one."

"I have been honest with him, but he repeatedly compares me to my cousin Urraca, and does nothing but insult me."

"Be yourself and leave the rest to providence," the doctor murmured. "By the way, you have a staunch ally in Yusuf. Since he discovered Aiya is with child he's been pouring down blessings on your head daily. He desires another son, you see, but so far he has been presented with four girls. His boy was only two years old when he was murdered by Leonese soldiers and his wife abducted. He was badly wounded and left for dead. God knows what that poor girl endured before Valentín brought her back. We never knew – she died a week after her return."

Madelon's hand was trembling so violently she had to put down her cup. It was too much of a coincidence surely for Valentín to have rescued two Moorish women who had been abducted.

"What was her name?" she asked faintly.

"Yasmin. Valentín told you about her then? It was tragic."

Madelon sat in a stunned silence. Valentín and Yusuf were like brothers. It would be natural for the former to pursue the soldiers who had stolen his friend's wife. But why had he not told her the whole story? A vision of his marble features rose up before her eyes and she knew he had been too proud to answer the cruel accusation she had heaped on his head.

"Would you like to see Aiya?" Abraham asked her, when she had drunk another cup of kahwi. She said she would and he took her through the camp to a small tent erected close beside Yusuf's.

Aiya was reclining on a narrow couch surrounded by a bevy of veiled women, enveloped in their dark coloured cloaks. Whenever they left the sanctuary of the harem, it was decreed they must be covered from head to toe so that no man might look on their beauty.

Abraham ben Canaan clapped his hands and ordered them out. Laughing and chattering the women brushed past him and Madelon watched them being escorted back to the harem by two black eunuchs.

"I have brought someone to see you, Aiya."

The girl's black eyes fastened on Madelon and she was silent, then her face broke into a smile.

"The angel of mercy whose intervention saved me from my lord's anger," she said in Arabic. "Aiya is your servant. May you always walk in the shadow of Allah. Please tell her of my gratitude, El Hakim."

"She understood," Abraham replied. He smiled at Madelon. "I will be in my tent when you have finished here."

Madelon moved hesitantly to the couch as Aiya asked in wonder:

"Do you speak my language?"

"Yes."

"How wonderful. Where did you learn it?"

"In a convent."

"A what?" asked the girl mystified.

"A place where Christian women go to dedicate their lives to God – to Allah as you call Him. Sometimes young girls are sent there to have a good upbringing."

"Oh, then it is like a harem. We are taught many things too," Aiya said.

Madelon laughed and said it was not quite the same thing.

"How are you feeling after that awful beating?" she asked. Outwardly the Moorish girl showed no signs of ill treatment. She lay with a large platter of fresh fruit balanced on her stomach, popping juicy black grapes into her mouth at regular intervals. She wore a diaphanous robe of some wispy material which clung to the contours of her body. Her feet were bare and Madelon saw her toe-nails were painted a dark red to match her long nails. On her ankles and wrists were numerous bangles and bracelets.

"I have been whipped before," she murmured with an indifferent shrug of her shoulders, "but this time it was different. I carried my lord's child in my belly."

"He seems very sure it will be a son."

"My dreams have told me this will be so and they are never wrong. I dreamt of you several nights ago. I saw your whole life spread out before me. You don't believe me? Then it's of no importance, you will not want to know what I saw."

"But I do," Madelon protested. She did not believe in seers or second sight, but she did not want to upset the girl. Sitting down on the edge of the couch, she pleaded, "Please tell me."

"You are going on a journey to a place where many finely dressed women are gathering to watch men die. I saw the sun flashing on steel and there was blood – much blood and you gave your favours to the man you would one day marry."

"Who was he?"

"I could not see his face."

How romantic, Madelon mused, not believing a word. The tournament at Golpejerra was common knowledge in the camp. She had been told nothing out of the ordinary.

"You are sceptical of my powers?" Aiya was watching her through narrow eyes. "Come, I will look into your future."

Getting up she went across to a small polished coffer on a table and taking something from it, knelt beside the fire burning in the middle of the floor. Mystified, Madelon stood behind her and saw she was holding out towards the flames what looked like a smooth flat pebble. As the heat reached it, the colour changed from blue to red and then green. As it grew hotter, the colours mingled and threw off a strange glow. She watched fascinated, wondering how Aiya could keep her hands over the fire for so long and yet show no sign of pain from the fierce heat. Her eyes dropped to the Moorish girl's back, clearly visible beneath the semi-transparent material of her gown and with a start Madelon saw there were hardly any signs of the whipping she had received. Abraham ben Canaan's skill had not worked that miracle.

Aiya seemed to be going into some kind of a trance. Her eyes were rivetted on the bright hue of colours surrounding the stone. She began to sway over the flames, her face and body wet with perspiration.

"Two men will possess you, but you will give your heart to only one ... who will both love and hate you. His hatred will bring you near to death, but his love will give you a fine son. For every man there is only one woman chosen for him by fate – the same applies to a woman. If the two are destined for each other, nothing can keep them apart. Not they themselves – or the will of others – despite everything they will be one." Her voice trailed off and she sat back on her heels, dropping the stone onto the soft earth beside her. When she looked at Madelon, her expression was slightly contemptuous. "Remember what I have told you. Believe it."

Madelon was too shaken to reply. Wordlessly, she looked down at Aiya's hands. They looked red and painful, but there were no blisters. As if to prove they did not hurt her, the Moorish girl rose and produced a jar of salve and proceeded to rub some vigorously into her skin. Madelon was convinced.

The sound of many horses galloping into the camp drew both women to the entrance of the tent. Aiya gave a glad cry.

" 'Tis my lord returning."

As two riders detached themselves from the others and rode in their direction, she hurriedly ducked back out of sight for she was not veiled. And then across the path of the oncoming horses appeared a tiny child, barely able to walk. Tottering unsteadily, she faltered and fell. With a woman's scream ringing in her ears, Madelon leapt forward. The deafening thunder of hooves was in her ears as she scooped up the little girl and tossed her to safety. She felt a sharp blow on her shoulders, another on her temple. She pitched forward and then there was only blackness.

CHAPTER
EIGHT

"My God, I thought I'd killed you," Valentín exclaimed hoarsely as Madelon opened her eyes.

He was bending over the bed where she lay, pressing a wet cloth to her forehead. She winced as a pain tore across her temples and Valentín restrained her when she tried to sit up.

"Lie still, you are in my tent, it was the nearest. Abraham has just gone to see the child."

"Is she all right?" Was it the pain making her feel so faint, Madelon wondered, or the way he was looking at her? His anguished features swam before her blurred vision.

"Shock, most likely. It's you I'm worried about. You gashed your head as you fell and there was blood all over the place." He drew back from her and Madelon saw how pale he was. "I thought I'd killed you," he repeated harshly.

"Why should the death of a whore concern you?" she asked icily, determined not to be swayed by this apparent change of attitude. He had tricked her once before. Valentín grew even paler beneath his tan.

"I was wrong. I admit it."

"How noble of you, gracious lord." Madelon pulled herself upright despite the restraining hand he laid on her shoulder. Before her haughty expression, it fell away and the protest he intended to make died unuttered on his lips. Staring out through the entrance, Madelon was dismayed to find darkness had fallen.

"Paco will have missed me, I must leave at once," she insisted.

"You are in no condition to ride. You will stay here tonight and we will return together in the morning."

"No. I demand you allow me to leave this instant."

When he made no answer and did not move, Madelon gave an angry sigh and clambered off the bed. She would not have thought a man could move so swiftly, yet he was around the other side of the bed in time to catch her as her knees buckled and she fell forward with a moan of pain.

"I understand your impatience to return to your brother, but in your present condition you couldn't manage the journey," Valentín said, depositing her back on the bed. "Lie here and rest. We will have something to eat and then see how you are feeling. Do I have your promise you will not try to leave when I go?"

"Yes," Madelon answered weakly. The pain in her head was so intense she felt sick and faint. Turning her face into the pillows she drifted into a state of semi-consciousness. She fancied Valentín returned to her side some while later, and that his hand gently caressed her cheek and he murmured. "Sleep, *shafra sha'r*. I will stay beside you." But in that strange world of shadows nothing was real. Perhaps she only imagined it.

When she awoke, the squire Stephen was preparing the table for a meal. He had obviously been told not to make any unnecessary noise for she noticed how carefully he moved about. She lay watching him drowsily until he finished his task and slipped silently away. A moment later Valentín came in with Abraham ben Canaan, who despite her protests she was feeling better, insisted on examining the cut above her temple.

"Hmm ... not serious, but you'll need to take it easy for a day or two. The child merely suffered slight bruising. You were very lucky. If Valentín hadn't managed to swerve, you would have both been killed."

"It appears I must thank you for saving my life a second time," Madelon said, gazing across to the couch where the Castilian sat, a goblet of wine in one hand, the other resting on the hilt of the jewelled dagger nestling in his belt.

"Doña Madelon wants to return to the castle tonight," Valentín said. "What do you think, Abraham?"

"Definitely not – unless you intend to carry her most of the way."

"The idea appeals to me, but not to the lady," Valentín chuckled.

He watched Madelon stand up, somehow managing to remain upright without any support. Her face was ashen and in the light of the wall torches, the cut on her forehead was beginning to swell. His fingers tightened around the goblet he was holding until the knuckles grew white as he visualized her falling beneath his horse's hooves. Thank God, Conquistador was trained to respond to the slightest touch or she would have been crushed to death. He thought she intended to argue with the doctor, but instead she turned to him.

"Don Valentín, I am appealing to you to take me back. My presence here will anger my brother as it is. I acted without thinking, I admit, and I don't want to provoke him further. Heaven knows what he will believe if I don't return before tomorrow."

"I can imagine," Valentín returned humorously. "Loath as I am to disregard your advice, Abraham, I think if we are to avoid trouble, we must go. I'll arrange something."

"Then I will leave you to your food," Abraham said. "Good-bye, Valentín. I will see you when you return from Golpejerra."

"If one of Alfonso's knights doesn't stick me with his lance," Valentín laughed. "Good night, old friend."

"Good-bye, Doña Madelon." The old man held Madelon's hand for a long moment, as if to remind her if she ever needed a friend, he was available.

"I shall always remember you. I hope we meet again soon," Madelon said. "Good-bye."

"Come and eat some food," Valentín ordered when they were alone. "I refuse to even consider leaving here until you do."

She sat down beside him and under his watchful eye she ate the sliced chicken he piled on to her platter and drank a full goblet of wine, followed by two cups of steaming kahwi.

"Not another mouthful," she protested as he began to fill her platter again. "Truly, I cannot eat any more."

"Some more wine then," Valentín insisted. "I don't want you fainting on me. If I walk through the door with an unconscious girl in my arms, your brother will probably do something stupid, like issuing a challenge."

Madelon's eyes clouded with apprehension. That was something she was frightened he might do anyway when he saw her riding back with his enemy.

"If he did, I wouldn't accept," Valentín assured her quickly. "I don't fight wounded men."

Madelon relaxed back on to the couch after the meal. Her head still ached, but she did not feel so faint. Whether or not she could stay on a horse was another matter, but she would try. Valentín moved alongside her. He was very close, his shoulder was pressing against hers. She felt rather warm and comfortable and did not want to move away, besides she had some apologizing to do. How wrongly she had misjudged him. It would serve her right if he rebuffed her.

"The doctor told me about Yusuf's wife," she said in a very small voice.

"Did he?" Valentín leaned forward to replenish his empty goblet and hers and then he turned and stared gravely down into her face. "So now you know I'm not the ogre you thought. I've had several Moorish mistresses, I don't deny it, but Yasmin was like a sister to me."

"I understand that now, but at first ... I was so afraid, confused ..."

"And I didn't help matters by comparing you to your cousin, did I? We have both made mistakes."

"You didn't lie about her, did you?"

"You will be able to judge for yourself when you reach Santa María de Carrion. My mother wants you to stay with us after the tournament. Would you consider it?"

"I – I don't know," Madelon answered, taken aback by the request. "Perhaps we should wait and see the outcome of the

tournament. When it is over will Castile and Leon really be
united under one king again?"

"Under the rightful king – Sancho," Valentín replied
mockingly.

She pursed her lips angrily, but he was right. Sancho was
the true king of the two kingdoms by the ancient Roman and
Visigothic customs which decreed the eldest son should inherit
his father's lands. Instead of adhering to this, however,
Ferdinand had followed the example of his father, Sancho el
Mayor, who had first introduced the dividing up of land and
property between the sons and daughters of the monarch.

To his eldest son, Sancho, whose magnificent build and
courage had earned him the name of "El Fuerte" – the Strong,
Ferdinand gave the kingdom of Castile. The second son,
Alfonso was allotted Leon. The smallest kingdom of Galicia,
renowned for possessing the shrine of St. James at Compostela
was passed to Garcia, the youngest – and weakest son.

Ferdinand also had two daughters, Urraca and Elvira. To
these he gave the lordship of several monasteries. The latter
accepted the state of celibacy in which her father had decreed
she should live, but not so Urraca, who had protested so
violently that the town of Zamora was added to her property.

Garcia, a weak, self-indulgent man, with no heart for king-
ship, had also been given the task of conquering the Moorish
kingdom of Badajoz, to the south of Galicia, but he had no
heart for fighting and it was his brother Alfonso who came to
his aid. Sancho immediately accused him of trying to steal the
kingdom of his younger brother and the first of many violent
quarrels took place which were to split the monarchs apart.
In the month of March in the year 1068, the armies of Alfonso
and Sancho faced each other on the fields of Llantada on the
borders of the two kingdoms.

The Castilians, led with great success by Rodrigo de Vivar,
soon overcame the Leonese soldiers. In accordance with the
bargain struck before the battle began, the vanquished king
should have surrendered his kingdom and gone into exile, but

Alfonso refused to accept defeat and successfully managed to escape and return to Leon.

Over the next two years however, the quarrel was forgotten. Garcia's control of his kingdom gradually passed into the hands of his two scheming brothers. Together Sancho and Alfonso laid conquest to the kingdom of Badajoz.

In 1071, Garcia, realizing too late his lands were being stolen from under his very nose, attempted to prevent Castilian troops from crossing his land. He was seized and imprisoned in a castle in the mountains of Leon and his two brothers divided his land between them.

The additional land was an added incentive for them to begin quarrelling again and for a second time, a time and place was arranged where they could meet to resolve their differences. This time there would be no battle, but a tournament fought between knights from both sides. It was the beginning of the year 1072 and the place chosen was the lush green fields of Golpejerra on the banks of the river Carrion, within sight of Santa María de Carrion, a fortified town belonging to one of the most influential families in Castile. It was here Madelon and Paco were to meet their cousins.

"Will you be fighting?" Madelon asked.

"Yes. Rodrigo too. Why, are you hoping to see someone avenge your wounded pride? I expect there will be many young hot-heads willing to accept your favour."

"No – despite the terrible things you have said and thought about me, I bear you no ill will."

"My God, how sweet and innocent you are, I must have been blind not to realize the first time I held you in my arms, that no man had ever kissed you before – let alone owned your body."

His reference to that time brought the colour surging into Madelon's face. She could feel the warmth of his skin through his doublet where his arm was pressing against her. He smelt of sweat and horses and she was suddenly seized with the wild hope he might take her in his arms and rain passionate kisses on her mouth until she surrendered.

Whether or not her thoughts were betrayed on her face, Madelon did not know, but Valentín leaned closer to her, his pale eyes glittering. They were not cold now, nor was his face void of emotion. The naked hunger in his eyes told her his feelings matched her own.

He reached out to lightly touch the painful swelling on her temple and then his fingers entwined themselves in her loose hair and she found herself being drawn slowly towards him. In a hoarse whisper he said something in Arabic. She had noticed he always used this language when conversing with Yusuf and even at times with Rodrigo, once she had heard him speaking to his mother in Arabic. It was as natural to him as his own tongue, probably more so, since he seemed to spend more time with his Moorish friends than anyone else.

Shafra sha'r – yellow hair. He had called her that again. Then it had not been a dream before. And then he had said, *I have a great longing for you.* Why had he used Arabic, she wondered, unless he was afraid she would scorn him after their hitherto tempestuous relationship. It appeared no one had told him she spoke the language fluently and she said nothing to enlighten him. Perhaps this way she would come to know him better.

Her face glowed with pleasure at his words. She relaxed a little more against the arm that had slipped around her shoulders and was allowing herself to be drawn still more tightly against him when the entrance to the tent was suddenly flung to one side and Yusuf's tall, cloaked figure marched in.

Madelon parted from Valentín as if struck with a red-hot dagger as the Moor's black eyes fastened on the two figures seated so close together on the couch, and a broad grin spread across his swarthy face.

"Am I interrupting something?" he chuckled, looking at Valentín who had stood up, but did not appear to be in the least embarrassed.

"Doña Madelon and I have just had a meal before we leave," he replied calmly.

Yusuf bowed.

"*Allah ywasslak bissalâmi*. May God let you arrive in safety," he said. It was one of the many courtesy phrases the Moors used for people about to undertake a journey.

"*Allah yhûn ma 'ak!* God be with you," Madelon answered, which was the correct way to answer his good wishes. Not until she saw the amazed looks on the faces of the two men did she realize she had spoken in Arabic. Yusuf's unexpected arrival had thrown her completely off guard.

"Excuse me, I will see about the horses," Valentín said. He did not look at her, turning quickly away. What he was thinking she did not want to imagine.

"One moment, my friend." Yusuf detained him. "I wish Doña Madelon to take a small gift with her, if you approve?"

"The lady has a mind of her own," Valentín returned with a shrug of his shoulders.

From beneath his red and white silk cloak Yusuf produced a jewel case and snapped back the lid. The array of shimmering gems displayed before her eyes, made Madelon gasp

"I cannot decide what will best suit you," he murmured. "Come, Valentín, you have excellent taste. What do you think?"

Madelon held her breath as Valentín's eyes scanned the contents of the box and then he selected a necklace of blood red rubies. Yusuf nodded delightedly and motioned him to put them around Madelon's neck. She was dreaming, she thought, as the magnificent stones nestled on her skin. Her eyes widened as Valentín selected yet another piece – this time a ring – an enormous pearl set in gold. It slipped easily on to her little finger.

"Well chosen," Yusuf said with great enthusiasm. "The fire of the ruby and the cold dignity of the pearls. You certainly have an eye for beauty. The keen eye of the eagle."

Valentín's pale eyes flickered over the jewels he had just bestowed on Madelon and then rested briefly on her face.

"Fire and ice – I wonder which is the stronger?"

The inference was only too clear. She instantly turned

away, pretending to admire her ring, hating him for the cruel game he was playing with her. One moment he was holding her in his arms, the next, he was a stranger.

"Aiya has told me of your visit to her. You have a kind heart, Doña Madelon." Yusuf said moving to her side when Valentín had left them. Looking down at her flawless skin he momentarily cursed the quirk of fate which had given her to his friend, the Lord of the Eagles and then, his envy disintegrating, he was pleased they had come together. Valentín deserved only the best and this woman, with her great beauty and the untold delights her soft body, could give a man who had never known true love, made her far superior to any woman he had ever encountered.

"Your gifts overwhelmed me, my lord," Madelon said breathlessly.

"Beauty must be graced with something of equal beauty. What do you think of Valentín's choice?"

"They – they are perfect," she stammered.

"He is a perfectionist."

"Is that why he prefers to be alone?"

"Perhaps. Eagles are solitary creatures and prefer to fly alone – only sheep flock together. Valentín is as free as his eagles – as dangerous – and as lonely. He has yet to find his mate." Yusuf gave a soft laugh and his eyes fastened on her amusedly. "I am forgetting, he has already found her."

To cover her rapidly mounting confusion, Madelon said she was feeling hot and would like to go outside. In fact she was feeling far from warm. There was a strange coldness creeping through her limbs that made her want to shiver violently. Yusuf escorted her outside. Almost immediately Valentín appeared on his stallion, with Stephen riding behind him. Madelon was looking expectantly for her own mount when the former said:

"We will ride double, Doña Madelon, you are in no condition to handle a horse for yourself. Conquistador can carry us both easily and you may be able to sleep for a while."

The sound of Yusuf's laughter came out of the darkness

behind Madelon. It was obvious what he thought of the suggestion. She bit back the sharp retort which rose to her lips, too weary to argue. And what he said was true. She was incapable of handling a horse.

She allowed him to pull her up in front of him on the elaborate Moorish saddle with its silver trappings, casting a quick look into his face before he turned away and gathered up the reins, but his expression was unreadable.

Both Abraham ben Canaan and Rebecca came out to wave good-bye to the departing couple. Madelon watched them until the darkness swallowed them up and the last of the tents disappeared into the blackness of the night. She was alone with Valentín. Stephen remained a discreet distance to the rear and might not have existed.

"Are you comfortable?" Valentín asked. There was nothing in his voice to tell her he had deliberately planned this close intimacy between them for his own purpose. She had not forgotten how soft his voice could be, as it had been that night on the battlements, in the tent only a short while ago and was bitterly disappointed it was now so casual.

"Yes, thank you," she answered and a silence ensued between them.

How Valentín managed to guide his horse successfully over the uneven terrain, Madelon did not know. The animal seemed to have an instinct of its own, or it was remarkably well-trained, for it rarely stumbled and the gentle, swaying motions, began to make her feel sleepy. But she was also cold and could no longer suppress the bout of shivering she had held back before. Held tightly in Valentín's arms, it was impossible for him not to feel the shudders which racked her slender body.

"Are you feeling ill?" he asked in alarm.

"I'm cold," Madelon answered through chattering teeth. Immediately he reined in Conquistador.

"Sit still, I have a cloak in my *khurj*."

A *khurj*, Madelon discovered, were the two wide bags made out of horsehair which, when sewn together, were placed across the horse's rear behind the saddle. On a journey they would be used for storing provisions and extra clothing. Valentín drew out a thick burnous and wrapped it around her. As he pulled the wide hood over her head, his hand lingered on her cheek and she heard him mutter an inaudible oath.

"I knew it was madness to venture out tonight. It's so damned cold in these mountains, by the time we reach the castle you will have a raging fever. I'm of a mind to turn back."

"No, you must not," Madelon cried, twisting round in his arms to look up at him

Pale moonlight filtered through heavy clouds gave her skin a beautiful, translucent kind of glow. She felt her hands on her shoulders and waited eagerly for his lips to claim hers, but they never did. Instead he drew her head against his shoulder and set his horse in motion again.

Angry at the turbulent emotions which had almost made her beg for his kisses, Madelon huddled against him and pretended to sleep and at length she did. Above her, Valentín's face bore a strangely tender expression as he cradled her close. He bent his head until his lips touched the soft wisps of blonde hair escaping from beneath the hood and then, unable to restrain himself any longer, he kissed her on the mouth. Madelon stirred but did not awaken and he quickly drew back, alarmed at the passions she roused in him.

He had not possessed her and yet she gave him more pleasure than any woman he had ever known. He liked to be near her, though it was an effort to be so and not to catch her in his arms and bend her to his will. It would be easy for a man of his experience. It was not the number of women he had known which gave him this experience, for compared to his amorous friend Rodrigo, and other knights he knew, he was a modest lover, but the fact he had learned the art of love in the arms of a Moorish girl. She had tended his wounds after a battle which had been so long ago he could not remember the name of it, but he remembered the girl and the skill which had brought him back to life. During his years as a soldier women had scarcely entered his life. He had neither the time nor inclination to waste on them and then suddenly he had been plunged into a world that he never knew existed.

Madelon was a child in comparison to the Moorish girl who had taught him so much, he mused, yet their ages differed little. Once she arrived at Alfonso's court she too, would find another world and despite his mother's prophecies, he was sure it would appeal to her. How could the attentions of handsome young courtiers not flatter and please a child who had been deprived of love and affection for so long? She would undoubtedly be the centre of attention and soon forget him. For him, it would not be so easy.

Madelon was awakened by a loud noise in her ears. Opening her eyes with a start she discovered it was the drawbridge being raised behind her. They had arrived back at the Castle de Aguilas.

Dismounting, Valentín swung her to the ground. She realized it must be almost dawn. There were no lights showing from the castle – only the torches in the deserted courtyard still burned. The patrolling sentries on the ramparts were the only visible signs of life.

"Go inside and kindle some torches, Stephen," Valentín ordered his squire, "and find Doña Madelon's maid and say her mistress has returned and has need of her."

"My lord, a moment," Madelon said as he took her arm to escort her inside.

"It's late and you should be in a warm bed. Whatever you want to say can wait until tomorrow."

"No, it can't," she protested. "You are angry with me, aren't you, because I speak Arabic and understood what you said to me?"

"My mother told me of your talent for languages some while ago, I forgot, that's all," Valentín returned casually. "I don't enjoy being made a fool of, but it was my own fault."

"You said you wanted me," Madelon swayed closer to him, her hands clutching at his arms. "I think you meant it." Her determination to remain aloof from men and so save herself the same heartaches as her mother and Rebecca was forgotten at the memory of the pleasure his kisses and embraces had given her.

Valentín's hand closed over her wrists in a grip of steel and her jerked her hands free of his sleeves.

"Don't act like a little fool. I was merely taking advantage of what I thought might turn out to be a very enjoyable evening. Of course I wanted you – any man in his right mind would want you and have acted the same as I did. Soft words and a few stolen caresses aren't a declaration of love, you foolish child, so stop looking so starry-eyed and get up to bed where you belong."

Madelon reeled back from him, her eyes dilated in horror. Unable to stand the sardonic smile tugging at his lips, she turned and ran up the stairs into the castle. The Great Hall was dark with shadows. Stephen had only paused to light two torches before going on his way to find Diya and Madelon was forced to cease her headlong flight in order to see where she was going. A long shadow slanted across her path as Valentín moved up behind her. Wordlessly she stalked on towards the staircase. A dark shape suddenly rose from a chair in front of her and she came to an abrupt halt with a cry of alarm.

"Where have you been until this hour?" Paco demanded harshly. She saw he was fully dressed and armed, both with sword and dagger. His expression was furious.

"I went to thank the doctor for all he did for you," she replied with a wildly beating heart. Behind her more torches flared to life, illuminating her brother's features more clearly.

"I prefer not to hold a conversation with a shadow," Valentín drawled as Paco glared in his direction.

"I'll not waste words with you," he snarled. "Cold steel is all you understand. Haven't you enough Moorish mistresses without seducing my sister?"

"There will be no fighting beneath this roof. You are my guest. Keep your brave words for the fields of Golpejerra,

Montevides. Besides I gave your sister my word I wouldn't fight you." Valentín's green eyes glittered dangerously, but he kept his own temper well in check.

"Did you now." Paco wheeled on Madelon with blazing eyes. "What else did he give you to make you run in here as if the devil himself were after you?"

"You are talking like a fool, Paco," Madelon cried. "You must have a fever to act this way with me. Of what am I accused, besides the error of not asking your permission to go to Yusuf's camp and of having enough manners to remember you would have died but for Abraham ben Canaan?"

"It's you who are the fool. I warned you what kind of man Maratín is. I can't altogether blame you. You are too young to protect yourself against such scum, but this won't happen again. You will remain in your room until we leave tomorrow." Paco seemed beside himself with rage and she was unpleasantly reminded of her father as he stood before her, his face contorted with anger. She knew it was not wise to argue. "Get upstairs," Paco shouted, "unless you want me to take a whip to you . . ."

His voice trailed off as he saw the look on Madelon's face and realized the memories he had evoked. "You know I didn't mean that."

"Didn't you? Why not, you have his temper? Just now you looked like him – sounded like him. I swear if you lay a hand on me, Paco, I'll . . . I'll," she faltered, knowing she loved him too much to retaliate whatever he did to her. She could pity him, but not hurt him.

"If he touches you he'll have six inches of my blade in him," Valentín growled.

He stepped up to her side and she was horrified to see his sword already more than half out of its scabbard. She caught his arm and hung on to it.

"No – no – you don't understand. Please don't interfere."

"Where did you get that?" Paco asked in a deadly voice. She saw his eyes were fastened on the ruby necklace around her throat, just visible beneath the burnous. She lifted a hand

and hesitantly touched the warm stones and in doing so revealed the ring on her finger. "And that?"

"The Moor Yusuf gave them to me," she said as calmly as she was able. She was really frightened now, for Paco was shaking with rage. He began shouting abuse at her and the man at her side until Valentín scornfully interrupted him, saying:

"Moorish custom demands a host gives his guest something to take away as a momento of their visit."

"A priceless necklace and a pearl ring bigger than even I've ever set eyes on before," Paco sneered. "God, Madelon, what have you done? Have you been bought with worthless baubles and sweet words as your mother was before you? Why didn't you heed my warnings? To give yourself to such a man as this ... I could forgive any other, but not him." Paco's voice rose to a shrill hysterical pitch. Without warning he threw himself at Valentín, taking him completely by surprise, and the two of them fell fighting to the floor. Madelon saw the flash of steel and screamed as Paco aimed his dagger at the other man's chest.

"Stop it! Please, Paco, you are wrong ... listen to me ..."
Her pleas went unheard. She heard a grunt of pain and through half-closed eyes saw Valentín had disarmed her brother. The blade of the weapon was against Paco's throat. To her tortured vision he seemed about to use it and she threw herself on her knees beside him pleading.

"No, Valentín ... spare him for the love of God."
Valentín looked up at her startled. Without hesitation he stood up and tossed the dagger across the far side of the room, contemptuously.

He said something briefly in Arabic, then as she sat staring up at him in a shocked silence, he asked harshly,

"Do you understand?"
She nodded, bright tears flooding her eyes and streaming unchecked down over her cheeks. "I do for you what I would do for no other – man or woman" he had said. He did care for her. He had known better than she what her brother's reaction

would be to a liaison between them. In trying to make her hate him, he had been attempting to save her from Paco's anger.

"Thank you." No other words would come, her heart was too full of happiness. Even if they were forced to part for ever, at least she knew. "Thank you."

"Don't grovel," Paco snarled from where he lay on the floor, nursing a badly bruised shoulder. The brief struggle had shown him how weak he still was. He would have to wait for his reckoning with Valentín Maratín but his day would come. Valentín bent down and hauled him unceremoniously to his feet.

"Don't forget to thank your sister for saving your life. Now get out of my sight."

"I want two horses for tomorrow."

"You will leave when I do – the day after tomorrow," Valentín retorted. "My men have orders to use force to stop you if you try to leave before then. We Castilians don't allow spies to wander our countryside alone."

Madelon went up to her brother and took him gently by the hand.

"Please, Paco, let us go."

"When you have given the Lord de Aguilas his gifts back."

Madelon's warning look silenced the reply which rose to Valentín's lips. Unfastening the necklace she took it off and placed it on the table behind her. Beside it she laid the pearl ring. Only then did Paco leave the Great Hall. She did not look at Valentín as she passed him.

Crossing to the table, Valentín stared down at the rubies. He touched them and felt they were still warm where they had rested against her skin.

Rodrigo Díaz stepped out of the shadowy alcove beneath the staircase where he had witnessed the fight and slowly crossed the hall. He had been en route to his room when the sound of voices raised in anger had brought him to investigate and he had been on the point of intervening in the dispute when Madelon had brought it to an abrupt end. He was surprised – and disturbed – by the murderous look on his friend's face and cast a disgusted look after the departing figures.

"One day I'm afraid you are going to have to kill that young pup," he growled.

Valentín barely glanced at him – he was still looking at the jewels he held in a tightly clenched fist.

"Yes," he muttered. "I will."

CHAPTER
NINE

THE day was heavy and oppressive. At dawn, when the riders had left the Castle de Aguilas, the plateau and the valley below had been shrouded in heavy mist which made the descent along the narrow trail slow and tortuous. The weather did not improve even when the Sierra de Gredos was far behind them. Black clouds gathered in the overcast sky threatening rain, but none came to relieve the terrible humidity which made clothes cling uncomfortably to perspiring bodies and seemed the lengthen the already long journey.

Francesca Maratín had given Madelon a cloak of sumptuous velvet, lined with fur to keep her warm. When the girl protested she could not take it, Valentín's mother had smiled and said she could return it on her next visit.

Remembering her words as she rode, Madelon touched the velvet resting against her cheek. She wanted desperately to go back to Valentín's home again, to get to know his mother and sister without Paco's disapproving eyes following everywhere, to be alone with Valentín so that she could put into words what her eyes said every time they followed him, but she knew it was impossible. As the journey progressed, she forced herself to accept the fact she would never return and she must put all of them out of her mind. Her brother's behaviour had not improved since the night in the Great Hall. The next day he had been confined to his room with an armed guard outside to ensure he did not leave. Madelon had remained in her room too, despite Teresa's attempts to get her to go riding on her last day and later, to dine with them. Madelon was infinitely relieved Valentín did not seek her out and try to change her mind. In a few days they would part – never to see each other again. He would return to his great castle and she would be with Paco in Leon. No two worlds could be further apart. Nor for one moment did she consider the possibility of Sancho of Castile being the victor at Golpejerra for it meant Paco would be imprisoned. She would be free to go her own way, to return to the Maratín family if she wished in pursuit of her own happiness while her brother languished in some filthy dungeon slowly wasting away – it was unthinkable.

When they had started out on their journey that morning Paco had demonstrated the skilful healing powers of the Jewish doctor who had cared for him, by starting a fight with the Sergeant-at-arms who was his escort. He had knocked down three men and seized a sword before he was overpowered by Rodrigo Díaz. His face a mask of fury, Valentín had ordered him to be bound on his horse and to have a constant guard of four men. Watching him Madelon thought he might be regretting his leniency of the other night. Wisely she held herself in check and did not interfere as she had done before.

For most of the morning she rode beside Teresa and Rodrigo in the middle of the accompanying soldiers, listening only half-heartedly to the other girl's eager chatter or to Rodrigo describing the excitement of a tournament. Her eyes repeatedly singled out the lone rider in front of them, clearly identifiable by the golden eagle on the back of his cloak. He had not spoken to her at all, but from time to time he rode past her down the column and she was comforted by the warmth in his eyes and the faint smile meant for her alone. Once she caught sight of Teresa and Rodrigo exchanging knowing glances, but she said nothing to disillusion them. They would realize their mistake soon enough.

Towards midday they rested on the banks of the Duero river. While the horses were being watered, Madelon tried to find some way to console her brother, but he only repeated his suspicions that Valentín intended to take them before Sancho as his prisoners. Madelon, equally determined he was not, went in search of the Lord of the Eagles, only to be told he

had ridden on ahead. She did not see him again until they had
been travelling for several hours and then there was no chance
to talk to him for he was with Rodrigo. It was as if he was
deliberately keeping out of her way, she thought.

In the afternoon the sun broke unexpectedly through the
clouds and within a short time, these had disappeared and
the sky was blue and completely cloudless. It was a blessed
relief for Madelon to remove her enveloping cloak and to feel
the warmth of the sun on her body. With the whole countryside bathed in bright yellow sunshine and the birds singing
in the trees, she found it hard to believe Valentín might have
lied to her, despite everything. As she reined in her horse
on the rise of a hill and looked down on the fields of Golpejerra, she found herself beginning to tremble. They had arrived.
Now Paco would be proved wrong – or else she would have to
admit the word of Valentín Maratín was worthless.

Below her were hundreds of silken pavilions of all shapes
and sizes. Some were striped, with different colours, others
were all one colour and very brilliant.

She noticed the tents were divided into two camps by a
long, narrow field where workmen were busily erecting
wooden stands for the most important spectators to watch the
tournament in comfort. A crowd of curious people had come
to watch and a pie seller, who had set up his stall nearby, was
doing a roaring trade with hot pies.

Madelon saw the scarlet flag of Alfonso of Leon waving in
the breeze on the largest pavilion furthest away from her. That
of her other cousin, Sancho, was displayed from the watch-
tower of the walled town of Santa María de Carrion.

The Counts of Carrion were proud of their claim to have
descended from a famous knight called Gomez Díaz and were
always known as the Beni-Gomez, or sons of Gomez. The
present Beni-Gomez were staunch supporters of Alfonso and
had opened up their town to him and his men. Not without
great reluctance they had also found quarters for Sancho and
his entourage. If the tournament went the wrong way and

the latter won, then it would be as well to be on the right side of the new monarch.

"Well, Doña Madelon, we have arrived."

Madelon was so lost in thought that she did not hear Rodrigo ride up. She turned to him, unable to hide the apprehension in her face from his alert eyes.

"And what now, my lord? Are we to be paraded through the town to your king?"

"I thought you knew Valentín better than that," Rodrigo reproved. "How many times has he told you, you are not his prisoners. Rather it is the other way around – he is yours."

"I wish it could be possible," Madelon sighed, "but I am no more free to follow the dictates of my heart than he is. His loyalty to Sancho who hates the name of Montevides. Mine is to my brother who hates Valentín – and you, lord Rodrigo. I am afraid he may try to kill you for our father's death."

"A father neither of you loved. Faith, what are you, a family of hypocrites?" Rodrigo demanded fiercely. "Follow your heart, let it lead you into the arms of a man who believes you are the most wonderful creature God ever created. Don't wait and hope he'll tell you, because he may never do so. Valentín has little use for words. He's a knight – a leader of men. You might find yourself bundled up and carried off one night."

And risk a clash with Paco? Madelon thought. No, he would not do that. Madelon was dazed by Rodrigo's words, but she knew Valentín would not come between her and her brother, no matter what his feelings were. The most wonderful creature God ever created ... did he really think of her that way. And then she recalled his words when she had asked him why he had called her a "golden savage". *Like a wild horse you have yet to be broken. The man who tames you will have gained himself a prize* ... ! He had broken her, not with a whip or cruel actions, but by the force of his personality. She had not been able to rid her thoughts of him since their first encounter. Despite all her determination not to become involved, he had taken her by storm and she knew she would never recover. She was not sure she wanted to.

Rodrigo sat silently admiring the flawless skin which had taken on a rosy tint beneath the ferocity of the sun. There was no denying she was beautiful and for the moment, as innocent as a new-born babe as far as men were concerned. In a short while she would be united with her cousins and then how long would it be before the innocence vanished under Urraca's expert guidance and Madelon was brought to realize what power her beauty could wield over men? A few months perhaps? No, not that long. A few weeks of careful coaching and Madelon del Rivas y Montevides could become as dangerous and as evil as Urraca herself. Paco Montevides was completely under the thumb of his mistress and would be helpless to intervene – he might not even want to. His sister's subtle use of her charms in the right quarters could bring her untold wealth – information useful to Alfonso – and for him there would be Urraca's gratitude.

Sweet Jesus! Rodrigo thought. Poor Valentín.

"Hola! Lord Rodrigo."

He became aware of a rider hailing him from the lower slopes of the hill, waving frantically as he galloped towards them and he recognized Teresa's betrothed, Cristóbal de Altamiras.

As the young knight reined in his panting horse and exchanged friendly greetings with Rodrigo, Valentín rode to Madelon's side. She cast a quick glance over her shoulder and saw Paco watching her. He was still heavily guarded.

"Valentín, it's good to see you. What happened, why are you so late?" Cristóbal enquired.

He was as good-looking as Teresa's description, Madelon thought, and was pleased for the young girl. He was barely more than twenty, but he had his spurs and made an impressive figure seated on a high-stepping charger, whose bridle was adorned by tiny silver bells which made a delightful tinkling sound as the horse pranced impatiently.

"Explanations can come later," Valentín returned with a

smile. "Tell me where Don Sancho is and you can be off to greet Teresa. I didn't think you rode out to welcome me," he chuckled as Cristóbal's face grew red with embarrassment.

"The king is at the house of the Beni-Gomez," the boy answered, adding with a distasteful grimace, "Don Alfonso is housed alongside him. The Beni-Gomez are making sure to be friendly with both of them until they knew which way the tournament fares, or else they intend a dagger for our king's back while he sleeps in one of their beds. I'm at the house of Colter, the vintner and I've held rooms for you and lord Rodrigo. I thought the setting would appeal to you both and I've even arranged for two of the prettiest ladies in town to be your companions at the feast tonight."

"Enough – slow down, for heaven's sake," Valentín interrupted. "Our lodgings will be fine as long as there's enough wine to satisfy my thirst. As for the female company, no doubt Rodrigo will be able to accommodate them both. Now, what's this about a feast?"

"It was Don Alfonso's idea that all the contesting knights and their ladies, with himself and our king at their head, should get together to prove their good faith."

"Good faith! Rot," Rodrigo growled. "We'll all be poisoned, or stabbed in the back."

"I don't think so, not yet anyway. Don't forget Don Alfonso is also staying in Santa María de Carrion of his own free will – I call that a show of good faith," Madelon glared at the three men. "Who will stop a Castilian, in his own land, from breaking the truce? You, Don Rodrigo – or you, my Lord de Aguilas ..." she broke off at the amusement mounting on Valentín's face.

Cristóbal de Altamiras gazed from one to the other in puzzlement, then at a significant nod from Valentín, he muttered a rapid "by your leave" and rode on to where Teresa was eagerly awaiting him.

"This is where we part company," Valentín told Madelon. "It will be best if you ride in with your brother ahead of us – alone."

"Thank you. Will I see you again?"

He smiled briefly, but his eyes had lost their warmth. They had come to the end of the road together – their two paths might never cross again except by chance. She smiled faintly and added:

"Perhaps not, that might be tempting providence – and my brother a little too far. It is better to part now – as friends."

Madelon did not look at Paco who had left his escort and ridden up to them, scowling fiercely. Valentín told him curtly where he would find his cousin and motioned him to ride on. He did so, with deliberate slowness.

Unexpectedly Valentín reached across to where Madelon sat and took both her hands in his and pressed her fingers to his lips. The searching look he gave her made her heart leap.

"*Insha'llah*," he whispered. "If it is written we are destined for each other, no force on this earth will be able to keep us apart. Go now."

His words, almost identical to those spoken to her by Aiya, brought the tears to Madelon's eyes. Valentín looked alarmed, then puzzled when he saw she was smiling too.

"You don't know what happiness you have brought me. Thank you."

He watched her riding swiftly after her brother, his face strangely troubled. Rodrigo gave a short laugh.

"Women! Why don't they say what they mean? Did you understand her?"

"No. I'm glad I didn't. In the past I've found it only too easy to understand women, my friend. Now I shall have a reason to seek her out again and find out what she meant, won't I?"

Madelon kept close behind her brother as they rode through the main gate for the streets were crowded with people who bustled along on both sides of the horses, dashing to and fro across their paths and threatening to separate them.

The streets were cobbled and uneven, forcing her to keep a tight rein on her horse. The smell was horrible. Most of it seemed to be caused by the foul rubbish lying everywhere. It was worse as they crossed over the town sewer which was little more than a ditch and lessened only slightly in the town interior. It seemed as if hundreds of people had invaded Santa María de Carrion for the tournament and already vendors had set up their stalls in the market places to attract and in most cases, dazzle the peasants with their wares. Madelon wished she could get near enough to Paco to make him slow down and let her inspect some of them. She glimpsed beautiful stitched gauntlets and belts trimmed with silver and hoped she could remember where the stalls were, so that she could visit them later. She had somehow to refurnish her whole wardrobe before the court assembled. On another stall there were shelves full of soft leather shoes with pointed toes in a variety of exciting colours and beside that, was a draper's stall with bolts of satin and velvet cloth – cloth of gold and silver from far-off Persia, decorated Cyprus silks and damask from Damascus. She had to have something really outstanding to wear at the tournament, Madelon decided, if only to make Paco proud of her so that he forgot her friendship with Valentín Maratín.

She had eaten nothing since starting out that morning, and she rode on, trying hard to ignore the emptiness in her stomach which was made worse by the delicious smell of baked bread wafting from a line of bakers' shops.

Most of the houses on the outskirts of the town, nestling beneath the fortified outer wall were of daub and wattle, with thatched roofs. These belonged to the poorer people and lower class merchants. An immediate improvement came as they rode past an inner wall into the heart of the town. There was far less garbage strewn about the streets and the buildings were of stone, mostly coated with white plaster which gave them a bright, fresh appearance. Several tall church spires soared above the roofs of other buildings. The sight of them was somehow comforting to Madelon and helped her put Yusuf, Prince of Tehlan, Aiya and the days she had spent at the Moorish camp, out of her mind. Nothing could ever change the fact that they were Moslems and she was a Christian. Paco would want to forget what was, to his mind, an unpleasant episode and she would have to do the same, or incur his anger.

Her brother drew rein before an impressive house which stretched almost the whole length of the street. A wide palisade of steps rose upwards to where two scarlet liveried servants stood in front of the massive doors. He dismounted and stood staring at the house completely forgetful of Madelon who was forced to dismount by herself.

"Is this where our cousins are?" she asked.

"Yes." He turned and stared at her coldly. "I would remind you, you are my sister and as such you will be expected to act with a certain degree of dignity. Any irregular conduct will not only sully my honour, but the name we both bear. That would make me angry, Madelon. Do I make myself clear?"

Madelon went white to the lips. So he expected her to act like a Montevides, did he? well, she could do that well enough.

"You have no cause to worry on my behalf, Paco. I won't bring any disgrace on any of the things you hold in such high esteem, but for the first time in my life I find myself wishing I was born of peasant stock. I envy the freedom of a girl who can surrender to her heart's desires and give herself to any man she pleases without bringing shame to those about her, who consider their honour so much more important than hers. May I take your arm, or am I to follow behind you like a lackey?"

Completely stunned before her contemptuous onslaught, Paco offered his arm and together they ascended into the house.

The first thought which struck Madelon as they entered the royal presence was that the Beni-Gomez, with all their pride of ancestry, did not possess a house as comfortable as Valentín Maratín. The thought gave her great satisfaction.

Her cousin Alfonso had changed little over the years. He was a man of medium height and build, in his late twenties. His dark hair was cut rather shorter than was fashionable and

his neat beard was trimmed to perfection as always. Madelon
hoped he would not bestow the honour of a kiss on her as he
had done the last time they had met for his beard had so
tickled her cheek she had wanted to burst out laughing.

"Sire, forgive my late arrival, it was unfortunately not of my
doing." Paco went down on one knee before his king and
kissed the jewelled fingers extended beneath his nose.

"How so, Don Paco? I seem to remember you were to meet
us here four days ago. How can there be a tournament when
one of my best knights is gallivanting around the countryside
with a wench – even such a comely one?" Alfonso's eyes
fastened on Madelon's impassive face. Deliberately she remained standing, meeting his gaze with matched candour. If
Paco was to forgive her, she must make a lasting impression
on her cousin, she thought. She heard a murmur run through
the courtiers crowded into the small chamber where the
audience was held at her boldness. Slowly she sank into an
elaborate, faultless curtsey and then, raising her head, she said
with a mocking smile:

"My king pays a great compliment to his cousin."

At Alfonso's side a woman who was surrounded by hand-
somely-clad men and women, turned to look at her. She was
breathtaking. Her raven hair plaited into one thick coil and
wound on to her head was adorned with a jewelled coronet,
over a pale coloured wimple. Jet black eyes studied Madelon
with growing interest. Her skin had an ivory sheen to it and
her red mouth was full and sensuous. With a shock of surprise,
Madelon realized this was her cousin, Urraca.

Suddenly she was ashamed of her own appearance. Dust
clung to the hem of her skirt, her face was flushed and wisps
of hair had escaped from her plaits to fall untidily around her
shoulders. She hardly represented a dignified picture and her
confusion turned into anger as she heard an amused titter
from somewhere behind. All the women around her were
lavishly dressed and heavily jewelled and Urraca was the most
outstanding of all.

Her tight-fitting gown was of scarlet velvet, the hem

bordered with ermine and sewn with diamonds. The neck-line, slashed low across her breasts was bolder than any other in the room. She had only to crook her little finger and immediately the young men clustered around her in force, each hoping he would be selected to do her bidding. Now she had seen her again, Madelon knew why she was reputed to hold such sway over men and she was envious of her power, although at the same time, a little frightened by it.

"Why, I do believe it is our little cousin, Madelon," Urraca murmured. Her voice was rather low with husky undertones. Her brilliant eyes wandered over the faces around her, all smiling because they expected her to come out with one of her witty remarks. Urraca's accuracy at shooting down her enemies or rivals with words was renowned throughout the court. There was a stunned silence as she rose to her feet, disdainfully ignoring the many hands outstretched to help her and descended to where Madelon stood.

"Come, cousin, kiss me," she said with a soft laugh and enfolded the amazed girl in her arms. Strong perfumes invaded Madelon's nostrils as she obeyed and pecked dutifully at Urraca's cheeks. "I vow you'd do better than that with a handsome man," Urraca murmured stepping back. "We shall have to find you one and see, won't we? My poor girl, you look exhausted. Why didn't Paco take you straight to your apartments?"

Madelon looked almost desperately at her brother.

"I thought it best to come directly here, to present my sister to her benefactress," he said somewhat stiffly.

"And subject her to the pathetic witticisms of my brother's courtiers? Look at her, for God's sake, she looks more like a peasant girl than a Montevides. Where are all the gowns she was to have had made?"

"They were stolen," Madelon broke in before Paco had time to answer. "We were almost captured by Moors. My clothes were lost and my ladies-in-waiting taken prisoner – and Paco was hurt ..."

Urraca's dark eyes swiftly scanned Paco's unsmiling face, silently questioning him.

"I am quite recovered," he murmured. "It was only a scratch."

Madelon opened her mouth to dispute the bare-faced lie, but something in his expression stopped her.

"I want to hear this story in full," Urraca said to Madelon. "Come with me."

Under the eyes of the astonished courtiers who fell back to allow her through, Urraca took Madelon by the hand and led her from the room. Behind them Madelon could hear Alfonso laughing, but she did not understand why.

Diya fell into step behind her mistress as they began to ascend a long, wide staircase to the upper part of the house.

"Who are you?" Urraca stopped and stared at the Persian girl in her dark-coloured burnous.

"My maid, Diya, she is invaluable to me," Madelon said quickly for fear her cousin was disturbed by the sight of the Moorish girl and might decide to find her a Christian maid instead.

"We'll see the truth of that statement when she has dressed you tonight," Urraca said, moving on.

She led Madelon to a room overlooking the street where merchants were shouting and bartering with customers. Her lips curled in digust as she looked down at them, then turning to Madelon who stood looking rather lost in the middle of the room, she studied her intently.

"What do you say to a bath?"

"Yes, please," Madelon replied enthusiastically.

"Good, I'll have one brought up for you and you can tell me all about this narrow escape you've had. I want to know everything, mark you. I have a tidy mind which doesn't like loose ends."

"You may not like all of it," Madelon said, wondering how her cousin would react to the news that her brother's enemies had been involved.

"Let me be the judge of that."

Madelon began her story. Seated on the edge of the bed, Urraca listened with half-closed eyes. Not once did she interrupt, not even when Madelon mentioned Valentín or Rodrigo Díaz or the fact she had been a guest of a Moorish prince.

A huge copper tub arrived and was filled to the brim with hot and cold water alternately, brought by a bevy of servants who moved in and out of the room so swiftly that Madelon's head began to ache from watching them. A gleam entered Urraca's eyes as Diya disrobed her mistress and helped her into the tub, but she made no comment and continued to listen intently until Madelon had finished talking.

"So you've taken the eye of the Lord of the Eagles, have you? What do you think of him?"

"I'm not sure," Madelon lied, with wildly beating heart. "He is a strange man. You are mistaken in thinking he found me interesting – he saved my life – but . . ."

"But he didn't tumble you?" Urraca laughed. "It wasn't for lack of trying on his part. I'll warrant. Stand up – let me look at you. I want to see which of my gowns will best suit that fair colouring. Tonight you will show those twittering idiots who were stupid enough to laugh at you, that you are not only a Montevides, but the most desirable woman at court – after me, that is. Come now, don't be shy. Did you hide behind a towel when Maratín was around?"

Blushing fiercely Madelon allowed the towel to fall away from her. Still dripping wet she stood in front of Urraca. Admiration crept into the woman's eyes as they wandered over the pure white body and the slender legs. The gently curving hips and upwards to the tiny waist and the perfectly rounded breasts.

In a low fierce whisper, Diya muttered something about her mistress catching cold and flung the towel around her again. Urraca hardly noticed. She had satisfied herself as to Madelon's usefulness. With or without Paco's help, she would become a talented spy, especially now that she had associations in the enemy camp. Once she had tasted the delights of love, the pleasure her body could bring a man and the satisfaction she herself would receive, she might even become Urraca's right hand. Her first lover would have to be picked with great care. She would need not only a man of experience, but one who possessed enough patience to lead her gently into the first affair and not be so overwhelmed by her beauty he would think only of his own satisfaction.

Urraca smiled at Madelon and rose to her feet. She knew the ideal man. She might even arrange for him to marry Madelon, whose dowry she knew consisted of her mother's lands near Salamanca and a vast amount of money. With that in her hands and a husband ruthless enough to bend Madelon to his will should it become necessary, she would be well pleased.

"I have just the right gown for you," she said. "It will be sent to you with whatever else you require. Tomorrow we must think about what you will wear for the tournament."

"I have a few clothes. I'm sure I will be able to find something suitable," Madelon protested.

"Very well." Wisely Urraca did not press the younger girl. There would be time for that once she had been at court a few days. After the tournament was over and her beloved brother was king of both Leon and Castile, she would give her innocent little cousin her full attention.

At the door she turned suddenly.

"I want to ask a favour of you, my dear."

"Anything." Madelon could have bitten off her tongue for answering so quickly.

"How sweet you are. It's a very small favour really. Tonight I want you to make peace with your cousin Sancho on Paco's behalf. Your brother is far too stubborn for his own good, lately he has become even worse and he flatly refuses to make the first move."

"And you think I should?"

"Sancho is your cousin and he has an eye for a pretty face. One look at you and he'll forget what the quarrel was all about. Do you know, by the way?"

Madelon shook her head. The rift had happened while she was away from home and Paco had never spoken of it.

"Paco may not want me to interfere."

"Think about it, my dear. Better to make peace with Sancho now – before the tournament. If his knights should win, God forbid, it will be too late. Paco holds a very special place in my heart. Do it for me, if not for him," Urraca said, bestowing on Madelon one of her most captivating smiles.

Completely taken in Madelon nodded. When it was put to her that way, what harm was there? Later on however, when she had rested, she began to wonder if there was not an ulterior motive to Urraca's "little favour"? Had her agreement not placed her just that little bit under her cousin's thumb, exactly where Valentín had said she would be as soon as they met?

Valentín! What would his reaction be when she presented herself before Sancho and asked for her brother to be reinstated in the king's favour? They had parted as friends; was this to part them again and evoke his old suspicions about her?

CHAPTER
TEN

As soon as it began to get dark, the streets became filled with people. Madelon sat watching them from her window, her chin resting on her hands. On the bed behind her lay the dress Urraca had sent her to wear that evening. It was of flame-coloured silk, the bodice sewn with hundreds of tiny pearls. Madelon did not like the colour and would have preferred something softer, but she dared not offend her cousin by refusing to wear it.

Diya too voiced her dislike of the dress as she helped her mistress into it.

"It makes you look too pale," she protested, "and as for that neckline . . ."

Madelon gazed down at the neckline which was cut low across her breasts, revealing more of them than she had ever allowed before.

"It's the fashion, Diya, don't make such a fuss. Until we can go out and buy more material ourselves, this will have to do."

She slipped her feet into the red leather shoes which had arrived with the dress, but deigned not to wear the items of jewellery Urraca had sent because she did not like the settings. How she wished she still had her ruby necklace.

Diya pulled her hair back into a severe line from her face, covered it with a dainty coif of the same material as the dress and brushed the loose tresses down over Madelon's shoulders. The simplicity of styling enhanced Madelon's delicate bone structure and made sure all eyes would be envying the golden hair cascading from beneath the coif.

Sounds of great revelry reached Madelon's ears as she

descended the stairs and stood hesitating outside the hall
where the feast was taking place. Through the half-open door
beside which stood two stone-faced servants in richly embroidered livery, she could see most of the people inside. On
the left were the King of Castile and his entourage – opposite,
the King of Leon and his. Madelon saw Urraca seated on the
right-hand of Alfonso, surrounded by the usual bevy of
fawning courtiers. She was dressed completely in black, the
severity of the colour broken only by a dazzling diamond
necklace at her throat. No one else was dressed so boldly,
except Madelon herself, and she began to wonder if the
comparison was deliberate.

Her eyes were drawn to the dais where Sancho of Castile
sat, deep in conversation with Rodrigo, in the place of honour
beside him. A little further down the table sat Valentín. But
who was the lovely girl at his side, leaning close against him
to whisper intimately in his ear? Madelon grew cold with the
realization this was Raquel Vargas, his ward. From the way
she was laughing and holding his hands, it appeared they
were not as estranged as Teresa had wanted her to believe.

Dragging her eyes away, she glanced along the faces until
she recognized Teresa, looking exquisite in pink satin, seated
beside Cristóbal de Altamiras and she inwardly sighed at the
look of adoration on the girl's face. Would she ever worship
a man with such blind adoration? If there were no obstacles
to overcome and she was in Valentín's arms again, would it be
the same? Could he rouse her to the same heights of passion,
or would she discover the thrill had gone forever? What was
love? How would she know when she loved a man – if she
ever did?

A soft step on the stairs made her turn. Paco stood for a
moment in silent admiration, then came forward and kissed
her on both cheeks.

"Madelon, you look lovely."

"You don't think this dress is too bold?" she asked.

"Not at all. You will have the eyes of every man in the room
following you wherever you go. Urraca has superb taste."

Of course, he likes it because it had been chosen by his mistress, Madelon thought and was surprised to find she was angry. Surely she couldn't be jealous of her cousin's liaison with her brother? Was this how Paco had felt when he caught her with Captain Rodriguez and Valentín? Now she could understand a little better.

With a bright smile she laid her hand on Paco's arm.

"Are we friends again?"

"How can I be angry with you when you look so delightful. Alfonso was quite taken by you – and as for Urraca ..." He had spent the last few hours in the arms of his mistress, listening to her compliments on Madelon's beauty and manners and of the perfect way she had conducted herself while with their enemies. Madelon had been unable to convince him her friendship with Valentín Maratín was innocent, but Urraca had succeeded.

"Yes, Paco, what kind of impression did I make on cousin Urraca?"

Her brother stared at her, aware of an oddness in her tone, but she was still smiling and he dismissed it as imagination on his part.

"Once you have had a chance to settle to court life, she's talking of making you one of her companions. It's an honour she doesn't bestow on many people. She has only two companions at the moment, both middle-aged and from very important families."

"Does it mean I shall be staying at court with you?" Madelon stammered.

"Yes, isn't it marvellous?"

His sister nodded, not daring to speak. Paco's face glowed with such enthusiasm, she did not have the heart to tell him she did not want to remain.

Unaware of the gloomy cloud he had cast over his sister's head he escorted her into the banqueting hall. Madelon was aware of the excited whispers coursing around the room as she walked and of the many eyes which fastened on her.

Before leading her up to the dais where Alfonso and

Urraca, sat, Paco brought her before the long table where Sancho sat still talking with Rodrigo Díaz and bowed respectfully. Madelon made a low curtsey.

Sancho glanced at them briefly and signalled with a wave of his hand for them to go to their places. Madelon saw the momentary scowl on his face as he recognized Paco's downbent head. Flushing at the deliberate snub, for Sancho had been receiving guests all evening with a smile and a few words of greeting, her brother straightened and joined Urraca. Not until he had seated himself did he realize his sister had remained where she was in a determined effort to force Sancho to acknowledge her.

Rodrigo touched the arm of his king and whispered to him. The King of Castile turned and looked down at the woman in red who had ignored his dismissal. He was a broad-shouldered man who wore his royal ermine trimmed robes with an air of great authority. His hair and eyes were as black as his sister's and his handsome face as dark as any Moor. Only the faint shadow of grey at his temples betrayed he was older than his youthful countenance implied.

"By Sant' 'Iago, what have we here?" he demanded.

Deliberately he allowed his bold gaze to linger on the exposed part of Madelon's breasts until the colour surged into her cheeks and then he lifted his eyes to her face with a satisfied smile. That would teach the impudent minx a lesson. She looked too much like her mother for him not to have recognized her, but Paco's presence had made him refuse her his recognition. Her stubbornness both surprised and pleased him. So, despite the whipping she had endured and the years of convent life, she still had a will of her own. Valentín had only briefly mentioned her. It had been Rodrigo who filled in the details and Sancho had been annoyed that one of his best knights had fallen into the trap of a woman's smile – and a smile from a Montevides at that.

But now he had had seen her, he forgave the Lord of the Eagles. Valentín was taken aback when Sancho looked down the length of the table at him, his face wreathed in smiles.

Was this a sign of approval, he wondered, or was the crafty fox already weighing up the advantages of having an ally in the enemy camp?

Drawing herself upright, Madelon stared challengingly into her cousin's dark eyes. The light from the wall torches caught the brilliant colour of her gown and to the silent onlookers she looked like a golden angel surrounded by fire.

"Have I altered so drastically that my gracious lord does not recognize his cousin?" she asked sweetly.

Sancho's mouth quirked sardonically.

"You are the image of your mother in looks, but I'll wager you didn't inherit the sting to your tongue from one so sweet and gentle as she was. You have been too long with pious old women. Come, cousin, sit beside me," he motioned to the empty chair on his left. "Perhaps I can find a topic of conversation to make you feel more friendly towards me. If I cannot, I know of someone who can."

It was a royal command and Madelon dared not disobey. Out of the corner of her eye she saw the look of astonishment on Paco's face. Urraca, who had not taken her eyes off the figure in red since she entered the room, was smiling and Madelon realized she was thinking this had all been deliberate to get a chance to talk to Sancho. As if in a dream she mounted the dais and seated herself beside her cousin. She was the chief topic of conversation for the remainder of the evening. The atmosphere, although outwardly cordial, gave Madelon the impression it was false, and she was relieved when Alfonso decided to leave the banquet early for that meant she would be able to leave too. Sancho had talked to her often, but she noticed how trivial his chatter was, as if he did not want to be drawn into any lengthy conversations. It was a sign that she was not wholly in favour yet despite her sitting beside him and she wisely did not press her brother's case. Further down the table Valentín and his ward had been enjoying themselves with great gusto. The girl's high-pitched laugh often reached Madelon's ears and had successfully ruined her appetite.

"Will you not remain with us a while longer, cousin?"

Sancho asked when Madelon asked to be excused. "No? A pity, run along then, your watch-dog is waiting."

Madelon thought he was referring to her brother, but as she reached the door of the banqueting room, Urraca was beside her.

"Congratulations, my dear, you have Sancho in the palm of your hand."

"I wouldn't exactly say that," Madelon protested.

"Did you speak to him, about Paco, I mean?"

"No, I didn't think the time was right. If he is as courteous to me tomorrow, I will try then."

"How wise I was to leave the matter in your hands. Come and see me tomorrow. I have something I want to discuss with you."

Urraca was gone before Madelon could reply. She stood alone in the doorway feeling as if she had been used to take part in a cheap façade. Life at court was so different to what it had been three years ago, or had she merely been seeing everything through the eyes of a sixteen-year-old girl – a starry-eyed girl at that? Tomorrow she would definitely speak to Sancho, she decided. If Paco was returned to favour, he might be grateful enough to allow her to go home. The desolate castle near Salamanca had suddenly become very inviting.

"Are you waiting for anyone in particular?" Valentín's drawling voice caused her to start violently. He emerged from the shadows beside her and in his outstretched hands she saw the ruby necklace and pearl ring Yusuf had given her. He had been carrying them with him all evening, waiting and hoping she would make an early appearance which would enable him to return them before too many curious eyes were around. "I come bearing gifts as a peace offering for ignoring you all evening. It would not have been wise to have acknowledged you," he added.

Madelon's heartbeats quickened at the admiration which blazed out of his eyes.

"Urraca has a rival, *shafra*," he murmured at great length.

"You are mad," she said breathlessly. Then, as Raquel

Vargas's shrill laughter reached her ears, she said, "Will your friends not be missing you?"

Valentín laughed, understanding her at once.

"Are you jealous of poor little Raquel?"

"I? No, course not." Madelon was glad it was too shadowy for him to see her face or he would have seen she had lied.

"I see. The emotion doesn't attack you as it does other women then?"

"I have no reason to be jealous," Madelon retorted.

"No," Valentín murmured. "Indeed you have not."

Madelon cast a furtive look over her shoulder, terrified her brother or cousins might re-appear and misinterpret her standing with this Castilian.

"Don't worry about Paco, he's probably out in the moonlight telling Urraca how wonderful she is," he said and the note of contempt in his voice made her wince. "Forgive me, but I did warn you how it was here and you chose not to believe me."

"I do now – at least I think you have spoken the truth. Oh! I don't know. Urraca has been so kind and Paco loves her. He couldn't love her if she was as evil as you say."

"He's only a man, *shafra*. Come, take your jewels before he comes along to find you. Will you wear them?"

Madelon nodded and turned around for him to clasp the necklace around her throat. The light caress of his fingers against her neck made shivers of delight run up and down her spine and only with an effort did she stop her thoughts from showing in her expression.

Almost as if he read her mind, Valentín slipped the ring onto her finger and pressed his lips to the cold stone.

"If you accept my mother's invitation, you need fear no interruptions," he whispered and his pale eyes glittered as he felt the reaction which ran through the slender fingers he was clasping so possessively. How he longed to be alone with her, to re-awaken passion in her as he had done before, secure in the knowledge no man had touched her before him.

"Please don't ask me again," Madelon pleaded. "When you

know there can never be anything between us, why do you make things so difficult?"

The catch in her voice told him of the conflict raging inside her. For a moment longer he held her, allowing himself a last, long look at her lovely face before he allowed her to leave him.

"Very well, for the moment I will respect your wishes, but when the tournament is over, my patience will be at an end. So too, I hope, will your excuses."

Madelon disengaged herself, growing pale.

"When the tournament is over, Don Valentín, we will go our separate ways. For a while I thought something other then friendship could have happened between us, but I was being foolish and unrealistic. I can't hurt my brother – I won't. He needs me moré than you realize, besides I have personal reasons for not wanting to become involved with you – or any man."

"Do you really believe you have a choice?" Valentín demanded harshly.

"Yes. My mind is made up. Please, let us remain friends . . ."

"Friends! My God, what a child you are. I suppose this decision to remain uninvolved, as you call it, cutting yourself off from reality, is because of what your father did to you. Rebecca told me of your hatred for him, but I didn't realize it dominated you so completely." He stepped towards her, an angry light blazing out of his eyes. "I don't believe it does. At Yusuf's camp your eyes begged me to take you – to awaken in you what no man has ever achieved – as I did on the battlements, remember, *shafra?*"

Madelon's body tensed, resisting him as he pulled her against him, knowing if he kissed her she would weaken. He pressed her back against the wall, holding her gently, but quite firmly with the weight of his body. Cupping her face between his hands he kissed her very slowly and with great expertise, intent on drawing a résponse from her cold lips.

"Take your filthy hands off my sister, Maratín," a voice thundered behind them.

Madelon tore herself free from Valentín's embrace with a frightened cry and over his shoulder her eyes met those of her brother. He stood in the doorway leading to the street, his face slowly turning purple with rage. Urraca was beside him.

"Go, please," Madelon begged her companion.

If Paco had seen her struggling with Valentín he might well lose control of his temper. If he had not, and he thought she was willing, the result could easily be the same. Her fears were confirmed as Paco stepped forward and struck the Castilian in the face with such a savage blow that a trickle of blood began to flow from the corner of the other man's lips. Madelon reeled back against the wall, her eyes dilating. No, dear God, not another fight, she prayed. Now a public challenge had been issued, she could not interfere.

"You will give me satisfaction," Paco growled.

Valentín did not move and the onlookers who were crowding behind Paco, from the street and the banquet hall were surprised to see a smile flit across his pale features. Those in the crowd who were his friends and knew his different moods, were well aware he was most dangerous when he did not lose his temper.

"Do you think your luck will be any better than the last time?" he drawled contemptuously. "I wouldn't count on your sister's help to stop me again."

"Are you refusing to fight?" Paco demanded. "Do you hear, Madelon, he's a coward as well as a lover of Moors."

"No Castilian ever refuses to fight," an angry voice declared from the rear of the banquet hall. A sudden hush fell and people stepped back as Sancho strode through the ranks. At a single glance he took in Madelon and Valentín side by side, faced by the furious Paco. No one needed to tell him what the quarrel was about. At the sight of the mark on Valentín's face, he wheeled on his Leonese cousin with an angry bellow. "If you want the blood of one of my men, Montevides, you'll have to wait until the tournament begins. Even then the only blood you'll see will be your own. The two of you will meet in the first encounter, in single combat. Agreed?"

"I accept with the greatest of pleasure," Valentín said stonily.

He did not look at Madelon as he spoke, not even when his words brought a dismayed cry to her lips. Paco, on the other hand, could not drag his gaze away from his sister's tortured features. She had met the Castilian again despite all his warnings and now she would see the consequences of her foolhardy action. He had to protect her against herself. Urraca had been right when she said Madelon was too lovely for her own good and needed protection. This time he would protect her. Then, he would consider Urraca's suggestion that she be found a husband.

"Agreed," he said between set teeth. "No quarter to be asked for – or given."

Sancho threw him an amused glance. Was this challenge supposed to worry Valentín – one of his most skilful fighting men?

"You really are determined to get yourself killed, aren't you? Very well, no quarter, as you wish. And now perhaps I can return to the food and entertainment. Valentín, join me, it's been a long time since we got drunk together." It was an order, not a request.

Madelon's eyes filled with tears as Valentín returned to the feasting without so much as a smile for her. Proudly she began to ascend the stairs, ignoring both Paco and Urraca and the few curious spectators who still lingered. Then, half-way she stopped, looked down at her brother. He could see the tears flooding her eyes.

"I think it is only fair you should know how I feel in this matter, Paco," she said in a calm voice. "If you go ahead with this fight to satisfy your own stupid pride, and Valentín Maratín is harmed, I swear I will never forgive you. Not because I have any feelings for him, but because you have done a terrible injustice to a man who saved not only my life, but yours too."

She ran the rest of the way to her room and threw herself across the bed sobbing bitterly. Whatever the outcome of the combat, Paco's love for her, if any still remained, could never be the same. She had kept silent, allowing him to believe she had been a willing participant to the scene he had witnessed instead of clearing herself by telling the truth. By morning both Castilians and Leonese would know what had taken place and she would be the centre of speculation and very unpleasant gossip.

Rolling over on to her back, she stared out tearfully at the star-laden sky just visible through the window. Was it true everyone had a special star which watched over them during their lifetime? If it was, what compelling force radiating from hers had promoted her to start so forcefully along this new path from which there was no turning back and treacherous pit-falls at every bend? Where it would lead her only providence knew. She suspected her future had already been decided by a force greater than anything on earth.

The words Valentín had spoken to her as they parted that morning returned to bring momentary comfort.

"*Insh' allah.* If it is written ..."

CHAPTER
ELEVEN

THE tiny chapel was very quiet and deserted except for the slender figure kneeling in prayer in one of the benches in the shadows. Madelon had been there since early morning, praying fervently to the richly robed figure of the Virgin standing beside the altar with hands outstretched, waiting to receive those who came to her seeking guidance.

Madelon was clothed from head to toe in jade green velvet. The brilliant colour not only enhanced her fair colouring, but successfully distracted attention from the dark shadows beneath the blue eyes which lacked their usual lustre. Around her throat was fastened the ruby necklace Yusuf had given her. She wore the pearl ring too, as if in defiance of anything her brother or anyone else would be thinking when she took her place in the spectator's stand for the beginning of the tournament that morning. She had not slept since Paco had savagely struck Valentín Maratín across the face in front of a large audience, and demanded satisfaction. Was he fighting to defend the honour of his name, Madelon wondered, or because of the anger he felt towards his own sister, believing she had deliberately sought the company of the enemy Castilian.

Madelon had not seen her brother since the incident, except for a brief glimpse of him from the window of her room where she had remained for two long, miserable days, dreading the encounter she would be forced to watch. At first she had thought of pretending to be ill, but the excuse would be such an obvious lie and an added insult to her brother's pride, that she put the thought aside and decided instead to follow her cousin Urraca's example. Boldness – that was what was needed. Boldness in appearance and manner and contempt for the people who thought they were going to look down their noses at her.

She had prayed for some miracle to happen which would avert the combat between Paco and the man who had saved her life, but none had been forthcoming and she had been forced to accept the fact that the duel would take place and she must watch it.

Accompanied by Diya, who had been a wonderful companion during the two frustrating days, Madelon went out into the streets of Santa María de Carrion to visit some of the stalls she had seen on her entry into town. Recognition by Leonese and Castilians alike was unavoidable and after the first moments of embarrassment, caused by their bold stares and whispered comments, had passed, she returned their curious looks with a haughty gaze that made many turn away.

She took great care to avoid bumping into Rodrigo Díaz or Valentín, both of whom she saw on several occasions. She saw Urraca too, escorted by the usual crowd of courtiers, riding out of the West gate and quickly hurried down a side street to avoid being seen.

Madelon slowly lifted her head and stared into the serene face of the Virgin, her lips moving in a final, silent prayer. Then she left the chapel and joined Diya who was waiting in the street outside.

The little Persian girl was no longer dressed in her flimsy clothes with the usual abundance of coins. She had taken a fancy to a bright blue satin robe among her mistress's wardrobe and had been trying it on when Madelon had come in unexpectedly. Far from being annoyed, she had been amazed at the transformation which presented to her, not a sultry slave girl, but a dusky-skinned beauty of surprising elegance, and Diya had been delighted to be told she could keep the dress and purchase more materials if she wished to have other dresses made. She wore her hair in a thick plait secured on the top of her head, but had found the addition of a head-dress far too cumbersome and instead, her headpiece if it could be called that, was a gold coin secured by a fine gold chain worn in the midst of her forehead.

Both Leonese and Castilian courtiers had been preparing to leave for the meadows of Golpejerra when Madelon left for the chapel. She was relieved to find most of them had gone during her absence. Horses were saddled and waiting for them. The stable-lad looking after them helped Madelon to mount and then did the same for Diya, looking at her with more than just a casual interest on his face. She would have to watch her maid, Madelon decided. There was a new appeal about her that would attract men like flies and with her Eastern upbringing, she might not be too hasty in repulsing their advances.

"Come, Diya," Madelon said firmly and turned her horse about, only to pull it up short as a voice called out:

"Wait, Madelon, I will ride with you."

Urraca appeared in the courtyard and immediately the groom brought out a chestnut mare which had been saddled and waiting inside the stables. Mounted, Urraca rode across to join her cousin.

"Where have you been, I've been looking everywhere for you?"

"I – I went for a walk."

"Paco was sure you were hiding somewhere afraid to show your face." Urraca's face broke into an amused smile as she contemplated the calm, superbly dressed girl by her side. "He's a fool, doesn't he know his own sister?"

"He hasn't had much of a chance, has he?" Madelon said, somehow forcing a smile to her stiff lips. Whatever happened she was determined to not give way to tears or temper.

"I wasn't sure about you until this moment," Urraca said. "It was foolish of me to think you couldn't take care of yourself. I congratulate you Madelon, you and I think alike. When in doubt, don't hesitate – attack. By the way, Sancho was asking for you. You've made quite a hit with my dear brother – and Valentín Maratín. One moment you pretend to me there is nothing between you and then you are caught in his arms. Poor Madelon, I do understand how difficult it was to

resist his charms. I've heard he is a very experienced lover –
and you are so young. Paco had no choice but to challenge
him and it's no more than the wretch deserves. No doubt he
took advantage of the gratitude you naturally felt because he
saved your life . . ."

Madelon, whose cheeks were burning fiercely with embarrassment could stand it no longer and burst out,

"He did no such thing. I have no idea what Paco had told
you, cousin Urraca, but Don Valentín has not seduced me –
or even attempted to do so. I find your suspicions sordid and
unfair." She had used those same words to Valentín when he
had remarked on the affair between Paco and her cousin, she
remembered.

Urraca's eyes gleamed with triumph. How easy it was to
trick the little fool into telling her everything she wanted to
know. So despite Paco's fears to the contrary, she was still a
virgin. Urraca intended to take great pains to ensure she
remained that way until she put her own plans into action.

It seemed as if everyone was turning out to attend the
tournament. The streets were filled with people, all heading
in the same direction and it was extremely difficult for a rider
to break through the heavy throng. Urraca urged her horse
on regardless of the people milling around her. Her obvious
contempt for the unfortunates who had to leap for their lives
to avoid being trampled made Madelon flush with shame and
she was glad when they had passed through the outer gate and
could make more speed. Ahead of them lay the fields of Golpejerra. Madelon could see the flags fluttering in the breeze
and was unable to drag her eyes away. She grew paler as they
approached their destination and sat tensely in the saddle.
Urraca threw her a searching look and then said in a fierce
whisper:

"You lied to me. You are in love with the Lord of the Eagles.
Look at you – near to throwing a faint at the thought of him
getting hurt."

Madelon bit back a sharp retort and lowered her eyes before
Urraca's probing gaze.

"My concern is for Paco, no one else."

"Nonsense. The way you sprang to Maratín's defence the other night was quite delightful, my dear, but it gave you away completely," Urraca argued. What a stroke of luck this could turn out to be. Madelon was not only still a virgin, which would be a tempting bait for Gaspar Vivaldes, the man Urraca had chosen as a suitable husband, but the little fool had fallen in love with the Lord of the Eagles. The prospects from such a liaison, suitably nurtured by Urraca herself, were endless. She veiled the delight in her eyes and forced her tone to be reprimanding as she said, "You have brought all this unpleasantness upon yourself, you know. If Paco is hurt you will only have yourself to blame – and I will never forgive you. Personally I hope he kills Maratín, the man annoys me. Whatever the outcome of the combat, I hope you know where your duty lies."

Madelon dragged her eyes away from the hundreds of flags and pennants and looked at her cousin.

"Yes, you have made things quite clear to me. Thank you."

Urraca spurred her horse forward towards the crowd of richly dressed young men who had ridden out to act as her escort. Madelon allowed her horse to fall in behind the laughing, chattering cavalcade which surrounded her cousin the rest of the way to the stands. She was forgotten – and glad of it. Urraca had brought the issue out into the open and unwittingly had forced Madelon to accept the truth at last. Paco was her brother and she loved him, but she loved Valentín Maratín too. Was this strange ache in her heart really love? This longing to run to Valentín and confess what she had been too afraid, too ashamed to say before – to feel his arms crushing her against his chest, and his lips claiming hers, awakening her to all the untold delights her heart and body had never known before.

The long length of ground where the contestants were to engage each other was flanked at each end by the pavilions of the knights. Suits of armour were being busily polished by squires, horses groomed and practice bouts were in progress between friends. On each side of the lists were the spectators' stands, large enough to seat five deep. The centre seats were covered in velvet cloth and cloth of gold and a canopy over each bore the arms of Sancho, King of Castile and his brother Alfonso, King of Leon.

"Look, my lady," Diya whispered touching Madelon on the arm as they took their places beside Urraca. "Yonder."

Madelon looked across to where Sancho and his entourage were taking their places. Rodrigo de Vivar and Valentín were below the royal box. The former was busily talking to Teresa, but Valentín was staring at Madelon. She felt the colour rise in her cheeks as her cousin turned in her seat and stared at her angrily. The man at Urraca's side, a tall, heavily-set Leonese, whose finery far outshone any worn by the younger members of Urraca's admirers, also followed Madelon's gaze and his thick lips curved in disgust on discovering the cause of her interest.

Quickly Madelon looked away. When she risked another glance in Valentín's direction, she was disappointed to find he had his back to her and was talking with his sister. How proudly he stood, she thought. The arrogance that had at first angered her, now seemed doubly attractive. If Paco was the victor this morning and Valentín was killed, she would leave Santa María de Carrion at once and go to her mother's estates at Salamanca until the rift between them healed. If Valentín was wounded, she would go to him an stay by his side regardless of her brother's dictates – but what if Valentín killed her brother? The thought chilled her for a moment. No, he would not kill him. She felt confident after the way he had spared Paco's life in the Great Hall of the Castle de Aguilas, he would not deprive her of the only other person she cared for in the whole world.

Urraca left Madelon's side and moved by her brother. As they began to talk, the heavy set man carefully inspected the space provided before sitting down.

"We shall have an excellent view from here, Doña Madelon. You must be anxious to have this unpleasantness over and done with."

"You are too kind . . ."

The man chuckled as she searched her memory to put a name to him.

"We have never met. Urraca did intend that pleasure for the first evening you arrived, but you were otherwise engaged when we came upon you. Don't look so angry, my dear child, most women find Valentín Maratín attractive – in an animal sense I suppose. I find him crude, too Moorish in his ways and too damned arrogant, but here I am talking about a man neither of us cares about and who will shortly be dead anyway, when I would much rather be talking about you – and our our plans for the future."

Madelon stared into the strange face, speechless with amazement. "How can I share any plans with you – a complete stranger?" she asked breathlessly.

The man leaned forward, took one of her hands in his and pressed it to his lips. Madelon caught the aroma of strong perfume which was vaguely reminiscent of that used by Yusuf the Moor. She suppressed a shudder and tried to pull her hand free, but it was held too tightly. Words of protest died on her lips as she found herself being scrutinized by a pair of bold eyes. Something inside her warned her to be on her guard against this man, whoever he was.

"I won't be a stranger much longer, Doña Madelon," came the quiet answer. For all the softness of tone, there was something which hinted this man was not the fop he appeared. "Come now, don't be shy. I am Gaspar Vivaldes, Count of Segovia – your brother's estates and mine are practically alongside each other. For years all I've ever heard about is the beauty of his little sister, Madelon. He painted a picture of an angel, no, a goddess, and I never believed anyone could be so perfect – until I saw you. Paco has had you to himself long enough, it's time he let someone else have the delightful

pleasure of your company. Both he and your cousin Urraca
agree it will be a good match."

The heavy features broke into a smile – a smile Madelon
decided was meant to dispel the terrible fear rising inside her.
Gaspar Vivaldes was a liar. Paco had not seen her since she
entered the convent for the second time. It was impossible for
him to have praised her beauty. But why had this man lied
and what was this talk of a match?

"Are you implying you have asked my brother for my hand
in marriage?" She forced the words out through stiff lips. Oh,
no, she thought with growing dread, was Paco to act as their
father had done years ago? Was she to be forced into marriage
with this man she did not know or return to the convent for
the rest of her days, if she refused? He had promised never
to inflict his will on her to this extent.

"Not yet, Doña Madelon, but today, the instant he has
killed Valentín Maratín, I shall speak to him. Seeing you so
close, talking to you, touching you . . ." he attempted to caress
Madelon's hand and she jerked it free and buried it in the
wide sleeves of her gown. She did not miss the look of anger
which flashed across the Count's face and her fear mounted.
"The instant his combat is over, my dear," he murmured.

Urraca broke off her conversation and turned to the man at
her side. One look into Madelon's stricken features told her all
she wanted to know.

"Gaspar, you promised to speak to Paco first," she said,
feigning annoyance.

"So I did. So I did, but I have been overwhelmed by Doña
Madelon's loveliness. My choice could not have been more
perfect."

Urraca smiled, deliberately ignoring the appealing glances
Madelon threw her way. When it suited him Gaspar Vivaldes
had a tongue of velvet. He had often used it on women whose
husbands were in a position of importance and might well
prove useful to Urraca or her brother, Alfonso. She had
instructed him to use his best manner to soothe the natural

fears Madelon would feel when the news was first broken to her. When the time was right and she was his wife, the pose would drop and Madelon would discover she had married a man with an iron will which would be used on her ruthlessly.

From his seat in the royal box opposite, Sancho signalled his impatience for the first combat to begin. Alfonso followed suit and immediately the trumpeters clad in yellow and blue livery, advanced into the centre of the lists and gave several loud blasts on their golden trumpets to herald the commencement of the tournament.

A loud cheer went up all around Madelon as her brother appeared from his pavilion, mounted his horse and rode into the lists. Beneath his raised visor, his face was set in hard lines. He acknowledged first Sancho and then his own king, but he did not once look at his sister and Madelon was aware of the speculation his action caused. She herself was deeply hurt, but not for one moment did she falter beneath the spiteful glances being directed at her.

The next instant Paco's cruel gesture was forgotten, as Valentín came into view. His black armour, highly polished by young Stephen, shone in the strong sunlight. In his helmet danced two white plumes and the huge golden eagle of the de Aguilas family was emblazoned in gold on his white silk tunic. Madelon saw he was riding Conquistador, that wonderfully trained horse which would respond to the slightest touch of his beloved master. The silk caparison covering the stallion's body was heavily embroidered in gold and silver thread. The saddle was silver mounted and all the trappings were also silver and conspicuously of Moorish design.

Madelon felt her heartbeats quicken as he approached and reined in beside her brother. And excited murmur ran through the onlookers as Urraca rose to her feet. Drawing a magnificent ruby ring from her finger she held it out towards Paco. He leaned forward and took it, slipping it on to his little finger and replacing his gauntlet. Not a word was spoken, but the smile which passed between them seemed to Madelon to be of the greatest significance and in that moment she remembered Paco was out to kill his enemy. They would not break four or perhaps six lances and then engage in friendly combat until one man yielded – this was to be a fight to the death. Paco had demanded "no quarter".

She felt Diya's hand clutch at her sleeve as she gained her feet, but she brushed it aside and stepped to the edge of the stands, unfastening the green scarf from her belt as she did so. She knew every eye was on her, but she saw no one but Valentín and no one else mattered.

"Will the Lord of the Eagles honour me by wearing my token?" she asked in a clear voice.

She saw the puzzlement which leapt to Valentín's face. His eyes held hers. They demanded silently why she would not admit to caring for him, yet was going out of her way to outlaw herself among her friends by bestowing on him her favour.

Please take it. Oh, don't refuse me, Madelon prayed in an agony of suspense as he sat unmoving on his stallion. Don't you understand what I am trying to tell you? You must understand ...

A smile touched Valentín' lean mouth. Leaning forward he plucked the flimsy material from her and tied it around his wrist.

"It is I who am honoured," he replied softly.

"My God! This is too much," Paco rasped, his face working angrily. "For this last insult you will surely die, Maratín."

Valentín barely gave him a glance as he swung Conquistador about and cantered leisurely back to the end of the lists where his squire waited with the first of his lances at the ready.

Madelon felt a fierce grip on her wrist as she sat down and found Urraca scowling at her. Conscious of the smirks and whispers all around her, it was all Madelon could do to keep an indifferent look on her face.

"Are you out of your mind?" her cousin hissed furiously.

"I give my favours to whom I please, cousin," she replied quietly, but with a dignity that quelled further comment.

Urraca drew back, restraining her anger. Let the little fool

commit herself. If Maratín died, Paco would be so furious over
her folly, he would agree to anything asked of him which would
rid him of her troublesome company. And if Paco died, that
in itself would not be so disastrous. Madelon had shown
everyone where her feelings – if not her loyalty – belonged and
Urraca would be able to make good use of that. The thought
of losing her lover did not bother her. There were others,
younger, more attentive than Paco, who was beginning to an-
noy her anyway with his possessiveness. By all means give
your favours to whom you please, Urraca thought with a
sidelong glance at her cousin, exercise that prerogative while
you may.

For Madelon there was no one at Golpejerra that day but
Paco and Valentín. Her brother and the man he was determined to kill. The Lord of the Eagles, his sworn enemy – the
man she loved. When the first lances clashed and one broke
she had to lock her hands tightly in her lap to stop herself
flinging them up in front of her horrified eyes. It was Valentín's lance which had broken, but he was not unseated and
both men returned to pick up their second lance.

The thunder of hooves filled her ears. The sun glinted on
Valentín's armour as he bore down on his opponent. She
heard the terrifying sound of a steel-tipped lance meeting
chain mail and for a moment both men reeled in their saddles
from the impact of the blows. This time she closed her eyes.
When she opened them Paco lay outstretched on the ground.
Valentín dismounted, drawing his sword and as the former
drew himself up on to his knees, he received a well-aimed foot
in the centre of the back and was sent sprawling again. The
next instant the Toledo blade of Valentín Maratín's sword was
against his throat. The fall had knocked Paco breathless and
his head was throbbing madly. Through pain racked eyes he
looked up into the face of his adversary and saw death in the
dark eyes which surveyed him.

"Yield," Valentín growled.

Paco's answer was to spit in his face.

There was a cry of utter disbelief as Valentín stood up and

sheathed his weapon. No one believed he could actually have allowed his enemy to live after such an insult until he halted before the spot where Madelon sat petrified with terror and lifted his visor.

For the first time she saw he was hurt. Blood was welling from a vicious gash on his cheek where Paco's first lance had struck him. Only the visor shield had saved him from a far worse injury – even death.

"I give you your brother's life, *shafra*. It is of no importance to me," he said shortly. "We Castilians are not butchers, as well you know."

Not giving her a chance to thank him, he bowed briefly before Alfonso and walked steadily across the grass to where his sister and Rodrigo were standing at the edge of the stands and behind them the whole Castilian court was applauding his unexpected chivalry.

Valentín acknowledged Sancho's congratulations with a reserved smile. He could not leave the field – and the tortured face of the lovely girl behind him – quickly enough and yet neither could he resist a last mocking taunt at his king's brother.

"If that is the best this tournament has to offer us, sire, we shall be crowning you in the cathedral in Leon before the week is out."

A hearty gust of laughter shook the Castilians and loudest of all was that of Rodrigo de Vivar, who laughed until the tears came to his eyes and his face was the colour of his flaming beard. Sancho's momentary disgust that Paco had been allowed to live quickly vanished. He was allowing personal feelings to cloud good judgement. At times it was sufficient to strike at a man's pride instead of his heart. His eyes rested on the green material still tied around Valentín's wrist and then lifted to the inscrutable face before him. Whatever thoughts passed through his mind he did not give light to them. I'm damned if he doesn't love the girl, Sancho thought. Aloud he said:

"Well done, Valentín. When you have rested and refreshed

yourself, come and watch Rodrigo give your Leonese friends another lesson."

Madelon did not stay to watch the next encounter between Rodrigo de Vivar and his opponent. She knew she had to face Paco's anger sooner or later, and preferring to get it over and done with out of sight, and earshot of the whole court, she went to his pavilion. She had decided to be honest with him, to admit she loved Valentín and face the consequences and to tactfully broach the subject of Gaspar Vivadles. Her well-rehearsed speech died unuttered in her throat as she entered her brother's presence and found he had a visitor. As she stood on the threshold of the pavilion in dismay, the Count of Segovia rose to his feet from the couch where he sat with Paco and bowed courteously.

"Doña Madelon, come in. We have been expecting you."

"I do not wish to disturb you, Don Gaspar, I can come back," Madelon said quietly. How she masked her alarm at finding him on such cordial terms with her brother, she did not know.

"Leave your maid outside and join us," Paco said. It was more of an order than a request and she obeyed instantly.

Paco's armour had been removed by his squire. She saw a large bruise on one cheek and noticed he limped as he stood up and stepped towards her, but words of sympathy died at coldness on his face.

"Come and sit down, I have something to say to you."

Madelon sank down on to the velvet-covered couch, conscious of the smile hovering around Gaspar Vivaldes's sensuous mouth.

"Have you satisfied your honour now, Paco?" she asked. "You have fought the Lord of the Eagles and lost. Am I to be held responsible for that too?"

"I was hoping you had come to beg my forgiveness. I see I was mistaken – as I have been all along where you are concerned. Giving your token to Maratín before everyone was the final straw. You have betrayed me for the last time, Madelon,

I am washing my hands of you. The Count of Segovia was named as a prospective husband for you when you first came to court, but I withheld my consent. I wanted you to prove my suspicions wrong, but you only added to them with your clandestine meetings with Maratín – and this final folly before the whole court. Have you no shame?"

The unjustness of the attack momentarily stunned Madelon, then she leapt to her feet, fierce colour rising in her cheeks as she realized what was intended for her.

"I will not be forced into marriage. I would rather go back to the convent."

"That worked with father, not with me," her brother retorted dryly. "Your betrothal will be announced tonight. This is not only my will, Madelon, it is by order of the king. Are you foolish enough to think you can disobey a royal command?"

Madelon swayed back from him and felt a supporting arm go around her shoulders. Strong perfume invaded her nostrils and she lifted her tortured gaze to meet Gaspar Vivaldes's smiling face.

"Come, Doña Madelon, am I so repulsive as all that? When you know me better ..."

Madelon felt her senses slipping away and it was some minutes before she had recovered sufficiently to push away the possessive arm encircling her. With a pleading expression she looked across at Paco, but the stony face registered no pity and she knew there would be no reprieve.

"If you do this to me I will never forgive you. Never!" she cried tremulously.

"I suggest you return to the town and compose yourself before this evening. I shall expect you to conduct yourself with a little more control when we next meet," came the cruel answer.

Madelon swept out of the pavilion blinded by tears. Diya's anxious questions fell on deaf ears and she ran after her mistress who was hurrying towards her horse, fearing the worst.

"Are you leaving us so soon? The fun has only just begun, cousin." Urraca's mocking voice sounded behind Madelon as she was about to mount. A satisfied smile touched her mouth as she moved closer and saw the unshed tears in the young woman's eyes. "Oh dear, has Paco been reprimanding you? You did rather deserve it, didn't you. Never mind, soon you will be away from this life you find so distasteful."

Slowly Madelon turned and stared into her cousin's beautiful face. Of course, Urraca had put the idea of marriage into Paco's head! A marriage which would bind her to the court – to Urraca. Valentín was right, she thought with a feeling of disgust overwhelming her, Urraca is evil and I am to be her pawn. Oh, Valentín, why didn't I believe in you a little more?

"So it was your idea to marry me off," she said coldly. Then with a brittle laugh, "I never took Paco for a fool before, but he is, or else you're a witch."

"I am a woman who uses her talents wisely," Urraca returned indifferently. "I suggest you do the same when you and Gaspar are married. He intends to take you to his estates for a long honeymoon. It is up to you whether that time is spent in instruction – or correction."

"What if I tell Paco of your plans for me?"

"He won't believe you, little fool. Giving your token to the Lord of the Eagles finished you in his eyes." Urraca's eyes narrowed thoughtfully as she stared into her cousin's pale features. "The only person who could help you now, is Valentín Maratín himself. I might find myself able to persuade Paco to forestall Gaspar's suit if your association with this man progressed to a more satisfactory stage – shall we say? Paco would know nothing about it of course. Well, which do you find the more attractive? The arms of the Count of Segovia – or Maratín? Here come my young men, Alfonso must have sent them to look for me. Think it over, cousin. If you choose Maratín, I will leave all the details to you and you can tell me about it when you return from the joyful reunion."

"And if I refuse?"

"Your betrothal to Gaspar is being announced tonight. A refusal will make you a married woman within the month. Consider it well, cousin."

Madelon rode back to Santa María de Carrion in a daze. For the rest of the day she remained in her room, touching neither food nor drink.

Diya was beside herself with anger when she heard her young mistress's plight and voiced all manner of threats against Urraca, from plunging a dagger into her scheming black heart, to having a spell cast on her which would cause her to die very slowly and in great agony.

Madelon lay on her bed, oblivious to the fiercely whispered comments. She was wishing she had never left the grim sanctuary of the convent

CHAPTER TWELVE

MADELON sat on a stool by the window watching a group of acrobats in the crowded street below, while Diya brushed her mistress's hair until the pale blonde strands shone like silk in the candlelight.

"How will you wear it tonight, my lady?"

"Hide it all, Diya, let none of it show," Madelon replied quietly.

Some while later when the maid had finished, Madelon rose from her seat and surveyed herself in the mirror on the wall. She was clothed from head to toe in black. Not one piece of jewellery broke the severity of her attire.

"Are you sure you want to go down there dressed like that?" Diya asked apprehensively. "Don Paco will be furious."

"Why should I consider his feelings, when he cares not one iota for mine?" Madelon retorted. "Let him think what he likes – let them all think what they will. Did you hear how the contests fared after we left?"

Diya's dusky face lit up with excitement.

"The Castilians are leading by two wins to one. When I went down to the kitchens they were laying wagers on Sancho being crowned king of both kingdoms by the end of the week. They say El Seid played with his opponent for the amusement of the crowd. Of course he was undefeated."

"I pray the Castilians are victorious," Madelon said. "Only cousin Sancho can help me now. If he is king he can overrule his brother's command and give me my freedom."

"But would he?"

"I will throw myself on his mercy. Beg, if necessary –

anything to be free of Gaspar Vivaldes. The marriage is a farce, Diya. I am to be married off and made respectable and then this man is going to train me as Urraca's pawn. I won't have it – I won't."

"There are many ways he can break your spirit, my lady and who will come between a husband and his rebellious wife. Not your brother – this is his way of ensuring you do not disobey him further and not the lady Urraca, for you will be very useful to her once you have been suitably trained. Of course, there is the alternative you mentioned."

Madelon wheeled on her with an angry expletive.

"To become Valentín's mistress and secure information for Urraca? Never! I would rather die than turn my love into such a sordid affair. It will be like dying, Diya, when the Count of Segovia touches me."

Tears welled into the maid's eyes at the sight of the desperation on Madelon's face. She flung her arms around her mistress as if to protect her and they clung to each other like small children.

"Don't be afraid, my lady, that man will never touch you, I swear it."

"Hush, you foolish girl. If you want to stay with me you must never give the Count any indication of the way you feel. If you are taken from me I shall be totally alone and friendless. Is that what you want?"

"Oh, no," Diya breathed, horrified. "I will do anything to make you happy."

"Happiness, it seems, is not meant to be mine," Madelon murmured with a sad smile. "You are the only friend I have, Diya. We must be patient and pray some miracle occurs to prevent this marriage. If not – I vow Gaspar Vivaldes will never make me his wife. I must go downstairs now. No, don't come with me, the less cousin Urraca sees of you the better. If anyone would think of parting us, it would be her."

With a brave smile, she went downstairs to join her brother and the rest of the court for the celebration supper Sancho was holding in honour of his victorious knights. It had been decided before the tournament began, that for its duration, which would be two or three days, the king whose knights had been victorious that day, would entertain the losers at supper.

As she reached the bottom of the staircase and steeled herself to enter the banquet hall, she heard the sound of laughter and quickly stepped to one side as Alfonso and Urraca came in through the street door, followed by Paco. The laughter was coming from Sancho who had been drinking steadily since Rodrigo, on whom he was leaning heavily, had provided such amusement by "playing" with his opponent for over an hour. Bringing up the rear was Valentín Maratín, resplendent in rich burgundy-coloured velvet.

Alfonso stared at the downbent head of the girl curtseying before him without recognizing her and then, as Urraca whispered something in his ear, anger registered on his sallow features. Before he could give words to his obvious displeasure, Sancho drawled mockingly,

"Is this the newest fashion for prospective brides, cousin?"

Madelon stood up and stared into Sancho's handsome features, unable to keep the bitterness out of her voice as she said:

"My attire matches my mood, sire."

"Madelon – tiresome wretch! Are you to embarrass me to the last?" Paco stepped towards his sister, glaring at her furiously. "Go and change this instant."

"No, Paco, it doesn't matter." Urraca laid a hand on his arm and moved closer to him. "The girl needs to be disciplined, but not by you. Leave her to Gaspar. I suggest she returns to her room and stays there until tomorrow. Come and enjoy yourself, she is no longer your problem."

"Of course, the Count of Segovia is to be the lucky bridegroom. How many tame lap dogs will you have when he is gone, Urraca?" Sancho asked with a sidelong glance at his sister. He was still smiling and swaying unsteadily as if the worse for drink, but Rodrigo who was nearest to him, saw the sudden wary look which sprang into his eyes. The grip on the

Seid's shoulders tightened. "Come Rodrigo, we are late for the celebrating."

In the doorway Valentín had been a silent onlooker to the proceedings. He followed his king into the crowded banquet hall, giving Madelon a faint nod of acknowledgement as he passed, but nothing more. After her actions at the lists that morning she had expected at least a smile to break from those berry-brown features and she felt sick with disappointment. Did he care nothing for her predicament? She noticed Paco's eyes follow the tall figure of the Lord of the Eagles into the room and saw the satisfied smile on his face as he turned to her.

"You see! Your gallant gesture this morning was wasted, he cares nothing for you. Urraca is right. It is best if I leave you to Gaspar. You are a great disappointment to me, Madelon, but I have only myself to blame for taking you out of the convent in the first place." For the first time in many days a little of the harshness faded from his features and Madelon was sure she glimpsed sadness in the depths of his brown eyes. "You are too much like our mother for your own good. Go to your room and try to remember you are the future wife of a Count of Segovia. We have nothing more to say to each other," he added quickly as his sister appeared to be going to speak. Taking Urraca's hand he led her after Alfonso into the hall and as the large doors closed behind them, Madelon found herself alone in the shadowy corridor.

Madelon was roused from a deep sleep by someone shaking her urgently by the shoulder. Diya's dusky face loomed over her, her eyes gleaming with excitement in the light of the candles she held. As Madelon opened her mouth to protest angrily at the awakening, the maid put a finger to her lips.

"Hush, my lady. You must get up quickly."

"Get up?" Madelon stared at her as if she had taken leave of her senses. It was still dark outside the unshuttered windows.

"He wants to see you," Diya hissed. "His squire is waiting to take you to him."

"He?" Madelon was so dazed with sleep it took some while for the full meaning of the words to penetrate her mind. She sat up in bed unbelievingly. "You – you can't mean Don Valentín?"

"Who else would risk your brother's anger by seeing you again? The squire says he's waiting in the stables below. Don't you want to see him?" she asked when her mistress did not move.

"Find me something warm to put on ... quickly," Madelon breathed, throwing aside the bedclothes.

Within minutes she was dressed and enfolded in a warm fur cloak, her face well hidden beneath the hood. Diya insisted on accompanying her, saying if anyone saw her and Stephen, the squire, together they would merely think they were lovers and not keeping watch.

Twice Stephen waved the two young women to hide as patrolling sentries came close, but thanks to his vigilance, the stables were reached without mishap. A shadowy figure moved forward to greet them, gave a quiet order to Stephen who immediately turned and left them, followed by Diya. She stared through the gloom, trying hard to distinguish the features of the man before her. She discovered she was trembling violently at the thought of being able to snatch a few stolen minutes alone with the man she loved.

"Don Valentín," she said in a whisper, "are you quite mad? If my brother should discover us ..."

"Are you not willing to take the risk?" Valentín's silky tones mocked her. "Perhaps you are not the same girl who handed me her token this morning or who showed such distaste at being forced into an unsavoury marriage. I thought your brother would burst a blood vessel when he saw that black gown."

"I wanted to hurt him. I am not proud of it," Madelon replied, a catch in her voice. "Once we were close."

"Come, we cannot stand talking here. Give me your hand and we will go up into the loft. I chose this place because it

is the last spot anyone will search for you if you are missed
– but I regret it is not the most comfortable."

Strong, lean fingers fastened over Madelon's wrist and
guided her to the ladder at the far end of the stalls. Valentín
climbed up first and then helped her negotiate the ladder,
chuckling infuriatingly as she repeatedly trod on the hem of
her dress.

"Pray what do you find so amusing?" Madelon demanded,
when she stood beside him at last. Bright moonlight was
flooding through the open window embrasure behind them
and she saw his face was wreathed in smiles.

"You, *shafra* – and my own stupidity. Why I don't carry
you off to my mountain fortress and let Paco go to the devil,
I really don't know. Here I am in love for the first time in
my life and yet I've done little – or nothing to tell you how
I feel or to get you out of Paco's care and into mine." With
a soft laugh he picked her up in his arms and laid her down
behind several bales of hay and then knelt beside her, smiling
at the incredulity on her face. "You are young, *shafra*, only
nineteen, and I am thirty, perhaps that's why I have held back
my feelings for so long. I've known enough women in my
thirty years to know what I feel for you is real; the most
wonderful thing I've felt in my life. If you don't feel this way
too, or if you are not sure, then be honest with me. We can
part as friends, if nothing more. If it is the Count of Segovia
you really want, then I'll even give you my blessing."

Madelon's senses reeled under the shock of his words.
Reaching out her hands, she touched the velvet of his doublet,
slowly, wonderingly, as if afraid it was all a dream and when
it ended she would find herself in bed and not in the company
of her lover. Her eyes, bright with tears, shone like two
brilliant sapphires as she stared up at Valentín. Freed from
the confines of the hood, her hair streamed past her shoulders
like a golden cloud. To Valentín, she had never looked more
beautiful. His golden savage was suddenly an angel again.

"Whenever men have looked at me I have been flattered,

sometimes amused, but never moved as I am when your eyes
are on me," she confessed quietly. "When I am with you –
Oh, Valentín! I have no words the describe the depths of my
love. I only know when you hold me in your arms and kiss me
I feel as if I am being transported to another world. I love you
– and I am not ashamed to offer you proof if you need it."

"At last we are honest with each other," Valentín muttered.

Catching a handful of her loose hair he pulled her into his
arms and kissed her hungrily, allowing himself for the first
time, to give way to the tumult of emotion raging within his
breast. Madelon melted immediately in his embrace, fired to
a response only the unleashing of a deep, suppressed love could
bring. Her skin burned like fire beneath his caresses and she
pressed closer to him with the eagerness of an unawakened
child, returning kiss for kiss, touch for touch, until she was
seized in a tide of passion and swept towards inevitable surrender, unable to deny the love she had hidden for so long.
This ache in her heart was love. This longing to stay crushed
against Valentín's chest for the rest of her life. It was wonderful,
frightening and she wished the moment would go on forever.

Valentín pressed her down into the hay and had unfastened
her bodice before she was aware of what he was doing. Her
young body trembled and was awakened by the gentle,
exploring hands on her breasts. Madelon knew she was near to
surrender, but nothing seemed to matter while he held her
and whispered soft endearments in her ear. She knew it could
not last for she was not free to follow the dictates of her heart,
but that did not make it any the less wonderful. She felt the
hard muscles of his shoulders beneath her hands and clung
to him with a cry that was as much out of despair as it was
from passion.

Raucous, drunken laughter drifted up to them from the
courtyard below, followed by a lewd comment from a soldier
who had come upon a couple making love in a doorway.
Madelon felt Valentín stiffen. For a long while he was still,
then slowly he drew away from her. Even with her limited
knowledge of life she knew how easy it would have been for

him to take her and she could not understand why he had not done so, until she saw the fierce colour flooding into his cheeks. Slowly he shook his head.

"Not this way, *shafra*, though if our soldier friend outside had not given vent to his feelings, I would have taken you and not regretted it for an instant."

Madelon drew herself up and laid her head against his shoulder, content to watch the handsome profile shadowed above her in silence. She felt drained of all strength, but at peace.

"You were right about cousin Urraca," she said at length. "Gaspar Vivaldes is to be not only my husband, but my tutor. I am to be Urraca's pawn, just as you said. How can anyone be so evil, Valentín, so cruel as to try and manipulate another person's life? Paco is completely under her thumb. She is horrible. She even offered me a way out of the marriage, but it was too awful to contemplate."

Valentín looked down at her, his expression growing alarmed. Silently he cursed Urraca and wished her dead for the tenth time that day.

"What way?"

Madelon baulked at telling him, but she had gone too far to back down.

"She said if I allowed our friendship to – to develop into something – more – more binding – and I used it to get information for her ..."

"In other words you were to become my mistress?"

"Yes."

"And you find the suggestion too terrible to contemplate?"

Madelon's fears for his reaction were dispelled by the laughter in his voice.

"I can no more lie to you than I could become the wife of that awful man."

"You won't be his wife. Tomorrow Alfonso will be sent into exile and you and I will be on our way to church."

"You make it sound so simple," Madelon whispered. "What if it is Sancho who is exiled?"

"Then you and I will leave this town under the cover of darkness and by the time our absence is discovered we will be well on our way to my home. I'm not letting you go now, my love, and I'll kill anyone who stands in our way. Anyone, do you understand me? I've allowed him to live twice – there will be no third time."

Madelon nodded and clung to him, gaining strength from the arms which held her so possessively. Paco's anger would dissolve once she and Valentín were married and safe from everyone in the Castle de Aguilas. She would have to take the chance anyway. She had put her love for him before that for Valentín too many times. If he really cared for her he would not be so ready to surrender her to his mistress's choice of a bridegroom. Was he so blind that he could overlook the gossip which flowed through the court about the Count of Segovia and the women he had seduced on the orders of the king's sister? Madelon had been appalled by the lurid details and a natural loathing of her future husband had turned to fear.

"Take me away tonight," she pleaded. "Valentín – I'm afraid if I leave you, I shall never see you again."

Valentín's mouth on hers effectively dispersed her agitation. She felt herself begin to grow drowsy crushed so close against him and was quite content to lie against him without thought to the lightening sky outside the window. Valentín's hand with the strange star-shaped birthmark slid lovingly over the satin softness of her breast and then was withdrawn abruptly.

"You must go now, sweetheart." He stood up and drew her to her feet. Moving to the edge of the loft he stood surveying the empty floor below while she refastened her bodice and rearranged her cloak about her shoulders, then he helped her down the ladder and they crept to the outer door. As if by a prearranged signal, Diya and Stephen materialized from the shadows. Madelon was too happy to mind if her maid and the squire had been enjoying a few stolen kisses.

Valentín caught Madelon up in his arms and kissed her so hard she was breathless when he let her go. Stephen led the way back to her room and left her at the foot of the stairs.

Safe once more in her own room, with the door securely bolted, Madelon tore off her dress uncaring even when she heard it rip at the seams and tumbled into bed suddenly feeling exhausted. Diya tucked the clothes around her as if she was a little baby, smiling in satisfaction at the glow in Madelon's cheeks. Never before had she seen her mistress look so radiant.

"And what made you choose Gaspar Vivaldes as a prospective husband for my sister?" Paco demanded.

He was in Urraca's chamber, watching her being dressed by her maids to attend the tournament that day. They had spent the night together, but he had got drunk at supper after giving the Count of Segovia his consent to the marriage and had fallen asleep before Urraca joined him. She seemed to sense the ugly mood he was in for she had not berated him for the insult to her pride. As Paco sat on the edge of the bed watching her selecting pieces of jewellery to wear, he realized he would not have cared if she had. He refilled the empty goblet in his hand with more of the heady wine he had been consuming the previous evening, ignoring the warning look she sent his way.

Dismissing her attendants, Urraca studied herself for a long moment in a mirror, then remembering that Paco had asked her a question, she turned and looked at him.

"Why Gaspar? Why not? He has fine estates not far from your own, which will ensure Madelon is not lonely, so far from her friends. We shall be able to go and visit them. Of course Gaspar will bring her back to court eventually – when she has learned how to be a good wife."

"I won't have her used, damn you." Urraca was suddenly alarmed at the angry glint which appeared in Paco's eyes. "I admit she needs a strong hand to control her, but she needs kindness and gentleness too. If Vivaldes uses his position as her husband to turn her into a docile pawn for you, I'll kill him – and you."

"Really, Paco, what is the matter with you these days?" Urraca gave a soft laugh and sat beside him, taking the goblet out of his hand and placing it out of reach. "You've had too much of this already. I don't want you passing out on our great day. For heaven's sake, leave Madelon to Gaspar, he'll be good for her. You'll see – in a few months you won't recognize her."

Paco looked into the beautiful face hovering near his, but was no longer seized with a wild desire to kiss those full lips offering themselves, as had been the case so often since the first day he came to know her. Urraca's power over him was fading rapidly. The knowledge gave him no pleasure, only a dull ache in his heart. He would always love her in a way, even though he knew she had never loved him and had used him ruthlessly to serve her own ends, rewarding him with her favours whenever the fancy took her.

"Do you know why I agreed to this marriage?" he asked harshly.

"To stop her providing us with further embarrassing situations, I suppose," Urraca replied, "like the affair with Valentín Maratín. She saw him last night, you know – or should I say early this morning. One of my servants saw her leave her room and followed her to the stables. She remained in there until it was almost light while Maratín's squire and that Persian maid of hers kept watch outside."

Urraca expected anger, but none came. Instead Paco buried his head in his hands with a loud groan. When he looked up again his expression was utterly dejected.

"She must be married soon – before she disgraces the name of Montevides as my mother once did," he muttered fiercely.

"You haven't told me about that little family skeleton," his mistress murmured. She caressed Paco's worried face with long, slender fingers. "What burden do you carry on your shoulders, Paco? I've never seen you so utterly miserable."

Urraca's unexpected sympathy had the right effect. Paco needed a confidant. For fifteen long years he had carried the secret with him in silence, although on more than one occasion since Madelon had left the convent he had been sorely tempted to reveal everything to her.

"When I was nine years old, my grandfather – mother's father died after a long illness. Mother and I had been with him for two months. After the funeral we started out for home again, but we never reached there. We were captured by Moors and sold in a slave market in Toledo to the Sultan of ..." he paused, seeing the sudden interest in Urraca's eyes. "It doesn't matter where. My mother was installed in his harem. Very soon I heard she had become his favourite. I was treated with every respect, I must admit, and given private tutors as if I was the Sultan's own son. His servants said he loved her very much and that she – she loved him. I saw very little of her until my father ransomed us and took us home. Madelon was born the following year."

"Fathered by a Moorish sultan?"

"Exactly. She thinks father hated her because she was born a girl, but of course, that isn't true. Every time he looked at her he wanted to kill her because he knew she had been born out of love – not the necessity for an heir, as I was." Paco stared into Urraca's astounded face with a bitter smile. "I once heard my mother tell father if it had not been for me she would never have asked to be freed. He never forgave her and when she died he turned all his hate and anger on to Madelon."

"You are afraid Madelon is as worthless as your mother, aren't you?" Urraca asked softly. "From the way she has acted with Maratín, I think you may be right. Paco – I've just thought – is this what caused the rift between your family and Sancho? Does he know?"

Paco nodded, his mouth tightening.

"He and my mother were very close. He was with her when she died. No one else, not even I was allowed in her room – only Sancho. God only knows what lies she told to condone her wanton behaviour and the consequent birth of a love-child, but from that day, he and I have been as strangers." In a harsh tone he added, "The sooner Madelon is married, the better. I fear Sancho will rescind the marriage order if he comes to the throne."

"Then you have nothing to worry about. Tonight you and I will be celebrating my brother's accession to the throne of Castile. Once that has happened we can deal with the Lord of the Eagles and that upstart friend of his, the Cid."

"You sound very confident," Paco said, looking at her with suspicion.

"While you were sleeping off your over-indulgence, I was busy assuring victory for us today," his mistress returned, her eyes flashing proudly. "Unfortunately I couldn't deal with one knight, a Castilian called Altamiras; he dined with Maratín and Sancho last night, but the other two were well take care of by two of the most experienced courtesans in town."

"How well taken care of? Dead?"

"And have Sancho accuse us of murder? I am not a fool, Paco. The courtesans were well paid to wine and dine the knights and to ensure they slipped a certain drug I gave them into their drinks. Somehow I don't think the Castilians will have much heart for fighting today. The drug affects the mind. They will be like sleepwalkers."

"Sancho will suspect foul play, he is no fool either. What if he questions the women."

"He will never find them."

Paco's lips curled in disgust. That could mean they had either left town under cover of darkness, or they were dead. He gave little thought to any harm which might have befallen two women of fortune, but the drugging of the Castilians left a sickly taste in his mouth. He had lost his encounter with Valentín Maratín, but at least it had been a fair fight, which he might have won if he had not been so full of anger. Abruptly he rose to his feet.

"I am going to change and then visit Madelon. I think I will go with her today."

Urraca's expression registered displeasure. "I expect you to accompany me," she said stiffly.

"Do you begrudge me spending a few hours in the company of another woman – even my sister?"

"Last night you could not stand the sight of her."

A flicker of pain crossed Paco's face at the thought of Madelon standing before him in her sombre black dress. What a marvellously bold gesture that had been. She had the beauty of their mother and the temperament of the Moor who had fathered her. He doubted if Gaspar Vivaldes would ever tame her and he was beginning to regret the angry impulse which had made him agree to Urraca's proposals. If only there was another way, but there wasn't. If the Count of Segovia did not marry her and take her away from the court and the influence of Valentín Maratín, she would probably elope with her lover. God only knew what kind of a life she would have to endure with that man, who delighted in taking Moorish women as his mistresses and treating heathen infidels as his friends, Paco thought sourly. Probably most of her time would be spent in the camp of Yusuf, in the company of the Jewish doctor, Abraham ben Canaan and in a few years, that way of life would become more natural to her than anything else; just as it had for their mother. The comparison was enough to harden Paco's heart again.

"In the short time Madelon has left to her, she will have need of me," he returned, moving towards the door. "I will join you tonight for our victory celebrations."

"I want Gaspar to escort Madelon," Urraca said, a faint hint of colour rising in her cheeks. "It's time she accepted the fact she is to be his wife and today is as good a time as any to begin. You can tell her and then come back to me."

"No." Paco's voice was quiet, but firm. "Thanks mainly to you – and me, Madelon has been the subject of speculation since the first day I brought her to court. Despite her behaviour, she is still my sister and my presence with her today will put an end to the gossip for it will show she has not only agreed to marry the Count of Segovia, but that we have been reconciled."

"You fool!" Urraca was beside herself with rage and having great difficulty in containing it. The last thing she wanted was to have Paco and his sister reunited. It could spell disaster for her plans, especially the difficult way Paco was acting of late. Crossing to his side she put her arms around his neck and kissed him full on the mouth. There was no reaction and she drew back, veiling the fear in her eyes.

"We mustn't quarrel, Paco. Not now victory is so near. If I was the jealous type I might begin to think I was losing my attraction – preferring the company of your sister to mine."

Paco reached up and drew her arms away. He was shocked at the way her kiss had affected him. It was like being touched by Death – and he felt inexplicably cold and could barely suppress a shudder. Urraca saw an unfamiliar gleam enter his eyes and the suspicion that she was fast losing her hold on him grew stronger.

"Never force the choice on me, Urraca," he said, in a low, fierce whisper.

CHAPTER
THIRTEEN

"Tomorrow, you and I will be on our way to church."
Madelon remembered Valentín's confident words as she sat
beside her brother watching the last combat. It proved to be
more bloody than the two which had gone before and ended
in victory for the Leonese knight. She sat stunned, deafened
by the enthusiastic cheering going on all around her. Three
wins for Alfonso's knights. It was unbelievable. Young Cristóbal de Altamiras had been the only man to put up any sem-
blance of a fight. He had been wounded while engaging his
opponent with a battle-axe and carried unconscious from the
field. Madelon had watched sympathetically as Teresa had run
to his pavilion. Now she realized how lucky he had been. He
had lost, but at least he was still alive. Both the other Castilians
had been killed in ghastly spectacles that brought roars of
approval from the Leonese court. So much for her dreams of
a life with Valentín, Madelon thought sadly. Now Alfonso's
knights were supreme champions, Sancho must concede
defeat and go into voluntary exile. His favourite knights,
Rodrigo and Valentín among them, would probably be sent
into exile, or – and she inwardly shuddered to think of the
alternative – flung into a dungeon and forgotten.

"Are you all right?"

She found Paco's brown eyes on her and nodded weakly.

"I should be glad we have won because it means you are
safe, but it was so horrible. Those poor men didn't stand a
chance."

"No, they didn't, thanks to Urraca. They were drugged,"
Paco answered grimly.

Madelon looked at him in horror. Urraca again! Was her
cousin to wreak havoc on her life forever? Her brother's

expression softened slightly as he stared into her pale face.

"Would you really care if anything happened to me? After the misunderstandings we've had, I mean."

"Of course. You are my brother and I will always love you. We were close once – it is not your fault our lives are not our own."

Paco flushed and quickly looked away.

"When you are happily married, you will forget the unpleasantries," he muttered.

"Come now, Paco, at least let us be honest with one another. I love Valentín Maratín, nothing, not even my marriage to another man will change that," Madelon said tremulously. "In your eyes I have committed a terrible sin and perhaps you may never forgive me, but I must tell you how it is between Valentín and myself. No, I will not be put off," she added quickly as Paco opened his mouth as if to silence her. "I am not his mistress despite your fears. Valentín has always acted honourably towards me and he loves me. Yes, he does, he told me so last night. I met him. It was not planned and he did not make love to me, even though I wanted him to. For the first time he told me of his love and of his wish to make me his wife. Had cousin Sancho been the victor here today I should have gone with him and been wed to him before night-fall." She shrugged her slim shoulders and a sad smile touched her lips as she gazed across to the pavilions of the Castilians and the group of people advancing towards them. "Sancho comes to concede defeat. He has my sympathy, Urraca and Alfonso will crow over this moment for years to come. I am returning to my apartments. Are you coming?"

"In a while. I suggest you spend some time in choosing a more suitable gown to wear tonight. The Count of Segovia expects you to be his supper companion," Paco said, with a warning glance. Her revelations seemed neither to have angered nor surprised him and she wondered why. In the past it had only taken the mention of Valentín's name to make him fly into a rage.

Madelon turned away without answering, but at the edge

of the steps leading from the stands down to the grass, she
paused to glance back at her cousin Sancho. He stood before
his enemies wearing a most contemptuous smile on his face.
She had known he would not ask for mercy, he was too proud,
but she was amazed at the indifference with which he accepted
his defeat. Valentín and Rodrigo who stood beside him,
their faces closed against the anger in their hearts, both had
their hands on the hilts of their swords. Their eyes scanned the
sneering expressions before them and Madelon knew they
need no excuse to start the warfare all over again.

Despite a muttered protest from Rodrigo, Sancho stepped
up to the dais where his brother and sister sat enjoying their
moment of triumph, withdrew his sword and set it down before
them.

"Victory is yours – for the moment, my brother. What are
your plans for me now? A dark little dungeon somewhere, or
a knife in the back from an assassin as I leave?"

"The air in the mountains of Leon is very invigorating,"
Urraca snapped. How she hated the smiling, handsome man
before her, so full of confidence even in defeat. Alfonso had
always been weak, perhaps that was why she had taken his
side so long ago when the quarrelling first began. She was
strong, like Sancho, and clever too. The power Alfonso had
secured today would never really be his, but hers. She could
never sit on the thrones of Leon and Castile, but she would
be the power behind them and in a way that would be far
more satisfactory. She was amazed when the contemptuous
expression on Sancho's face grew.

"Don't tell me I am to be incarcerated with young Garcia?
Heaven forbid, Urraca, at least use your imagination. I'm sure
you can come up with something really unpleasant if you try."

"You will be delivered into the hands of my Sergeant-at-
Arms and escorted to Santa María de Carrion where you will
be confined until I have decided what to do with you,"
Alfonso retorted, objecting to the way the conversation was
flowing over his head. "Your retinue will disarm, only then
may they accompany you. All other Castilians will encamp

outside the town walls and remain there, under guard. I think it necessary to add a strong warning. Any attempt by anyone to leave the town without permission, to communicate with Castilians outside the walls, or with you will result in your immediate death."

"Do we have your word nothing will happen to our king while he is in your custody?" Rodrigo demanded in an insolent tone.

Alfonso glared at him balefully.

"My word is my bond, Rodrigo de Vivar, you will do well to remember it in the future, or you may not have one."

Rodrigo muttered an oath under his breath. Both he and Valentín stepped forward simultaneously as if it was their intention to cut down the upstart king before them. One of Sancho's hands fastened on each of the arms nearest to him. He was no puny being and his grip was strong enough to halt both men in their tracks. He spoke in a quiet tone, too low to reach beyond his companions.

"Gently, my impetuous friends. Rodrigo, let go of your sword, man, I have need of you alive. And you, Valentín, do you want to be cut down before the eyes of the woman you love?"

Valentín's pale eyes held his for a moment surprised, angry, rebellious, then slowly they singled out the slender figure standing by the steps and his fingers slid slowly away from his sword.

"They mean to kill you," he muttered.

"I know, but we are prepared for it, are we not? Use your time and your talents to find out from my little cousin, how the outcome here today came to be in favour of Alfonso."

"She may not know. If she doesn't, she'll find out for me," Valentín promised.

Madelon spent some time shopping at the many stalls just inside the walls of Santa María de Carrion. She bought several lengths of beautiful green velvet and some yellow silk, matching the colours with dyed fur and dainty leather shoes with silver trimmings. She did not know how long the court would remain in the town. Whether it was a day or a week, she was in desperate need of new clothes.

Many spectators were beginning to drift back from the fields of Golpejerra as she made her way towards her apartments and the streets were once more packed to capacity. Looking into the faces milling past her she realized they did not all look overjoyed by the outcome of the tournament. There would be celebrating tonight for some, but in other quarters such pleasures would have to wait until Sancho was free again.

Her horse reared violently as a rider galloped up from behind and almost cannoned into her. As she fought to control the frightened animal the rider wheeled about, caught the reins and dragged the horse off the street and into a narrow alleyway. Madelon was about to give vent to her anger when Valentín swung round in the saddle and grinned at her. With a cry of relief she threw herself into his arms. Diya, who had followed her mistress into the alley believing she was being abducted by celebrating Leonese soldiers, took one look at the couple locked in each other's arms and quickly turned about, positioning her horse so that no one could pass by. Stephen rode out of the crowd and edged his mount close to hers, completely blocking all view of the alley.

"What were you buying those beautiful silks for?" Valentín asked Madelon with a slow smile. "Your wedding?"

"Don't tease me, Valentín, you know all my clothes were stolen. Is it safe for us to be here?"

Valentín motioned to their two watchdogs and Madelon's heart warmed towards her maid and the young squire as she saw the protective shield they had set up.

"We have little time," Valentín murmured. "Listen to my plan. Tonight Alfonso intends to throw a large banquet for his court and all the prominent people of the town. He means to get on the right side of them from the start, for he's going to introduce new taxation tomorrow, to pay for his coronation. Sancho will be there, he has no choice. Alfonso means to keep him within seeing distance until all Castilians have been disarmed and dispersed."

"You sound as if you mean to try and rescue him," Madelon breathed and her eyes widened fearfully at the thought of him taking such a terrible risk. He gently touched her cheek with loving fingers.

"You didn't think Sancho would surrender himself without us having a ready-made plan, did you? But that is not for you to worry about. You must think of yourself – of us."

"Of us," Madelon faltered, "but it's impossible now."

"Only if you don't have the courage to do as I say," Valentín replied, his eyes quickly searching her face. "I don't intend the Count of Segovia to have my woman, nor do I expect her to give herself into his hands like a lamb. The town tonight will be in chaos – my men mixing with the townsfolk will make sure the celebrations are successful. Prepare for the banquet as if nothing is amiss. As you come downstairs there will be a group of acrobats outside the house. Go and watch them, step out into the street and then lose yourself in the crowd. Stephen will bring you to me. Once in the safety of our camp you will join Teresa and young Cristóbal – he's recovered enough to ride – and leave for the Castle de Aguilas. I shall be sending a dozen men with you. You will have no trouble reaching there safely."

"But ... but Alfonso said ... What about the guards?"

"They will not detain you, I promise," Valentín said with a soft chuckle. "Urraca is not the only one who can mix an effective potion."

"So you know."

"It was a shrewd guess. How did you know?"

"Paco told me. Urraca had two of the town courtesans entertain your men last night. I think Paco was quite disgusted with it all. He seems more reasonable today, more like his old self."

"Does that mean you wish to stay with him?" Valentín asked, his voice suddenly strained.

Madelon reached out and clasped his hand, her eyes bright with unshed tears, but with determination in her lovely face.

"No, my love of little faith, I want to be with you. After tonight I will be – for always."

Madelon swung away from the mirror, her eyes alight with excitement.

"How do I look, Diya?"

The Persian girl made a last minute adjustment to Madelon's blonde hair, secured in a loose coil of curls high on her head, then she stepped back and studied the exquisite little figure in pink brocade and satin. Madelon had taken great care in the choosing of the dress and matching slippers for she wanted to look her best tonight. Not for the Count of Segovia, but for her beloved Valentín. Her cousin Urraca had talked incessantly of her plans for the forthcoming wedding and Madelon had remained discreetly silent. It no longer mattered what plans were made for her, they would never be fulfilled.

"If you continue to look so radiant, your brother will suspect something," Diya said anxiously, but then her face cleared and she hugged Madelon. "I am happy too, my lady, so happy. Soon you will be away from this terrible place, cared for by the Lord of the Eagles. Once in his castle you will be safe from Don Paco, the king's anger and everyone who wants to harm you."

The Castle de Aguilas, Madelon murmured. Her eyes shone at the thought of the impenetrable fortress high in the Sierra de Gredos and the gentle Francesca Maratín who had already accepted her as a prospective daughter-in-law. How wonderful it would be to be surrounded by people who loved her. If only Paco . . . no! It was impossible and she must put him out of her mind.

"I can see a group of acrobats coming this way," Diya called from the window and Madelon flew to her side eagerly.

"They must be the ones we were told to watch for. We must go down now, but remember to keep your eyes open for Stephen."

Diya flashed a wicked grin that made Madelon wonder how far the relationship between her maid and the squire had developed. "I will, my lady. I promise."

Almost at the entrance of the banquet hall, Madelon stopped and turned in the direction of the street door, as if attracted by the acrobats and players, performing on the steps.

"Oh, Diya, aren't they clever," she cried pointing to a couple of jugglers near the doorway. "I must watch for a while."

Threading her way through the courtiers heading for the banquet, she stood on the steps pretending to watch the entertainments and gradually edging her way closer to the packed street. Diya lightly touched her arm and hissed:

"Yonder, the man in the brown cloak standing by the wine cart. I'm certain it's Stephen."

Madelon's eyes quickly singled out the man who turned sufficiently in their direction for her to glimpse a familiar freckled face. Holding tightly to Diya's hand she stepped quickly into the crowd and was immediately lost from the view of anyone in the house. As they reached Stepehen's side, he turned and disappeared into an equally crowded side street. Diya pushed and cursed at people who jostled them, threatening to separate her from her mistress and to cut them off from their guide. It was almost dark. People appeared carrying torches. Someone thrust one into Madelon's hand. She hastily passed it on to someone else, frightened that her face might be recognized in the flickering light. Stephen continued to dodge ahead of them, down narrow foul-smelling alleys, past crowded stalls where merchants were taking advantage of the celebrations to peddle their wares at double the normal price and she realized he was heading for the little used south gate. Madelon's heartbeats quickened with the anticipation of encountering Valentín at any moment.

Diya came to a sudden halt and Madelon pulled at her hand impatiently. Already Stephen was out of sight. As she turned and saw her maid struggling in the arms of a burly soldier, a man's hand closed over her wrist, another over her mouth, and she was dragged backwards beneath the overhang of a building. A torch was thrust close to her face and a voice declared matter of factly:

"Yes, this is her. Take her back to the Doña Urraca and don't let her make a scene. Cover her with a cloak. I don't want her recognized."

Madelon's struggle tailed off weakly and she sagged in the arms of her captor at the mention of her cousin's name. She had been followed – trapped – hysteria seized her at such a cruel trick of fate and gave strength to renew her attempts to free herself. She struggled so violently against the arms which held her that it took two men-at-arms to subdue her. The sergeant in charge stared stony-faced at the dishevelled, panting girl being hoisted unceremoniously on to a horse where she was held in the grasp of a red-faced soldier. A heavy cloak was wrapped around her head and body, obscuring her face from curious onlookers.

"You'd best calm yourself, my fine lady, or you'll end up bound and gagged. And you!" He glared at Diya who was swearing in a most profound fashion at the man who held her. It was in her own language which made it sound doubly offensive. At a glance from Madelon she fell silent.

Madelon's relief at Stephen's prompt disappearance was shattered by the sight of the boy's unconscious form being slung across a nearby horse. She felt sick with disappointment and fear and offered no further resistance as her captor turned his mount around and headed back into the centre of the town. Her last chance to escape marriage with Gaspar Vivaldes was gone. The realization left her dazed and totally without hope of ever being reunited with Valentín again. She prayed he would not try to find out what had happened to her. If Urraca had had someone following her, it was possible she also had a watch kept on Valentín too. One wrong move and his life would be in danger.

In her misery she did not notice the curious stares of the townspeople or the uncomfortable ride. She was lifted from the horse outside a side entrance and pushed roughly into the house. The sergeant pushed past her on the stairs and led the way to the floor where Urraca had her apartments. He knocked on the door and disappeared inside, to reappear almost immediately.

"Inside," he ordered Madelon. "You, stay outside and guard the other prisoners," he ordered the escort.

Urraca was not alone, Paco was sprawled in a chair. Beside him on a table were several bottles of wine and a full goblet. He stared at his sister and said nothing. After a moment he drank his wine and refilled the vessel.

"You may go, sergeant, I will reward your diligence as soon as I have dealt with my little problem here." Urraca smiled warmly into the weatherbeaten face of the soldier, allowed him to kiss the tips of her jewelled fingers and waited for him to withdraw. As the door closed behind his retreating figure, she turned slowly on Madelon, her eyes glittering with satisfaction at her appearance. The beautiful pink satin had been ripped in several places during the brief but hectic struggle and Madelon's hair hung down her back in wild disarray. Paco blinked at her over the rim of his goblet.

"You look like our mother," he mumbled.

"Be quiet, you drunken fool," Urraca snapped.

"Why have I been molested by your men-at-arms like a common whore? Why have I been brought here?" Madelon demanded with immense dignity. Her fear had gone and anger had come in its place. Anger for the brother who sat staring at her in silence, neither condemning her nor siding with her – and anger for the beautiful, scheming cousin whose plans she had tried so hard to destroy.

"If you act like one, my dear Madelon, you must expect this kind of treatment. Here you are about to become a bride and yet you sneak off to meet a lover."

"I was watching the entertainments in the street when I was suddenly grabbed and bundled back here. I demand an explanation."

Urraca relaxed down on to the couch and leaned back amid velvet cushions, her face breaking into a sneer.

"I wonder how the young man outside, Maratín's squire, or your maid would tell the story – under torture."

Madelon blanched. She suspected they would both die rather than betray them, but she knew she could not allow either of them to be touched. She shrugged her slim shoulders.

"Very well, I was on my way to see Valentín Maratín. I – I was going to ask him to take me away with him."

Paco uttered a stifled groan and poured himself another drink. He was not drunk, as Urraca thought, but the constant drinking had revived memories he had put out of his mind for many years. Madelon, standing before him in her torn gown, was as proud and defiant as their mother had been in the slave market at Toledo. One hand had clutched the remnants of her clothes about her as best she could, the other hand held Paco's tiny fingers tightly in hers. She had borne threats and beatings as an inducement to let him go, but they had not been parted since their capture. Among so many other bitter memories he had forgotten the way she had clung to him and protected him without any thought to her own safety. She had loved him once ... they had been close, just as he and Madelon ... He ran a hand through his hair and then wiped it across his wet mouth, and continued to drink ... all the time waiting and watching and listening.

"Tomorrow the court leaves for Burgos," Urraca was saying. "Alfonso will be crowned in the cathedral there. The day after we shall both be at your wedding. Do you understand me, Madelon?"

"You will have to drag me to the church," Madelon declared defiantly, "I will not go of my own free will. If Paco beats me I will wear sackcloth and let everyone see the bruises on me."

Did she really think he would sink so low as to beat her, as their father had done, Paco wondered and inwardly shuddered to think of himself bruising her soft skin. His eyes suddenly fastened on her arms and saw several unpleasant-looking marks he had not noticed before. She had not lied when she said she had been manhandled by the soldiers – Urraca's men, acting on her orders. The smiling face of his mistress grew even more loathesome to look at. Damn her, she was enjoying Madelon's discomfort. He stifled the impulse to leap from his chair and plant his fist in those attractive features. Her turn would come. He did not know when or what form his revenge would take, but somehow he knew he was going to have the pleasure of seeing Urraca stripped of her powers – as defenceless as all her victims. It no longer mattered if he fell with her, so long as her corruptness was destroyed.

Urraca gave a low amused laugh as if she considered the sight of Madelon in sackcloth would be highly enjoyable.

"For disobeying the command of your king, you could be stripped of all lands and titles, dragged through the streets on a rope like a common peasant and then thrown into a dungeon to await his pleasure."

"Or yours, cousin," Madelon retorted. "I'm not afraid of your threats. I don't care what you do to me."

"Then a finger won't be laid on you," Urraca said. She contemplated her long polished nails and changed several rings on to other fingers. "I shall simply have Valentín Maratín executed."

"No!"

The pitiful cry which came from Madelon's lips brought a cruel gleam to the older woman's eyes.

"Yes, Madelon, yes. I shall call in my sergeant in a few moments and give him instructions to take a detachment of men to the lodging house where Maratín is staying. He will arrest your lover and bring him back to the excellent dungeons beneath this house. A night with my private executioner may persuade him to reveal a few of Sancho's secrets. If not, it does not matter, he has a strong will and my executioner will enjoy trying to break him. Tomorrow, before my brother's coronation, I shall have him beheaded. Did you know that's the way the Moors deal with their Christian captives? They cut off their heads and nail them over the archways over the roads leading into their towns. Perhaps I shall have the head of the Lord of the Eagles decorating the door of the church in Burgos. An appropriate end for a man who is a follower of the Moorish way of life, don't you agree?"

Madelon gave a soft moan and began to sway unsteadily. Paco came out of his chair with surprising swiftness and steadied her. He sat her down and put his goblet to her lips, waiting while she drank deeply of the honeyed wine and recovered her composure.

"You bitch." He glared at Urraca with hate-filled eyes. "You were fathered by the devil himself."

"I like that, Paco, your sense of humour is returning. The devil's daughter and a Moor's bastard. We should be good company for each other."

Madelon raised her head and stared at Urraca with horrified eyes. Her mind was still so full of visions of a headless Valentín that she could scarcely take in this new development, yet instinctively she knew the remark had been directed at her, not Paco. Beside the chair, her brother had become like a frozen statue. His hand, still holding hers, was like ice.

"What does she mean, Paco?"

"Nothing – she only wants to hurt you."

Urraca ignored the wildness growing in Paco's expression. One way or the other she would make sure Madelon married Gaspar Vivaldes.

"Don't look so tragic, cousin," she purred, "no one but Paco and I know the truth – and Sancho, of course, but he is in no position to cause any trouble."

Madelon felt as if she was going out of her mind. She leapt to her feet with an anguished cry.

"For the love of God, what is it I don't know? Paco, why am I like my mother? Why do you always compare us? Do we look alike, is that it?"

Mutely Paco nodded. While he floundered desperately for words – the right words, gentle words, to explain, Urraca rose to her feet and poured herself some wine.

"Your mother was taken in a Moorish raid and sold as a slave in Toledo. She was bought, according to Paco, by a Moor of some repute, though the name escapes him. You are a result of that liaison."

Madelon did not move or speak. Her face was so white, her expression so shocked, that Paco put his arms around her shoulders, half afraid she would faint, but she appeared not to notice. Hundreds upon hundreds of thoughts flashed through her mind as she stood there. How clear everything was now. Her father had hated her not because she had been born a girl, but because she had been fathered by another man – a Moor! His violent quarrels with her and his hatred for her poor mother, his desire to marry off his unwanted bastard and rid the house of her presence, it was easy to understand now. There was Moorish blood in her veins, blood of men like Yusuf. She glanced down at the slim hands clasped tightly in front of her. They were the same – she was the same. Whatever was in her now had always been in her, nothing had changed. Her fingers sought Paco's hands, firm on her shoulders and clung to them.

"I am grateful to you, cousin Urraca, you have opened the door to many secrets which have been kept from me," she said calmly. "My only regret is not knowing sooner."

"Some day I will kill you," Paco muttered, glaring at Urraca. He turned his sister gently in his arms and pressed his lips to her forehead. "Forgive me, I should have told you, but when you met Maratín and it became obvious there was an attraction between you, my hatred of him overruled everything else. I was wrong to keep it from you, to force you into marriage with a man who isn't fit to kiss the hem of your gown. Our mother was forced into marriage too, perhaps that's why she found pleasure in the arms of another man. I was a fool to condemn her."

"Paco, oh, Paco, does that mean I don't have to marry the Count?" Madelon breathed, hope dawning on her ashen face.

"It makes no difference whether Paco changes his mind or not," Urraca snapped. "The marriage is a royal command. Disobey it and I send my sergeant for Maratín this instant."

"I shall appeal to the king," Paco retorted.

"Against me?" Urraca laughed. "You have already lost favour with me, Paco, take care I do not have a word in my brother's ear. You may find yourself sampling the entertainments of my executioner – or even joining Maratín."

"Paco, please, it's no use," Madelon said quietly. "Thank you for coming to my help, at least tonight has brought us together again, but it's useless. If I must marry the Count of Segovia to save Valentín's life, then I will."

Paco's fingers tightened over her shoulders in a grasp which made her wince.

"Do you love him that much?" He was staring at her as if she had taken leave of her senses. "Can you really go through with this marriage and risk not only his anger, but his contempt and the loss of his love too?"

"At least he will be alive," Madelon murmured with a faint smile. "I think I am like my mother, Paco, I may not love wisely, but I love sincerely. What must I do to ensure his safety?" she asked, turning to Urraca.

"You say you were on your way to see him. He was expecting you, wasn't he?"

"Yes."

"Good. Then the answer is simple. Write him a note and tell him you have decided not to run away with him after all, but to stay and marry the Count of Segovia, that you have been reconciled with your brother and he has made you see things in their right perspective. I will leave the wording of it to you – you know him so much better than I."

The implication was not lost on Madelon. She knew just what she had to say and every word cut her heart like a knife thrust. Urraca took the completed letter from her and a ripple of laughter broke from her lips as she read aloud:

"Dearest Valentín,"

"Once you told me what you felt for me was the most wonderful thing you had ever known, but that if I did not feel that way we should part as friends, before we hurt each other too deeply. At the time I believed my feelings to have matched yours, now it grieves me to have to tell you, that was not so. I have thought on it for a long while and I know now I must face the fact I do not love you – and never did. I cannot therefore join you tonight. I belong here, with Paco and the day after tomorrow I am to be married to the Count of Segovia. Forgive me if I have hurt you."

"You might have signed it with something a little more endearing than just 'Madelon'. Oh, well, it will do. What charming little heart-to-heart talks you two must have had. Maratín's squire can take this to him. I suggest you warn him what will happen to his master if he attempts to see you again."

Madelon barely suppressed a cry as Stephen was pushed into the room. His face was cut and bleeding as if he had been continually punched and kicked about the head. She held the sealed letter out to him, thankful that her hands were no longer trembling.

"You will take this to your master for me," she said firmly.

Stephen looked at her curiously, oblivious to the two silent figures on either side of her.

"Are you not coming too, my lady?"

"No, Stephen, I am remaining here. You will deliver my letter and if you value your master's life, you will say nothing of what has happened tonight. We met in the street and I gave you a letter, that is all."

At the mention of his master's safety Stephen's freckled face grew grim. He nodded acquiescence and was quickly bustled out. Urraca gave a sigh and said in a relieved voice.

"Well, that's that. Are you coming down to the banquet, Paco, or do you intend to stay here and play the doting brother? It's a little late, don't you think?"

"Go to the devil," Paco retorted through clenched teeth. Only Madelon, holding on to his arm, prevented him from striking out at her smiling face.

"No, my dear, I shall go and enjoy myself. I shall leave several men outside to ensure both you and Madelon reach your rooms safely."

As the door closed behind her, Madelon turned her face against Paco's chest and began to cry weakly.

CHAPTER
FOURTEEN

THE sound of great revelry from the banquet hall beneath Madelon's room refused to let her sleep. She lay in the huge canopied bed, staring out of the open windows at the night sky. It was an uncomfortably close night without even a slight breeze to ease the heaviness of the atmosphere. The noise from the street was almost as rowdy as that coming from below, but with the window shutters closed, the heat would have been unbearable.

An untidy, threatening Diya had been waiting for her when she returned and as Madelon related how she had been forced to give her promise to marry the Count of Segovia to save Valentín's life, the maid called upon all the gods she could think of to strike Urraca dead upon the spot. Madelon did not try to soothe the furious girl. She felt the same way herself, but was unable to give way to her feelings so colourfully. Diya said everything she thought, but could not put into words.

Paco had held her close and kissed her before they parted. He was suffering too, she realized. He both loved and hated Urraca now and she began to fear for his safety. His disgust at the whole situation and particularly the way he had allowed himself to be used might prompt him into doing something foolish.

Madelon gave up trying to sleep. Pulling on a silk robe, she stepped carefully over the figure of the sleeping Diya, stretched out at the foot of the bed, and sat on a stool by the window, watching the townsfolk below who were still celebrating despite the lateness of the hour. Valentín would have received her letter by now. What was he doing, she wondered sadly, sitting in his lodgings hating her, or trying to forget the plans they had made in the arms of another woman or with a bottle? Aiya, Yusuf's favourite wife had been wrong, she and Valentín were not destined for each other. With a sigh she leant her aching head against the window frame and dozed from sheer exhaustion.

The sound of shouting from below jerked her into awakefulness. There were soldiers in the street below. Her eyes widened as she saw the emblem of Sancho of Castile emblazoned on their tunics. Castilians! But that was impossible, the moment the news of their entry into the town reached Alfonso, he would order his brother's death. Who had commanded the soldiers to enter so openly and with such lack of thought for their imprisoned king? She strained her ears for sounds of fighting from below her room. How strange – the sounds of revelry from the banquet hall had ceased. No laughter – no shouting – no sounds of fighting. What was happening? At the heavy tramp of footsteps on the stairs she jumped to her feet and shook Diya into awakefulness.

The door was flung open and Castilian men-at-arms crowded in, their weapons menacing the two women who stood clasped protectively in each other's arms.

"What do you want? How dare you force an entry into my room, don't you know who I am?" Madelon cried indignantly.

"They know, Doña Madelon." A giant of a man with a flaming red beard pushed his way through the men to confront her. For a long moment Rodrigo de Vivar stared into the lovely face of the woman who had, so he believed, deceived his best friend, and his lips curled into a contemptuous twist. "You will be confined in this room until morning," he growled.

"So Valentín had a plan after all," Madelon murmured. "We are prisoners then, Don Rodrigo?"

"That you are, prisoners of King Sancho."

"Thank God!" To Rodrigo's surprise Madelon sank down on to the bed, relief flooding into her face. Bright tears sparkled in her eyes as she looked up at him. "Valentín is safe?"

"Safe and well. He's with the king. Tomorrow Sancho accepts the fealty of Santa María de Carrion and that of his brother Alfonso and his treacherous subjects. Then we leave to crown him in the cathedral at Leon. Why should you care anyway?" He stepped close to Madelon, his eyes blazing furiously. "If I had my way I'd – I'd – never mind, it would be unpleasant anyway. Do you know what your lies and deceit have done to him? Overnight he's changed so that even I don't recognize him. He won't even talk to me – his best friend."

"I deserve your anger and Valentín's too," Madelon answered, "but what I did was to save his life. If you will send your men away I will tell you everything, on the condition you keep it to yourself."

Rodrigo glared at her. He did not want to stay and listen to more carefully concocted lies, but the sight of Madelon's tear-streaked face was enough to move even the hardest man and Rodrigo, despite his rough exterior, had the softest of hearts. At his command the room was cleared. Madelon told him all that had happened to her since the last fateful meeting with Valentín, sparing neither herself nor Paco in the detailed explanation.

"If this is true, then Valentín must know," Rodrigo muttered when she had finished. He was not altogether sure it was true, but was more than half-way persuaded. Although he no longer regarded her as a scheming adventuress, he could not forget the terrible look of pain on Valentín's face as he had read Madelon's letter, which he had burnt directly afterwards without showing it to his friend. The wound was deep, too deep to heal perhaps.

"With Sancho on the throne of Leon, Valentín's safety is assured," Madelon said. "What would he think if I went to him now and said I loved him? No, Don Rodrigo, I must remain with my brother and await the king's decision on our future."

"It may not be a favourable one, you realize that, don't you? He is your cousin, but he has no love for your brother.

No harm will befall you, of that I am certain, but him . . . you had better be prepared for the worst, Doña Madelon."

"I know it and I am quite prepared." Madelon rose to her feet. In the flickering candlelight her face was pale and tired, yet she had never looked more proud, more courageous. Even Rodrigo was impressed by her bearing and promised Diya would be allowed to come and go from the room unhindered so that Madelon would not be inconvenienced. He even kissed her hand before leaving.

"You are mad," Diya gasped. "Here you are with all your problems solved and you don't take advantage of the situation."

Madelon slipped off her robe and climbed into bed. Were her problems solved, or just beginning with Paco's uncertain future? If Sancho ever comes to the throne I shall be thrown into the deepest dungeon they can find and the key tossed away, he had once joked.

"I'm tired," was her only answer and she fell into a deep sleep the moment her head touched the pillow. A determined expression came over Diya's face as she watched her. Making sure she was comfortable, the maid opened the door and stepped out into the corridor. The sentry posted in the corridor stepped forward to halt her, but then recognizing her as the personal maid of the woman he was there to watch and remembering Don Rodrigo's specific instructions, he stepped back and allowed her to pass without a word. Diya slipped silently down the stairs, praying she would be back before Madelon awoke.

Diya came back from the kitchens next morning, full of gossip obtained from the servants. The whole town was buzzing with the news of the great banquet Alfonso had held to celebrate his victory – a banquet where the food and drink had been liberally dosed with a strong sleeping potion. By the time Valentín Maratín and Rodrigo appeared at the head of a specially chosen band of Castilian soldiers some hours before dawn, the whole company was fast asleep. Even

Sancho, not wanting to appear suspicious, had sampled enough food to make him almost insensible. The few Leonese soldiers in the town gave little fight once they learned not only their king, but the whole of his court was in Castilian hands. From the camp outside the town came the remaining Castilians and by morning not a Leonese flag or soldier was to be seen anywhere.

"It's said when the Doña Urraca awoke this morning, she flew into such a rage her maids fled in terror and when they went back they found she'd torn up all her gowns," Diya laughed. "She will have to borrow one she lent you to appear before the king this morning."

The smile vanished from Madelon's face as the moment of amusement passed. She, too, had to face Sancho this morning, along with Paco and all the other members of the Leonese court. Nothing drastic would happen to her, of that she was sure. Sancho might banish her to her estates, or even send her back to the convent, but neither of these things were as terrible as the punishment he would mete out to Paco for being Alfonso's right-hand and Urraca's pawn.

"Help me to dress, Diya. No, not the black, cousin Sancho will not be swayed by my appearance. The yellow satin Doña Francesca gave me will do very well. And my rubies and the pearl ring. No, nothing else. Leave my hair loose. Wait, there is something else." From the coffer where her clothes were kept, Madelon took out her mother's ring with the Moorish inscriptions on it. Somehow it seemed appropriate to wear it now. With a smile she slipped it on to her finger.

She had just finished dressing when there came a knock on the door. She expected a soldier, or the Cid, and was surprised and delighted when Paco came in. She glimpsed three men-at-arms stationed outside before the door closed behind him. With a glad cry she threw herself into his arms and smothered his pale face with kisses.

"Paco! They haven't harmed you, have they? Oh, I was so worried."

Paco held her at arm's length, unable to conceal the astonishment he felt at seeing her. When Rodrigo de Vivar had told
him she too was under guard he had not believed it.

"Why aren't you with him?" he demanded harshly.

"Because you have need of me," came the quiet answer.

Shame flooded into Paco's face at her sacrifice. When she
needed him he had turned his back on her, but now at least
a way had presented itself for him to end the unfavourable
alliance with the House of Segovia and also to end his affair
with Urraca. At the same time it could result in his death or
imprisonment for an unpleasant number of years, but if
Madelon was free to live her own life, at least he would have
made some atonement for past mistakes.

"You are like our mother," he murmured gently, "and you
should be proud of it. It has taken me all these years to realize
what a wonderful person she really was."

He wanted to say so much more, to put her mind at rest, but
the door opened to reveal the Sergeant-at-Arms with an armed
escort, who announced Paco's presence was required in the
Great Hall below. The sight of them made Madelon feel
decidedly uneasy. Sancho obviously had no intention of
allowing his prize prisoner a chance of escape. With a defiant
little smile, she tucked her arm beneath Paco's and together
they left the room. Ahead of them were Alfonso and Urraca,
also heavily guarded. As they walked the long corridors
and descended the stairs, they argued violently, causing
much amusement among their escort who gained great
pleasure and satisfaction from the sight of their enemies
glaring at each other and each blaming the other for the
disaster which had overtaken them. Madelon felt a little sorry
for the weak-willed Alfonso, who was utterly cowed beneath
his sister's spasmodic outbursts of temper. For Urraca she felt
nothing. Her cousin would no doubt find a way out of her
difficult position.

At the end of the long passageway leading to the Great
Hall where she could see Sancho seated on a magnificent
throne covered in rich blue velvet, waiting to receive the oath

of allegiance from his new subjects, stood a tall figure dressed in dark green. Madelon's steps faltered as she saw the huge golden eagle embroidered on the man's doublet and she felt Paco's grasp tighten on her.

Valentín allowed Urraca and Alfonso to pass him without a word. Signalling the soldiers guarding Paco to fall back, he stepped towards them, blocking their way into the room. Madelon's nerves were near to breaking point. She had been dreading the encounter she knew must come some time, and Paco felt her begin to tremble.

"You have no business with us, Maratín," he said in a low, fierce whisper. Through the half-open door he could see Alfonso kissing Sancho's hand and faintly Urraca's voice drifted back to him as she began a speech. She would be as as eloquent as always – and as devious, he mused.

"I have something to say to your sister," Valentín retorted coldly. He stepped closer to Madelon and for a moment she thought he meant to wrench her out of her brother's grasp, but his hands fell away and his face became unreadable. "Did you mean everything you wrote in your letter?"

Madelon clung tightly to Paco's arm, feeling suddenly faint. Why had he chosen this moment to force a showdown? She was in a state of nervous exhaustion which caused the tears to start to her eyes at the slightest upset.

"Yes," her voice was hardly audible.

"Then the story you told Rodrigo was pure fabrication?"

"He ... he told you. He gave me his most sacred oath ..." Madelon cried.

"Your maid paid me a visit early this morning while you were asleep. She doesn't think your brother is worthy of the sacrifice you are making. She explained a great many things." Valentín's pale eyes held hers and the expression in them made her grow weak at the knees. He loved her still – it blazed out of his eyes for all to see.

"Then you know why I wrote that letter," she whispered, "and why we must forget the plans we made. Circumstances are different now."

Valentín's gaze flickered over her shoulder to Paco's stony face and his mouth tightened into a grim line. With a low oath he caught Madelon's arms and pulled her against him, kissing her with a fierce possessiveness that made her senses reel. Paco stood helpless to intervene, hemmed in by men-at-arms the moment he had stepped forward towards his sister.

"Well?" Valentín demanded as Madelon withdrew trembling from his embrace. "Are you still ready to turn your back on my love to stand by a man who was willing to abandon you to his mistress's schemes, willing to toss you into the arms of Gaspar Vivaldes to be used and humiliated . . ."

"It's no use," Madelon broke in quietly. Somehow she held back the tears and ruthlessly squashed the wonderful feelings Valentín's kisses had roused in her. "As readily as I was willing to save your life, so I am now prepared to stand by my brother in his hour of need. If you truly love me, Valentín, don't make this any more torturous for me." Quickly she broke from him and followed Paco to the door of the Great Hall. On impulse she stopped and looked back into Valentín's disbelieving face. "I love you," she whispered. "I will always love you, no matter what happens here today."

In the Great Hall a long table stretched across the far end filled with Castilian nobles and soldiers of high rank. In the midst of them was Sancho and Rodrigo de Vivar seated on his right. The chair beside the latter was empty. This was probably Valentín's place, Madelon thought. She waited for him to move past her and sit down, but he did not do so. Instead he followed her into the room and stood a few feet to one side of her, a determined expression on his dark features. Did he mean to make a scene, she wondered? He was high in Sancho's favour now – his position at the table was proof of that. He could ask for the death penalty for his enemy and probably get it.

As Paco bowed respectfully before his new king, she swept down in a low curtsy. A page advanced towards her brother holding out a sword on a silk cushion. It was the Sword of State. Rodrigo rose to his feet and glared balefully at the man before him. He was almost hoping Paco would not put in an appearance, thus proclaiming his rejection of his new monarch and also signing his own death warrant. A quick way to solve Valentín's problem and rid the country of a troublemaker.

"Paco del Rivas y Montevides, kneel." Paco knelt and the hall was suddenly quiet. "Do you swear as God is your witness, to give your loyalty to Sancho, eldest son of Ferdinand, rightful king of Leon and Castile and to no other?"

"I so swear."

"Kiss the sword and may God strike you down if you have lied."

Paco touched the cold steel with his lips and quickly straightened, to encounter Sancho's piercing gaze. Taking a deep breath he said in a harsh tone:

"If you are waiting for a plea for mercy, sire, you will wait until eternity. I have done nothing for which you can condemn me. I am a soldier and I have been loyal to my king. If that is a crime in Castilian eyes, then I am guilty."

"I am your king," Sancho snapped. "How will you serve me?"

Paco was silent. He had sworn an oath of loyalty and he would keep it, but Sancho would never hold the same sway over him as Alfonso had done – there was too much personal enmity between them.

"You know the answer to that as well as I," he returned.

Madelon grew pale at the sight of the grimness which settled over Sancho's face, knowing he was about to pronounce some terrible sentence. She ran to her brother's side and caught his hand.

"Paco, for my sake, bend a little," she pleaded.

"To Sancho? You don't know what you ask of me. I am his kinsman, but it carries no weight. We hate each other too much."

"But why?" Madelon was oblivious to Rodrigo calling her name or to the interested speculation among the Castilians. She had eyes only for Paco who seemed determined to throw his life away. "As boys you were close."

"Jealousy, perhaps. I've resented him ever since the day our mother died and he was the only one she wanted to see. Me – her own flesh and blood she shut out of the room. Sancho was alone with her when she died. I should have been there, shouldn't I?"

Madelon nodded, hastily brushing away the tears which blurred her vision. Poor Paco, how tormented he must have been for years. She wheeled away from him in a swirl of yellow satin and stood before her cousin.

"Your Majesty, may I speak?"

Sancho's expression darkened. He had watched and prayed she would not interfere. She had suffered too much in her young life and he did not want to add to it. He had promised her mother he would look after her if the time came when she needed protection and Paco was unable to give it. Even if she went down on her knees he would not relent in his determination to rid himself of Paco. He was too dangerous to remain alive. He sent a withering glance at Urraca, then said coldly:

"My head is still full of my sister's constant whining. Am I to be plagued by another tearful woman trying to appeal to my better nature? Believe me, cousin, you are wasting your time."

"Beg, sire?" A faint smile crossed Madelon's face. "I will not beg. You are too hard a man to be swayed by tears or the sight of a woman on her knees, so I will save you that ungainly sight. Paco has spoken the truth. He is guilty of only two things: loyalty to his king and love for a heartless woman who has scorned and betrayed him. I know it is in your mind to take his life and I know why. Consider carefully, sire, is it your intention to have him executed because he is your enemy, or because he failed my mother? I ask you to spare him – in the name of all you once shared with her."

For a moment Madelon thought she had gone too far. A heavy buzz of conversation broke out all around her, she was half aware of the incredulous stares being cast in her direction and of Valentín moving closer as if to give her moral support, but it was Sancho who held her attention. The colour fled from his face, then returned in a heavy flush which stained his neck and cheeks a dark red. She watched his fingers tighten around the carved arms of his chair until the knuckles grew white.

"You go too far," he said between clenched teeth. "Have a care or you may share your brother's fate for this act of folly."

"I am prepared even for that," Madelon answered proudly. She had seized her opportunity and it seemed she had lost, but the next moment her heartbeats quickened as Sancho leant across the table demanding:

"What if I exiled your brother to Zamora with the rest of the Leonese court, are you willing to go with him, to be his jailer? Can you swear to me he will never plot against my person or my kingdom?"

Madelon was silent. From one side of her she heard a hoarse whisper – "No! In the name of God, no!" – and knew it came from Valentín. She did not turn around. Sancho began to smile, confident she would not give up a bright future to go into exile.

"Your Majesty has forgotten I am to be married to the Count of Segovia. I cannot be a wife and my brother's keeper."

"The choice is yours."

"Then I will accompany my brother," Madelon replied simply. She was free! Safe from the clutches of Gaspar Vivaldes, of Urraca, and Paco still had his life. "Thank you, sire ..." She sank into a curtsey and found her legs were trembling so violently she could not rise. It was Paco who drew her to her feet.

"No," he said harshly.

Sancho's eyebrows rose sardonically and a courtier tittered.

"Be thankful you have your worthless life. Take your sister away and thank her before I change my mind."

"Yes, I have my life – at the cost of her happiness. The price is too high." A terrible look passed over Paco's face as his pride fought with his conscience. He put Madelon away from him and faced his cousin challengingly. "She would not beg, but I will. If I am to be exiled, let it be to my estates in Salamanca.

I have been away a long time and they are in need of my
attention. Besides," he gave a bitter smile in the direction of
his ex-mistress, "I no longer have a stomach for intrigue and
murder. There is nothing for me at Zamora."

"Such a weakness, I will gladly overlook," Sancho retorted.
He was unsure, wavering on the brink of a decision. His gaze
fastened on Madelon and on the tall, silent figure standing
nearby. "And your sister, what of her? Do you intend to drag
her off to that mausoleum as thanks for what she has done for
you today?"

"With your gracious permission Madelon will remain in
your care – or rather in that of Valentín Maratín whom she
loves deeply and who," Paco stumbled over the words ...
"who I now realize loves her."

Madelon felt someone's hands fasten over her shoulders and
knew it was Valentín. She leant against him weakly and felt
his lips brush the back of her neck.

At the table Rodrigo whispered something in the ear of his
king.

"If that old devil gives me any trouble, I'll cut off his
beard," Valentín muttered.

"It is settled then." Sancho relaxed back in his seat and
stared at Paco. "Paco del Rivas y Montevides, it is hereby
decreed you are to be exiled to your estates in Salamanca until
it pleases me to recall you to court. I need hardly warn you of
the consequences should you disobey my command. You will
leave Santa María de Carrion before the sun sets. You have
my leave to go."

Paco bowed and turned away, still a little dazed at his good
fortune. One day perhaps, he and Sancho would be able to
talk ... At the sight of the tears in his sister's eyes, he smiled
and gently kissed her.

"Tears, little one? Isn't this what you wanted? Come now,
dry your eyes and let me see you smile before I go. Will you
ride part of the way with me?"

"You are leaving at once?" Valentín asked in a quiet tone.

His dislike of Paco had not lessened, but in those last brief moments he had come to respect the enemy.

"Yes."

"Of course I will come," Madelon said, smiling bravely through a mist of tears. "I will change and meet you in the courtyard." Paco nodded and left them. She turned and looked into Valentín's face and her lips trembled. "There is something you must know ..." she began, but he laid a hand against her mouth and silenced her.

"Persian women are terrible chatterboxes," he murmured. "Did you think it would matter to me, *shafra*? I don't care who your father was, do you hear me? Now go and change and meet me by the stables. I am coming too."

Paco said nothing when he saw the man accompanying his sister. He helped her to mount and the three of them rode in silence through the streets of Santa María de Carrion towards the outer wall. A mile beyond it Paco reined in his horse and turned to face them. He was pale, but perfectly in control of his emotions and they could only guess at the tumult of feelings he was concealing.

Taking both of Madelon's hands in his he drew her to him and kissed her. She would have clung to him, but he put her from him into Valentín's hold.

"Good-bye, little sister, try to forgive me for being such a blind fool. Come and see me sometimes." He stared at Valentín for a long moment and his voice was strained as he said. "Make her happy, Maratín, she's had too little of it in her life."

Valentín nodded. This was not the time for speech-making and both men knew it. His arm tightened comfortingly around Madelon's shoulders as she began to weep. Paco's hand rested for a final moment on her cheek. As he withdrew it Valentín's hand snaked out and caught it in a grip too fierce for the other man to break free. Paco glared at him, but then his expression lightened and a smile softened the taut line of his mouth. His fingers fastened around Valentín's wrist in a firm clasp.

Before Madelon could grasp the significance of the incident, he had wheeled his horse around and was riding swiftly away from them. Valentín eased his horse nearer to hers. They sat close together, holding hands and watching Paco skilfully guiding his mount down a rocky incline to the valley below. A forest stretched out before him. As he reached it he urged his horse into a gallop and immediately, both horse and rider were lost to view.

**Millions of women
love Harlequin Romances**

**Millions of women
trust Harlequin Romances**

NOW
**Millions of women
can find that same love,
that same trust, in the**

NEW
HARLEQUIN
HISTORICALS

HARLEQUIN HISTORICALS bring you all the romance
and suspense, all the intrigue and mystery,
the excitement and adventure of an age long past.

HARLEQUIN HISTORICALS have the deep love and
sentiment you look for in Harlequin Romances.
They are about people you will care about. They
bring you other worlds and other times—all against
a background of pure romance.

Historical romances with the Harlequin magic

It was a time of lavish costume-balls . . .
of masked ladies in delicate folds of lace
and dashing cavaliers in pearl-trimmed satin . .
starry-eyed lovers cruelly kept apart
by the rigid rules of the nobility . . .
secret meetings in hidden, leafy bowers . . .
and the quiet, serene beauty
of everlasting love.

It was the age of romance.